Peace on Earth

OTHER BOOKS BY STANISLAW LEM

Stanislaw LEM

Peace on Earth

Translated by Elinor Ford
with Michael Kandel

A Helen and Kurt Wolff Book
Harcourt Brace & Company
New York   San Diego   London

Library of Congress Cataloging-in-Publication Data
Lem, Stanisław.
  [Pokój na Ziemi. English]
  Peace on Earth / Stanislaw Lem ; translated from the
Polish by Elinor Ford with Michael Kandel.— 1st U.S. ed.
    p. cm.
  Translation of: Pokój na ziemi.
  "A Helen and Kurt Wolff book."
  I. Title.
  PG7158.L39P5713   1992
  891.8'537—dc20   91-47970

Designed by Lydia D'moch
Printed in the United States of America
First edition
A B C D E

Contents

Doubled

I don't know what to do. If I could say "I'm miserable," it wouldn't be so bad. I can't say "We're miserable" either because I can only partly speak for myself even though I'm still Ijon Tichy. I used to talk to myself while I shaved but I had to stop because of my left eye's lewd winking. Coming back in the LEM, I didn't realize what happened to me just before lift-off. The LEM, by the way, doesn't have anything to do with the American NASA module manned by Armstrong and Aldrin to collect a couple of moon rocks. It was given the same name to disguise my secret mission. Damn that mission. When I returned from the Calf constellation, I intended to stay put for at least a year. But I agreed to go for the sake of mankind. I knew I might not come back. Doctor Lopez said my chance of survival was one in twenty point eight. That didn't stop me: I'm a gambler. You only die once. Either I come back or I don't, I said to myself. It never occurred to me that I might come

back but not come back because we would come back. To
explain I'll have to release some highly classified information but I don't care. That is, partly. I'm writing this too
only partly and with great difficulty, typing with the right
hand. The left I had to tie to the arm of the chair because
it kept tearing the paper out of the machine. It wouldn't
listen to reason, and while I was immobilizing it, it
punched me in the eye. It's because of the doubling. Our
brains all have two hemispheres connected by the corpus
callosum or great commissure. Two hundred million white
nerve fibers connect the brain so it can put its thoughts
together but not in my case. It happened on that range
where the moon robots tested their new weapons. I stumbled in there by mistake. I'd accomplished my mission, had
outsmarted those unliving creatures, and was on my way
back to the LEM when I had to urinate. There are no
urinals on the moon. They wouldn't work anyway in a vac-
uum. You have a little container in your suit, just like Armstrong and Aldrin, so you can relieve yourself anytime,
anywhere, but somehow I couldn't, not there in the full
sun in the middle of the Sea of Serenity. Not far from me
was a solitary boulder. I went over to its shadow. How was
I to know there was an ultrasound-inducing field there?
While I'm urinating, I feel this little snap. Like a crack in
the neck, only higher, in the middle of the skull. It was a
remote callotomy. It didn't hurt. I felt funny but the feeling
passed and I continued on my way. The strangeness I at-
tributed to an understandable excitement, considering all I
had been through. The right hand is controlled by the left
hemisphere of the brain. That's why I said I was writing
only partly. My right hemisphere obviously doesn't approve
of what I'm writing. And I can't say "I'm writing"—it's
my left hemisphere that's writing. I'll have to reach some
compromise with the opposition because I can't sit forever

with my hand tied. I've tried to appease it but nothing works. It's arrogant, aggressive, vulgar. Fortunately it can read only certain parts of speech, nouns mainly. I know this because I've been reading up on the subject. It doesn't understand verbs or adjectives, so while it's watching I have to express myself carefully. Will this work? I don't know. And why is it that all the civilized behavior is in the left hemisphere?

On the moon too I was supposed to land only partly, but in an entirely different sense, because it was before the accident, before I was doubled. I was supposed to circle the moon in stationary orbit, the reconnaissance to be accomplished by my remote, which even looked like me except it was plastic with antennas. I sit in LEM 1 and LEM 2 lands with the remote. Those war robots hate people. They will kill at the drop of a hat. At least that's what I was told. But LEM 2 malfunctioned and I decided to land to see what was going on because I was still in contact with it. Sitting in LEM 1, I suddenly had severe stomach pains, not in the flesh, that is, but by radio because, as I learned after landing, they broke LEM 2's hatch cover, grabbed the remote, and pulled out its insides. I couldn't disconnect because if I did, my stomach might stop hurting but I'd lose all contact with my remote and wouldn't be able to locate it. The Sea of Serenity, where the attack took place, is like the Sahara. Also, I got the wires mixed because even though each wire is a different color there are too many of them and I couldn't find the emergency instructions. Trying to find them with a stomachache made me so mad that instead of calling Earth I decided to land, even though I'd been warned I shouldn't do that under any circumstances. But retreat just isn't in my nature. Besides, the remote may have been only a machine stuffed with circuitry but I couldn't leave it in the clutches of those robots.

I see that the more I explain, the less clear it gets. I should probably begin at the beginning. Except I don't know what the beginning was because most of it is remembered in the right hemisphere, which I can't get to now. There's a lot I don't remember, and in order to obtain even a little of that information I have to speak to my left hand with my right in sign language but it doesn't always answer. The left hand gives me the finger for example, and that's one of its more polite indications of a difference of opinion.

I'd like to give it a good smack but the problem is, while the right hand is stronger than the left, the legs are equal, and what's worse, I have a corn on the little toe of my right foot and the left foot knows about it. When that trouble started on the bus and I shoved my left hand forcibly into my pocket, its foot took revenge by stomping on the corn so hard, I saw stars. I don't know if it's a loss of intelligence caused by the doubling but I can see I'm writing nonsense. The foot of my left hand is, of course, my left foot. There are times my unfortunate body falls into two enemy camps.

I interrupted my writing to kick myself. That is, my left foot kicked my right so it wasn't I, or it was only partly I, but grammar simply can't describe this situation. I started taking off my shoes but stopped. A person, even in such straits, shouldn't make a fool of himself. Was I supposed to twist my own arm to learn what the problem was with the wires and the emergency instructions? True, I had beaten myself in the past but the circumstances were different. Once in that time loop, when the today me was against the yesterday me, and once to counteract the poison of the benignimizers in that hotel in Costa Rica. I had beaten myself black and blue, but remained myself, indivisible. It wasn't so unusual. Didn't people in the Middle

Ages flog themselves? But no one now can put himself in my shoes. It's impossible. I can't even say that there are two of me because there aren't. Or there are but only partly. If you want to know what happened to me, you'll have to read this whole story, word by word, even when it doesn't make sense. The sense will come, though probably not completely because you can get to the bottom of it only by callotomy, just as you can't know what it's like to be an otter, say, or a turtle without being turned into an otter or a turtle, and then you can't communicate it because animals don't talk or write. Normal people, of which I was one most of my life, don't understand how a split-brain person can be himself and look like himself and speak about himself in the first person singular and walk normally and talk coherently while his right hemisphere doesn't know what his left hemisphere is doing (except for mushroom barley soup in my case). Some say that callotomy must have existed in Biblical times because it is written that the left hand needn't know what the right hand is doing, but I always thought that was a figure of speech.

One character followed me for two months trying to wring the truth out of me. He would visit me at the most uncivil hours to ask me how many of me there really were. The medical textbooks I gave him didn't help him any more than they had helped me. I loaned him the books only to get rid of him. How did I meet him? I had gone to buy shoes without laces, the kind with Velcro on the top, because if my left side didn't want to go for a walk, it was impossible to tie my shoes. As soon as I'd tie a shoe, my left hand would untie it. So I went to buy a pair of running shoes with Velcro fasteners, not that I'm one of those jogging types, I just wanted to teach the right hemisphere of my brain a lesson because at that time I couldn't communicate with it at all and I was furious and covered with bruises. I muttered something to the salesman to excuse my erratic behavior which wasn't actually mine. Then, as he knelt before me with the shoehorn, I grabbed his nose with my left hand. My left hand, that is, grabbed his nose, and I tried to explain this to him, the difference, figuring that even if he thought I was deranged (how could a shoe salesman know anything about callotomy?) he would still sell me the shoes. No reason for a madman to go barefoot. Unfortunately the salesman was a philosophy student working part-time in the shoe store and he was fascinated.

"Mr. Tichy!" he now yelled in my apartment. "According to logic, you're either singular or you're plural! If your right hand is pulling up your pants and the left hand interferes, it means that behind each stands a separate half of the brain that thinks its own thoughts and refuses to cooperate with the other. Because hands and feet don't go around fighting each other on their own!"

That's when I gave him the Gazzanigi. The best research done on the split brain and the results of that operation are in Professor Gazzanigi's book, *The Bisected Brain*, published in 1970 by Appleton Century Crofts, Educational Division, at the Meredith Corporation, and may my brain never grow together again if I'm inventing Michael Gazzanigi or his father to whom he dedicated his monograph and whose name is Dante Achilles Gazzanigi, also a doctor (M.D.). If you don't believe me, go to the nearest medical bookstore and ask for a copy.

The man who hounded me asking over and over what it's like living as two learned nothing from me. All he accomplished was to drive both my hemispheres to unanimous fury because I grabbed him with both hands by the neck and threw him out the door. This brief armistice of my dissociated being sometimes occurs, but I don't know why.

The young philosopher then telephoned me in the middle of the night, hoping that half-asleep I would spill my incredible secret. He asked me, ignoring the colorful language I was hurling at him, to place the receiver first to the left ear then to the right. He said it wasn't his questions that were idiotic but the state I was in, which defied all anthropological and existential concepts of man as a rational being conscious of his own rationality. He'd probably just finished his finals, that philosophy student, because he threw Hegel at me and Descartes (I think therefore I am, not we think therefore we are), and Husserl and Heidegger, to prove that my condition was impossible because it contradicted the greatest minds who for thousands of years, beginning with the Greeks, studied the conscious ego, and here comes someone with a severed commissure of the brain, as fit as a fiddle except his right hand doesn't know what his left hand is doing, likewise with the legs, and while some experts say that he has consciousness on the left side only and that the right is a soulless computer, others believe he has two consciousnesses but the right one can't speak because the Broca's area is in the left frontal lobe, but a third group proposes two partially separated egos. "You can't jump off a train in pieces," he yelled at me, "or die in pieces, and you can't think in pieces either!" I stopped throwing him out because I felt sorry for him. In his desperation he tried to bribe me. Eight hundred and forty dollars, he swore that was all he had, what he'd saved for a vacation with his girl, but he was prepared to part with it and with her as well if I told him *who* was thinking with my right hemisphere when *I* didn't know what it was thinking. I sent him to Professor Eccles, an advocate of left brain consciousness who believes the right side doesn't think at all, but the student didn't buy that, knowing that I had painstakingly taught sign language to my right hemisphere. He wanted me to go to Eccles and tell him he was wrong. The student now read medical papers instead of going to his classes in the evening. Learning that the nerve pathways are crossed, he searched through the fattest text-books to find out why in the hell that crossing happened so that the right brain controls the left half of the body and vice versa, but of course there was no answer to that question. The crossing either benefits us as human beings, he reasoned, or it doesn't. He read books by psychiatrists and found one who said that consciousness is in the left hemisphere and the subconscious in the right, but I was able to get that notion out of his head. I had read more than he, naturally. Tired of struggling with myself and now with this student burning with the thirst for knowledge, I left, I fled to New York—and jumped from the frying pan into the fire.

I rented a studio apartment near Manhattan and took the subway or bus to the public library to read Yozatitz, Werner, Tucker, Woods, Shapiro, Riklana, Schwartz, Szwarc, and Shvarts, and Sai-Mai-Halassza, Rossi, Lishman, Kenyon, Harvey, Fischer, Cohen, Brumbach, and about thirty different Rappaports. Almost every trip caused a scene, because I pinched the prettier women, particularly blondes. It was my left hand of course that did the pinching but try to explain that in a few words. Now and then I was slapped in the face, but the worst part was that most of the women accosted didn't seem to mind at all. On the contrary they considered it an overture, a pass, which was the last thing on my mind.

I could see I was getting nowhere trying to extricate myself single-handed from this nightmare, so I finally contacted a group of leading authorities in the field. These scientists were only too happy to study me. I was examined, x-rayed, scanned, subjected to positron emission tomography and magnetic resonance imaging, covered by four hundred electrodes, strapped to a special chair, and asked to look through a slit at pictures of apples, dogs, forks, combs, old people, tables, mice, mushrooms, cigars, glasses, nude women, and babies, after which they told me what I already knew: that when they showed me a billiard ball so that only my left hemisphere could see it and at the same time put my right hand into a bag with many objects, I wasn't able to choose the ball, and vice versa. They said I was an uninteresting case, but I said nothing about the sign language. I wanted, after all, to learn something about myself from them; I didn't care about adding to their knowledge.

I turned then to Professor S. Turteltaub, a loner, but instead of shedding light on my condition all he did was tell me what a pack of wolves, thieves, and parasites all the others were. Thinking his contempt for them was on scientific grounds, I listened with interest, but Turteltaub, it turned out, was angry only because they had rejected his project. The last time I saw Drs. Globus and Savodnisky, or whatever their names were—there were so many of them—they were offended when I told them I was seeing Dr. Turteltaub. They informed me that he had been expelled from their research group on ethical grounds. Turteltaub wanted to offer murderers sentenced to death or life imprisonment the chance to submit to callotomy instead. He argued that since callotomization was performed only on severe epileptics, it was not known whether the effect of cutting the commissure would be the same in normal people. And a normal man sentenced to the electric chair for murdering his mother-in-law, for example, would certainly prefer to have his corpus callosum cut. But Supreme Court Judge Klössenfänger spoke against this, because if Turteltaub murdered his mother-in-law in cold blood, that could be the decision of his left hemisphere alone, the right hemisphere knowing nothing about it, or knowing and protesting but being overruled, and if the murder occurred anyway after such an inner conflict, it would be difficult indeed to condemn one hemisphere while exonerating the other. In effect fifty-percent of the murderer would be sentenced to death.

Unable to obtain what he wanted, Turteltaub had to operate on monkeys, which were much more expensive than convicts, and as his grants were reduced, he feared he would end up with rats and guinea pigs, which wasn't the same at all. Added to that, the Animal Protection League people and other antivivisectionists broke his windows regularly. They even burned his car. The insurance company wouldn't pay, saying he had torched his own car in order to take the animal protectionists to court, besides the car was too old to be worth anything. Turteltaub was so boring that to shut him up I told him about the sign language my left hand had taught my right. A mistake. He called Globus immediately, or maybe it was Maxwell, to announce the presentation of a paper at the next neurologists' conference, a discovery that would crush everyone. Seeing what was coming, I left Turteltaub's without saying goodbye and went straight home. They were waiting for me in the lobby, their faces flushed and eyes burning with the unholy fire of science. I told them I would of course be glad to accompany them to the clinic, I just had to go up to my room to change first. While they waited for me in the lobby I climbed down the fire escape from the eleventh floor and grabbed a taxi to the airport. Since it didn't matter to me where I went as long as it was far from those researchers, I took the first plane out, to San Diego, and at a seedy little hotel there full of shady characters, before even unpacking my bag, I telephoned Professor Tarantoga for help.

Tarantoga, thank God, was home. You learn who your real friends are when the chips are down. He flew in to San Diego that night, and when I told him everything as succinctly and precisely as I could the good soul agreed to take me under his wing. Following his advice, I changed my hotel and started growing a beard, meanwhile he looked for a doctor who valued the Hippocratic oath more than the fame achieved by a rare case. We quarreled on the third day because he brought me some good news and I thanked him only partly. He didn't appreciate the sardonic winking from my left side. I explained of course that it wasn't I but the right hemisphere of my brain which I couldn't control. But this didn't mollify him; he said that even if there were two of me in one body, the sneering faces that half of me was making clearly showed that I must have harbored some animosity toward him in the past, which manifested itself now as black ingratitude, while he was of the opinion that one was either a friend or one wasn't. A fifty-percent friendship he had no use for. I finally managed to calm him down, and after he left I bought an eye patch.

The specialist he found for me was in Australia, so we flew to Melbourne. Joshua McIntyre, a professor of neurophysiology—his father and Tarantoga's father had been best friends—inspired confidence immediately. He was tall, with a gray crew cut, calm, sober, and, as Tarantoga assured me, decent. He would not use me or notify the Americans, who were frantic to find me. After the examination, which lasted three hours, he put a decanter of whiskey on the desk and poured a glass for me and for himself. When the atmosphere warmed up, he crossed his legs, thought for a moment, cleared his throat, and said:

"Mr. Tichy, I will address you in the singular, which is more comfortable. There is no question that your corpus

callosum has been severed from anterior to posterior commissure, though the skull shows no sign of trephi-
nation . . ."

"But I've told you, professor," I interrupted him, "the
skull wasn't touched, it was a new weapon, a weapon of
the future, designed not to kill but only to give the opposing army a total and remote cerebellotomy. Every soldier,
his brain severed, would fall like a puppet whose strings
are cut. That's what I was told at the center whose name
I cannot divulge. By accident I was standing sideways, or
sagittally, as you doctors say, with respect to the ultrasound-inducing field. But this is only conjecture. Those
robots work in secret, and the effects of the ultrasound
aren't clear . . ."

"Be that as it may," said the professor, looking at me
with kindly, wise eyes from behind his gold-framed glasses.
"Nonmedical circumstances need not concern us right
now. As for the number of minds in a callotomized individual, there are eighteen different theories, each supported
by experimental evidence, therefore none of them wholly
wrong and none of them wholly true. You are not one, nor
are you two, nor can we speak of split personalities."

"Then how many am I?" I asked, surprised.

"The question is poorly phrased. Imagine twins, who
from birth do nothing but saw wood with a two-handled
saw. They work well together, otherwise they would be unable to saw. Take the saw from them, and they become
like you in your present state."

"But each twin, whether he saws or not, has one and
only one consciousness," I said, disappointed. "Professor,
your colleagues in America gave me plenty of such metaphors. Including the one about the twins and the saw."

"Of course," said McIntyre, winking at me with his left

eye, and I wondered whether he too had something severed. "My American colleagues are as green as a field of corn and their metaphors are a dime a dozen. I mention the twins one on purpose; it comes from an American and is misleading. If we were to show the brain graphically, yours would resemble a large letter Y, because you still have a homogeneous brain stem and midbrain. It's the downstroke of the upsilon, while the arms of the letter are the divided hemispheres. Do you understand? Intuitively one can see—" the professor broke off with a groan because I kicked him in the kneecap.

"Sorry, it wasn't me, it was my left leg," I said quickly. "I didn't mean to . . ."

McIntyre gave an understanding smile, but there was something forced about it, like the grimace of a psychiatrist who pretends that the madman biting him is a fine fellow. He pulled his chair back a little.

"The right hemisphere does tend to be more aggressive than the left," he said, rubbing his knee. "Would you mind keeping your legs crossed, and arms too? It will make our conversation easier . . ."

"I've tried, but they go limp. Anyway that upsilon business, excuse me, doesn't explain anything. Where is the consciousness—under the division, on it, over it, where?"

"That cannot be precisely determined," said the professor, still massaging his knee. "The brain, Mr. Tichy, is made up of a great number of functional subsystems, which in a normal person connect in various ways to perform various tasks. In your case the highest systems have been permanently disconnected and thus cannot communicate with each other."

"And about subsystems too I've heard a hundred times. I don't want to be impolite, professor, or at least my left hemisphere, the one talking to you now, doesn't, but I'm still in the dark. I walk normally, I eat, read, sleep, the only problem is I have to keep an eye on my left hand and leg because without warning they'll misbehave. What I want to know is *who* is misbehaving. If it's my brain, why am I unaware of it?"

"Because the hemisphere that's doing it is mute, Mr. Tichy. The center of speech resides in the left—"

On the floor between us lay wires from the different instruments McIntyre had used to examine me. I had noticed my left foot playing with these wires. It looped one, thick and shiny black, around its ankle, but I didn't think much about this until suddenly the foot jerked sharply backward and the wire turned out to be wound around the legs of the chair upon which the professor was sitting. The chair reared and the professor crashed to the linoleum. But he was an experienced doctor and disciplined scientist because he picked himself up from the floor and said in an even voice:

"It's nothing. Please don't be concerned. The right hemisphere is the one with spatial ability, so it's adept at this type of function. I would ask you again, Mr. Tichy, to sit well away from the desk, the wires, everything. It will facilitate our deliberation as to the therapy indicated."

"I only want to know where my consciousness is," I replied, freeing the wire from my foot, which wasn't easy because the foot pressed hard on the floor. "Was it I who pulled your chair out from under you, and if not I, then *who?*"

"Your lower left extremity, governed by the right hemisphere." The professor adjusted his glasses on his nose, moved his chair farther away from me, and after a moment's hesitation stood behind the chair instead of sitting down. Which of my hemispheres suspected that the next time he might counterattack?

"We could go on like this until Judgment Day," I said, feeling my left side tense up. Uneasy, I crossed my legs and my arms. McIntyre, watching me carefully, continued in a pleasant voice.

"The left hemisphere is dominant thanks to the speech center. Talking with you now, I'm speaking to it; the right side can only listen in. Its capacity for language is extremely limited."

"Perhaps in others but not in me," I said, holding my left wrist with my right hand, to be safe. "It's mute, yes, but I've taught it sign language, you see. Which wasn't easy."

"Impossible!"

The gleam in the professor's eyes, I had seen it before in his American colleagues, and immediately regretted telling him the truth. But it was too late now.

"The right hemisphere can't conjugate verbs! That's been proved . . ."

"Doesn't matter. Verbs are unnecessary."

"All right, then. Ask it, please, I mean ask yourself, what it thinks of our conversation? Can you do that?"

I put my right hand in the left one, patting it a few times to pacify it, because that was the best way to begin, then made signs, touching the palm of my left hand. Its fingers began to move. I watched them for a while, then, trying to hide my anger, put the left hand on my knee, though it resisted. Of course it pinched me hard on the thigh. I didn't retaliate, not wanting to wrestle with myself in front of the professor.

"Well, what did it say?" he asked, imprudently leaning forward from behind the chair.

"Nothing really."

"But I saw myself that it made signs. They weren't co-herent?"

"Coherent, yes, very coherent, but nothing important."

"Tell me! In science everything is important."

"It said I'm an asshole."

The professor didn't even smile, he was so impressed.

"Really? Ask it about me now."

"If you wish."

Again I addressed my left hand, and pointed at the professor. This time I didn't have to pat it; it replied immediately.

"Well?"

"You're an asshole too."

"Is that what it said?"

"Yes. It may not be able to handle verbs but it can make itself understood. I still don't know *who* is speaking. Speaking with fingers or lips, it makes no difference. In my head, is there an I and an It as well? And if an It, how is it I don't experience what it experiences even though it's in *my* head and part of *my* brain? It's not external, after all. If my consciousness was doubled and everything confused, I could understand that—but this, no. Where did it come from, this It? Is it also Ijon Tichy? And if so, why do I have to speak to it indirectly, by signs, professor? And why does it cause me so much trouble?" No longer seeing any sense in reticence, I told him all about the scenes on the subway and the bus. He was fascinated.

"Blondes only?"

"Mainly. They can be bleached blondes."

"Is this still going on?"

"Not on the bus."

"Elsewhere?"

"I don't know, I haven't tried. I mean, I haven't given

it the opportunity. If you must know, I was slapped several times. It embarrassed and angered me, being slapped, because I wasn't guilty, yet at the same time I was pleased. But once a woman slapped me and the slap landed fully on the left cheek, and when that happened I didn't feel the slightest pleasure. I thought this over and finally figured out the reason."

"But of course!" cried the professor. "When the left-hemisphere Tichy was slapped on the cheek for the right-hemisphere Tichy, the right-hemisphere Tichy was pleased. But when the slap was wholly on the left, it didn't like that at all."

"Exactly. So there is some sort of communication in my unfortunate head, but it appears to be more emotional than rational. Emotions too are experience, though not conscious experience. But how can experience be unconscious? No, that Eccles with his automatic reflexes was all wet. To see an attractive girl in a crowd, and maneuver yourself close to her, and pinch her—that's a whole premeditated plan of attack, not a bunch of mindless reflexes. But *whose* plan? Who thinks it, who is conscious of it, if it's not *mine*?"

"It can be explained," said the professor, excited. "The light of a candle is visible in the dark but not in the sun. The right brain may have consciousness, but a consciousness as feeble as candlelight, extinguished by the dominant consciousness of the left brain. It's entirely possible that—"

The professor ducked, avoiding a shoe in the head. My left foot had slipped it off, propped the heel against a chair leg, then kicked it so hard that the shoe flew like a missile and crashed into the wall, missing him by a hair.

"You may be right," I remarked, "but the right hemisphere is damned touchy."

"Perhaps it feels threatened by our conversation, not fully understanding it or misunderstanding it," said the professor. "Perhaps we should address it directly."

"You mean, the way I do it? That's possible. But what do you want to say to it?"

"That will depend on its response. Yours, Mr. Tichy, is a unique situation. There's never been a person completely sound of mind, and not an ordinary mind at that, who underwent a callotomy."

"Let me make myself clear," I answered, stroking the back of my left hand to calm it because it was starting to move, flexing the fingers, which worried me. "I am not interested in sacrificing myself for science. If you or someone else enters into communication with It—you know what I mean—that could turn out to be harmful to me, let alone damned unpleasant, if, say, it becomes more independent."

"That's quite impossible," declared the professor, a little too confidently, I thought. He took off his glasses and wiped them with a piece of flannel. His eyes did not have that helpless expression of most people who can't see without their glasses. He gave me a sharp look as if he didn't need them at all, then immediately dropped his eyes.

"What happens is always quite impossible," I said, weighing my words. "The whole history of mankind consists of impossibilities, and the history of science too. A certain young philosopher told me that my condition is an impossibility, contradicting all established thought, which says that consciousness is an indivisible thing. The so-called split personality is essentially a consciousness that alternates between different states joined imperfectly by memory and a sense of identity. It's not a cake that can be cut into pieces!"

"I see you've been reading the literature," observed the

professor, putting on his glasses. He added something I
didn't hear. I was going to go on but stopped because my
left hand was putting its fingers into my right palm, making
signs. That had never happened before. McIntyre saw me
looking at my hands and understood immediately.

"Is It speaking?" he whispered as if not wanting to be
overheard.

"Yes."

The message surprised me, but I relayed it:

"It wants a piece of cake."

The joy on the professor's face made my blood run
cold. Assuring the left hand that if it was patient it would
have cake, I said to the professor:

"From your scientific point of view it would be wonderful if It became more independent. I don't hold that
against you, I understand how fantastic it would be having
two fully developed individuals in a single body, so much
to learn, so many experiments to run, and all that. But I'm
not thrilled by the thought of having a democracy established in my head. I want to be less plural, not more."

"You are giving me a vote of no confidence? Well, I
can understand that." The professor smiled sympathetically. "First let me assure you that all this information will
remain confidential. My professional oath of secrecy. Beyond that, I will suggest no therapy for you. You must do
what you believe is best. I hope you'll think it over carefully. Will you be in Melbourne long?"

"I don't know yet. In any case, I'll call you."

Tarantoga, sitting in the waiting room, jumped up
when he saw me.

"Well? Professor . . . ? Ijon . . . ?"

"No decisions have been made," said McIntyre in an
official tone. "Mr. Tichy has various things to consider. I
am at his service."

Being a man of my word, I asked the taxi driver to stop at a bakery on the way, and bought a piece of cake and had to eat it immediately in the car because It insisted, even though I wasn't in the mood for anything sweet. But I had decided, for the present at least, not to torment myself with questions such as *who* wanted the cake, since no one but me could answer a question like that, and *I* couldn't.

Tarantoga and I had adjoining rooms, so I went to his and filled him in on what happened with McIntyre. My hand interrupted me several times because it was dissatisfied. The cake had been flavored with licorice, which I can't stand. I ate it anyway, thinking I was doing it for It, but apparently It and I—or I and I—have the same taste. Which is understandable, in that the hand can't eat by itself and It and I do have a mouth, palate, and tongue in common. I had the feeling I was in a dream, part nightmare, part comedy, and carrying not an infant exactly but a small, spoiled, precocious child. I remembered one psychologist's theory that small children didn't have a continuous consciousness because the fibers of the commissure were still undeveloped.

"A letter for you." With these words Tarantoga brought me out of my reverie. I was surprised: no one knew where I was. The letter was postmarked Mexico City, airmail, no return address. In the envelope was a square of paper with the typed words: "He's from the LA."

Nothing more. I turned the paper over. It was blank. Tarantoga took it, looked at it, and then at me:

"What does this mean? Do you understand it?"

"No. Yes . . . the LA is the Lunar Agency. They were the ones who sent me."

"To the moon?"

"Yes. On a reconnaissance mission. I was supposed to submit a report afterward."

"And did you?"

"Yes. I wrote what I remembered. And gave it to the barber."

"Barber?"

"That was the arrangement. Instead of going to them. But who is 'he'? It must be McIntyre. I haven't seen anyone else here."

"Wait. I don't understand. What was in the report?"

"I can't tell that even to you. It's top-secret. But there wasn't much in it. I forgot a great deal."

"After your accident?"

"Yes. What are you doing, professor?"

Tarantoga turned the torn envelope over. Someone had printed in pencil, inside: "Burn this. Don't let the right sink the left."

I didn't understand it, yet there was some sense in it. Suddenly I looked at Tarantoga with widened eyes:

"I begin to see. Neither message, on the envelope or in the letter, has proper nouns. Did you notice?"

"So?"

"It understands nouns best. Whoever sent this wants to tell me something and not It . . ."

As I was saying this, I pointed to my right temple with my right hand. Tarantoga got up, paced the room, drummed his fingers on the table, and said:

"In other words, McIntyre is . . ."

"Don't say it."

I took a notepad from my pocket and wrote on a fresh page: "It understands what it hears better than what it reads. We'll have to communicate, for a while, in this matter, by writing to each other. My guess is that the things I didn't put into my report to the LA because I couldn't remember, It remembers, and that someone knows or at least suspects this. I won't phone M. or go back to him, because he's probably the 'he' in the letter. He wanted to ask It questions. Perhaps to interrogate It. Please write your reply."

Tarantoga read my note and frowned. Saying nothing, he bent over the table and wrote: "But if he is from the LA, why this deviousness? The LA can contact you directly, no?"

I wrote back: "Among those to whom I turned in NY there must have been someone from the LA. Through him they learned that I found a way to talk to It. But I left before they could try that themselves. If the anonymous letter is telling the truth, the son of the man who was your father's friend was supposed to take over. To find out, without arousing my suspicions, what It remembers. Whereas, if they turned to me directly, officially, I could refuse to submit to such an interrogation, and they would be up a tree because legally It is not a separate person and they would need my consent to talk to It. Please use participles, pronouns, verbs, and avoid simple syntax."

The professor tore out the page I had written on, put it in his pocket, and wrote: "But why is it that you don't want It to know what is now happening?"

"To be safe. Because of what was written inside that envelope. It can't be from the LA because the LA obviously wouldn't warn me about itself. Someone else wrote it."

Tarantoga's reply this time was brief:
"Who?"

"About what is taking place where I was and had the accident, many parties would love to know. The LA has plenty of competition. I believe we should avoid the company of kangaroos. Let's get out of here. It doesn't understand the imperative mood."

Tarantoga took all the pieces of paper from his pocket, rolled them into a ball with the letter and envelope, lit it with a match, and tossed it into the fireplace. He watched the paper shrivel into ash.

"I'm on my way to a travel agent," he said. "And what will you do now?"

"Shave," I said. "This beard itches like the devil and obviously is no longer needed. The faster the better, professor. Maybe there's a night flight. And don't tell me where we're going."

As I shaved in the bathroom and looked in the mirror, I made faces. The left eye didn't even blink. I appeared completely ordinary. When I packed, I looked at my left hand and leg now and then, but they behaved normally. At the last moment, however, as I was putting my ties on top of the folded clothes in the suitcase, the left hand took the green tie with brown dots, a tie I liked though it was quite old, and threw it on the floor. It, apparently, didn't like it. I picked up the tie with my right hand and tried to make the left hand take part of it so we could lay it neatly in the suitcase. What happened next had happened more than once before: the arm obeyed but the fingers didn't. They opened, and the tie fell on the bed.

"Hopeless," I sighed, stuffed the tie into the suitcase with my right hand, and closed the suitcase. Tarantoga appeared in the doorway, showed me two tickets without saying a word, and went to pack.

Did I have reason to fear my right hemisphere? I could think about this without worrying, because It couldn't know what I thought unless I told It by hand signals. Human beings are so constructed that they don't know what they know. What a book contains can be learned from the contents page, but there's no contents page in the head. The head is like a full bag; in order to see what's in it you have to pull everything out, item by item. Groping for a memory in your head is like groping in a bag with your hand.

Tarantoga paid the hotel bill, and as we drove to the airport at dusk and then waited in the terminal, I went over everything that had happened after my return from the Calf, to see how much I could remember. Earth had changed completely. There was total disarmament. Even the superpowers no longer had the money to continue the arms race. The more intelligent the weapons, the more they cost. That was the real reason for the Geneva Agreement. In Europe and in the United States no one wanted to enlist in the army. Men were replaced by machines, but one machine cost as much as a jet plane. Live soldiers surrendered the field to nonliving soldiers, who weren't robots, either, but simply small computers inserted into rockets, self-firing firearms, and tanks like giant bedbugs, flat, because no space was needed for a crew, and if its computer was knocked out, a spare took over. Since command communications were vulnerable to disruption, the machines were made more and more autonomous, and therefore became more and more expensive. I couldn't recall who came up with the idea of moving the arms race to the moon. Not in the form of weapon factories but through the so-called planet machines. These machines had been in use a couple of years for exploring the solar system. Remembering this, I noticed that a number of details were missing. Had I known them before or not? One usually knows, when one can't remember something, whether or not one knew it in the first place, but I didn't. I must have read about the new Geneva Agreement before my mission, but I wasn't sure. The planet machines were built by several companies, mostly American. They were unlike anything industry had produced before. Not factories and not robots but something in between. Some resembled giant spiders. Of course there was a lot of debate, a lot of protests that they shouldn't be armed but used only for mining and that sort of thing, but when it came to transporting the weapons to the moon, it turned out that the countries who could afford it already had self-programming mobile rocket launchers, cannon able to travel underwater, fire-throwers able to travel underground like moles, and laser artillery that could move like tanks and trigger, with salvos of intense radiation, nuclear fusion reactions that would vaporize everything, themselves included. Each country could program on Earth its own planet machines, which were then transported to the moon and placed in their respective sectors by the Lunar Agency, especially created for that purpose. The principle of parity was adhered to, how much of this and that could be put up there, and various international commissions watched over this whole military exodus. Scientists and generals from each country were allowed to verify that their devices were unloaded on the moon and in working order, then they all had to return to Earth together. In the twentieth century such a solution would have been senseless because the arms race wasn't so much a matter of production as of research, innovation, which in those days depended entirely on people. But these new machines worked on a different principle, one borrowed from the natural evolution of plants and animals. These were systems capable of auto-optimization, speciation, and ramification, which means they could change themselves and multiply. I was pleased with myself that I had been able to remember that. Was the right hemisphere of my brain, interested mainly in women's behinds and cake and hating green ties with brown dots, able to grasp such concepts? How could Its memory, then, be of value militarily? But if it wasn't, I reflected, all the worse for me, because I could swear up and down that It knew nothing but no one would believe me. They'd grill It, that is grill me, and if they didn't obtain what they wanted with the signs I taught It they'd use better teaching, better signs, and not let go for anything. The less It knew, the more trouble I was in. My life, even, might be at stake. This was not paranoia. I continued to dig into my memory.

On the moon, the electronic evolution of new weapons was to begin. In this way, despite disarmament, no nation would be defenseless, because it would own a self-perfecting arsenal. And any surprise attack by an enemy, war without declaration, was impossible now, because to commence hostilities a government first had to ask the Lunar Agency for permission to use its sector on the moon. There was no way to hide this, and the side threatened would also apply for permission, and that would begin the return of the means of annihilation to Earth. The whole point was that the moon be inaccessible.

Neither people nor probes could be sent to learn what military capability a given nation had at its disposal. A clever plan, but at first the project met with strong resistance from the generals and politicians. The moon was to be a testing ground and laboratory for military evolution within the sectors allotted to the various nations. The first order of business was to make sure there was no conflict between the sectors. If a weapon developed in one sector attacked and destroyed a neighbor's weapon, that would upset the balance of power. The day such news came from the moon, there would be an immediate return to the previous situation and very likely war, a war conducted with modest means at first but in short order the nations would all rebuild their arms industries. The programs of the moon systems, written by the Lunar Agency in conjunction with multinational commissions, contained locks to keep the sectors from attacking each other, but that protection was considered insufficient. As before, nobody trusted anybody. The Geneva Agreement had not turned men into saints or international diplomacy into a convocation of angels. For that reason, after the transporting was completed, the moon was declared off-limits to everyone. The Lunar Agency itself could not enter there. If a defense program in any of the testing ranges was destroyed or breached, all Earth would know about it in an instant, for each sector bristled with sensors that worked automatically and around the clock. They would sound the alarm if any weapon, even a metal ant, crossed the boundary into the belt that was no man's land. But even this wasn't guarantee enough. The guarantee was the so-called doctrine of ignorance. Each government knew that better and better weapons were being created in its sector, but it did not know their value vis-à-vis the weapons being created in the other sectors. It couldn't know, because the course of any evolutionary process is unforeseeable. This had been proven ages before, but the rigid politicians and generals were unreceptive to scientific argument. It wasn't logic that convinced them; it was the increasing economic ruin caused by the traditional arms race. Even a fool could see that one didn't need a war, nuclear or otherwise, to destroy oneself; the rising cost of weaponry could do that quite nicely. Since disarmament negotiations had been unsuccessful for decades, the moon project seemed the only solution. Every nation could feel it was powerful militarily because of its moon arsenal, but it had no way of knowing how its arsenal compared with those of the other nations. Since no one therefore could count on victory, no one would risk going to war.

The Achilles heel of this solution lay in the monitoring of it. The experts knew from the start that the first thing the programmers of each country would try to do is send to the moon machines capable of neutralizing the monitoring system. Not necessarily by attacking the surveillance satellites directly; it could be a more devious method, one more difficult to detect, such as invading the communication network and falsifying the data transmitted to Earth and the Lunar Agency. My memory of this seemed intact, so I felt calmer as I boarded the plane with Tarantoga. Settling into my seat, I again took to probing what I remembered.

Everyone understood that the peace depended on the monitoring, so the question was how to make the monitoring untouchable. An insoluble problem, it seemed, a *regressus ad infinitum:* One could devise a system to monitor a monitoring system, but that system itself would be vulnerable to attack, so one would have to monitor the monitor of the monitor, and so on, without end. But this dilemma was solved quite simply. They encircled the moon with two surveillance belts. The inner belt guarded the sectors; the outer belt guarded the inner belt. And the trick was: both would be independent of Earth. Thus the arms race could continue on the moon in total secrecy from all countries and all governments. The weapons would evolve, but the surveillance of them would remain unchanged for a hundred years. The whole thing, really, was quite absurd. An unknown arsenal was useless in politics. They should have simply disarmed without bringing the moon into it, but there was no mention of that possibility. Everyone knew where talk of disarmament led: nowhere. In any case, when the idea of demilitarizing Earth and militarizing the moon was accepted, it was clear that sooner or later an attempt would be made to violate the doctrine of ignorance. The newspapers from time to time ran stories under screaming headlines about surveillance machines that vanished upon detecting something; some said they were intercepted by satellites and captured. And governments accused each other of sending probes, but it was impossible to tell their origin because an electronic device is not a person: you can't get anything out of it if it's made properly. But then these anonymous scouts, these space spies, stopped appearing. And the human race sighed with relief, especially because of the economics, the fact that the moon weapons didn't cost a cent now. The energy was furnished by the sun, the raw materials by the moon. Which should also help limit the evolution of weapons, because there are no lodes of metal on the moon.

The generals had expressed the concern that weapons adapted to lunar conditions might not work on Earth. I couldn't recall how the gravity was increased, though they must have explained that to me at the LA. Tarantoga and I were flying BOAC. The night outside the windows was Stygian, and I thought, amused, that I had no idea where we were going. Should I ask Tarantoga? On the other hand, perhaps it would be better if we were to part company. In this awful situation, perhaps I should be silent and fend for myself. A good thing It couldn't read my thoughts. As if I carried an enemy in my head, though of course it was no enemy.

The reason the Lunar Agency, a supranational organization set up by the UN, turned to me? Its double-guard system had worked *too well*. We knew that the borders between the sectors had not been disturbed, but that was all we knew. In certain nervous, imaginative minds rose the specter of an attack upon Earth by the nonliving forces of the moon. The military sectors' inability to exchange information might be only temporary. The sectors might learn to communicate through ground tremors, seismically, making the vibrations in the rock look like natural moonquakes. The self-engineered and self-improving weapons might all join and one day unleash their monstrous power against Earth. Why should they want to do this? How would it benefit a nonliving army to reduce Earth to ashes? It wouldn't, of course, but cancer, everpresent in the organisms of higher animals and human beings, is an inevitable albeit disadvantageous consequence of evolution. People began to talk and write about this lunar cancer, and there were seminars, articles, novels, and films on the subject, and the fear of atomic annihilation, which had been dispelled on Earth, returned in a new form. The surveillance system included seismographs, and certain scientists reported that the frequency of tremors in the moon's crust was increasing, and seismic readings were analyzed for hidden codes, and fear grew. To calm the public, the Lunar Agency said in communiqués that the odds of this happening were one in two hundred million, but no one believed that calculation. The fear finally reached the politicians, and they began to demand periodic inspection of the sectors and not just of their borders. The Agency spokesmen explained that any such inspection could not rule out the possibility of espionage to learn the current state of the lunar arsenals. After long meetings and complex negotiation the LA finally received authorization to reconnoiter.

Reconnaissance, it turned out, wasn't so easy. None of the probes returned. Not a peep from them by radio. Specially armored landers were sent, with television cameras. The observation satellite showed that they indeed landed, and exactly on target, in the Mare Imbrium, in the Mare Frigoris, in the Mare Nectaris, and in the no man's land between the sectors. But not one of them sent back a picture. As if the ground of the moon had swallowed them. Understandably, this caused panic. A state of emergency. The papers urged that the moon be preemptively bombed with hydrogen bombs just to play it safe. But that couldn't happen unless a missile was built and atomic warheads again manufactured. Out of this fear and confusion my mission was born.

We were flying above thick clouds, their mounds tinged with pink from the morning sun still hidden below the horizon. Why, I wondered, did I remember the terrestrial things so well, while remembering so little of what happened on the moon? I knew some reasons. It wasn't for nothing that I'd read all those medical books when I got back. There are two kinds of memory, temporary and permanent. Severing the great commissure does not affect what the brain has already accumulated, but fresh memories evaporate, do not become permanent. What evaporates particularly is what the patient experienced shortly before the operation. Therefore I didn't remember most of what happened to me those seven weeks on the moon, when I went from sector to sector. All that remained in my head was an aura of strangeness, nothing I could put into words, into a report. Strangeness, and yet it was not threatening, or so it seemed to me. No dark conspiracy against Earth. I felt certain of that. But could I swear that what I felt and knew was the whole story? Perhaps It knew more.

Tarantoga was silent, only glancing at me from time to time. As usual on eastward flights, with the Pacific beneath us, the calendar tripped and dropped a day. BOAC was belt-tightening, apparently, because all we got to eat was chicken salad. We landed in Miami. It was early in the afternoon. Customs dogs sniffed our suitcases. We stepped out into the heat. Melbourne had been much cooler. A rental car was waiting for us; Tarantoga must have ordered it in Melbourne. We put our luggage in the trunk and set off down a highway full of traffic, and still said nothing, because I had asked the professor not to tell me our destination. Overcaution, perhaps, but I would stick to that policy until a better one suggested itself. And he didn't need to say anything, because after more than two hours on back roads we arrived at a large white building surrounded by pavilions, palms, and cacti, and I knew at once that my trusted friend had brought me to an insane asylum. Not a bad place to hide, I thought. In the car, I had looked over my shoulder now and then to see if we were being followed, but it never entered my head that I was such an important, valuable person that they would follow me by a method less conventional, not found in any spy novel. From a modern satellite not only can a car be observed but wooden matches counted on a garden table. That never entered my head—more precisely the half of my head that could understand without sign language the mess Ijon Tichy had got himself into.

Briefing

The worst mess in my life. I got into it quite by accident, while trying to see Professor Tarantoga after my return from Encia. He wasn't at home; he'd flown to Australia for some reason. He'd be back in a few days. Since he had a special kind of primrose that demanded constant watering, he asked his cousin to apartment-sit for him. Not the cousin who collects public-toilet graffiti around the world; another cousin, a paleobotanist. Tarantoga has a lot of cousins. I didn't know this one. When I saw that he was in a bathrobe and had just risen from a typewriter, I apologized and turned to leave, but he said no, I wasn't interrupting anything, I had arrived just in time: he was writing a difficult, trail-blazing book and he always liked to marshal his thoughts by telling someone, even a stranger, the idea of the chapter at hand. I feared he was writing some botanical treatise and would fill my head with weeds, bulbs, and perennials, but thank heaven it wasn't like that. It was actually quite interesting. From the dawn of history, he said, in the savage tribes there were unconventional individuals, no doubt considered mad, who tried to eat whatever their eyes fell on: leaves, sprouts, stems, roots both fresh and dried, and all kinds of vegetation. They must have dropped like flies because so many plants are poisonous. Which didn't deter the next generation of nonconformists, who carried on this dangerous work. It is only thanks to them that we know today how to use laurel leaves and nutmeg, that asparagus and spinach are worth the trouble, and that it's better to give wild berries a wide berth. Tarantoga's cousin acquainted me with the fact, ignored by world science, that to find which plant was the best to smoke, these Sisyphuses of antiquity had to gather, dry, ferment, roll, and turn into ash a good forty-seven thousand varieties of leaf before they discovered tobacco, because there was no sign on any sprig or branch that said *this* one will be good for cigars and snuff. Over many centuries whole armies of these prehistoric saints took into their mouths, bit, chewed, tasted, and swallowed everything that grew by a fence or from a tree, and this in every conceivable way, cooked and raw, with water and without, strained and unstrained, and in countless combinations, thanks to which we know today that cabbage goes with pork and beets with rabbit. The fact that in certain regions it's not beets but red cabbage that goes with hare Tarantoga's cousin attributes to the early rise of nationalities. One cannot imagine a Slav, for example, without borscht. Each nationality had its own experimentalists, and when they finally decided on beets, its descendants remained loyal to beets even though their neighbors turned up their noses at that vegetable. Tarantoga's cousin plans to write another book, later, about cultural differences in gastronomy and the influence of national character (the correlation between mint sauce and English spleen, for example, in the case of the loin chop). He will disclose in it why the Chinese, who have been so many for so long, eat pre-chopped food with chopsticks and always have rice.

"Everyone knows," his voice rose, "who Stephenson was and everyone honors him for his locomotive, his steam engine, but what is that banal relic next to artichokes, which will be with us forever? Vegetables do not age like technology . . ." The paleobotanist warmed even more to the subject. Was Stephenson risking his life when he put Watt's steam engine on wheels? Did inventing the phonograph place Edison in mortal danger? They risked at most their families' anger or bankruptcy. How unfair, that inventors of old-fashioned technology are all famous while no one even thinks about the great gastronomical inventors, or about raising a monument to the Unknown Chef as we do for the Unknown Soldier. And yet so many anonymous heroes fell in terrible agony after they made their brave experiments, with mushrooms, for example, where the only way of distinguishing poisonous from nonpoisonous is to eat and wait for the results.

Why are the schoolbooks full of kings who became king for no other reason than that daddy was king? Why do children learn about Columbus, the discoverer of America who discovered it only by accident, on his way to India, while there's not one word about the discoverer of the pickle? We could have managed without America, sooner or later America would have discovered itself, but not the pickle, and then there would have been nothing to sit on our plate beside a roast beef sandwich. No, gastronomy's nameless heroes were more heroic than those who found a soldier's death! A soldier had to charge the enemy trench or face a court-martial, but nobody ever forced a person to brave the danger of an unknown berry. Tarantoga's cousin would like to see a commemorative tablet over the door of every restaurant, with the inscription MOR-TUI SUNT UT NOS BENE EDAMUS.

The telephone rang. Tarantoga's cousin handed me the receiver, saying it was for me. I was surprised, because no one knew about my return from the stars. It was someone from the office of the Secretary General of the UN. He had called Tarantoga for my address, and the cousin short-circuited the call, as it were, by giving the phone to me. Dr. Kakesut Wahatan, plenipotentiary extraordinaire and adviser on global security, wanted to see me as soon as possible. We made a date for the next day. I jotted the time into my notebook, having no idea what I was getting myself into. But I was glad for the call, because it had interrupted the flood of eloquence from Tarantoga's cousin, who wanted to tell me next about spices and pepper. I took my leave, saying I had to go and promising (insincerely) that I'd drop in again soon.

Tarantoga told me later that the primroses died: his cousin, in his paleobotanical-gastronomical fervor, forgot to water them. A common phenomenon: he who devotes himself to the general does not concern himself with the particular. Thus the meliorists who would make the whole world happy but have no time for an individual.

I wasn't told straight off that I would be asked to risk my neck for humanity by flying to the moon to see what those intelligent weapons were up to. Dr. Wahatan received me with smiles, coffee, and old cognac. He was Asian, a perfect Asian, because I learned nothing from him: he knew how to keep a secret. The Secretary General, he said, intended to read me, but being so very busy, he wondered if I could recommend the ten books I felt were the most important. Seemingly by coincidence, a couple of people dropped by and asked me for my autograph.

It was hard to refuse. The talk turned naturally to robots, to the moon, but the moon mainly in its historical role: as a decoration in romantic literature. I learned much later that this was no normal conversation but a screening for security clearance, because the armchair in which I sat so comfortably was riddled with sensors that analyzed my reactions, through microscopic changes in muscle tension, to such key stimulus words as "moon" and "robot." The diagnostic situation since I left Earth for the Calf constellation had reversed itself: I was evaluated by computer, my human interlocutors serving only to gather data. The next day, I went again to the UN office, I don't know exactly why, and then they invited me again. They kept wanting to see me; I began having lunch with them in the cafeteria, which wasn't bad, but the reason for these appointments remained unclear. There was talk about the United Nations publishing my collected works in all the languages of the world: more than four and a half thousand languages. I am not a vain man, but that seemed like a good idea to me. These new acquaintances all turned out to be fans of my *Star Diaries*. They were Dr. Rorty, Engineer Tottentanz, and the brothers Cybbilkis, identical twins whom I learned to tell apart by their ties. Both mathematicians. The older, Castor, worked in algomathematics, which is the algebra of conflicts that end fatally for all parties. (This branch of game theory is sometimes called sadistics.) The other Cybbilkis, Pollux, was not a sadistician but a statistician and had the curious habit of suddenly interrupting a conversation with such questions as "How many people on earth at this very moment are picking their nose?" A phenomenal calculator, he could come up with answers to such things instantly. One of the four was always waiting for me in the vestibule as big as a hangar to take me to the elevator. We went either to the Cybbilkis' workshop or to

Professor Jonas Kuschtyk, who also loved my books and quoted from them, giving the page number and year of publication. Kuschtyk (like Tottentanz) worked with telefer theory, a new field of remote robotics. The telefer slogan: "Where a man can't go, a remote can." Kuschtyk and Tottentanz urged me to try remoting. It's quite an experience to have all your senses connected by radio to a machine.

I was willing. It was only much later that I realized they weren't Ijon Tichy fans at all but had read me strictly in the line of duty. Their task, with many other Lunar Agency people (whom I won't mention so as not to immortalize them), was to pull me gradually into the Mission. Why gradually? Because I could refuse, after all, and go home, taking with me all the secrets of the Mission. And what if you did? asks someone from the audience, a heckler. Would that be the end of the world? The point is yes, possibly, it would. The person selected from thousands by the Lunar Agency had to be both extremely capable and extremely loyal. Capable we understand, but loyal? And loyal to whom, to the Agency? Yes, inasmuch as it represented the interests of humanity. No nation or coalition of nations could be allowed to learn the results of the lunar reconnaissance, assuming it succeeded, because whoever knew the state of the weapons there first would gain, by that strategic information, immediate supremacy on Earth. The peace, in other words, was far from idyllic.

So the friendly scientists who let me play with the remotes as a child with a toy were actually dissecting my mind, that is, the computers were, invisible but analyzing our every conversation. Castor Cybbilkis, with his surrealist ties, was there as a theoretician of disastrous endgames, because precisely such a game was being played with me, against me. In order to accept or reject the Mission, I first had to learn about it, but then if I rejected it or if I ac-

cepted, returned, and then divulged the results of the re-
connaisance, known only to me, it would create a situation
the algomathematicians called pre-catastrophic.

The candidates were of different nationalities, races,
professions, and accomplishments. I was one of many
though I had no idea of that. The person selected would
be a delegate of humanity, not a spy—or potential spy—
for any country. His code name would be Missionary. But
I was kept in the dark as much as possible. When they
finally made me Missionary and I had crawled into the
rocket for the nth time only to crawl back out two hours
later in my space suit bristling with wires and tubes because again something had gone wrong during countdown,
I finally had time to think about the past few months and
put two and two together. I understood now the game the
LA had been playing with me for the highest possible
stakes. If not the highest for humanity and the world, certainly the highest for me: I didn't need algomathematics
and game theory to see that the simplest way for them to
ensure secrecy in this situation was to do away with the
pilot immediately after his return to Earth, as soon as he
made his report. Knowing that they *had* to send me now,
since I had shown myself to be the best of the candidates,
I told this to my dear colleagues, the Cybbilkis brothers,
Kuschtyk, Blahouse, Tottentanz, and Garraphizi (more
about Garraphizi later) who along with a few dozen communications technicians would be the ground support for
my selenological expedition, that is they would be for me
what Houston was for Armstrong and Co. during the
Apollo mission. To make those hypocrites as uncomfortable as possible I asked them if they knew who would take
care of me after my return as a hero—the Lunar Agency
itself or a hired gun?

That's what I said, in those exact words, to see their

reaction. If they had considered *that* scenario, they would understand me immediately. They froze. It made quite a picture: the small area in the cosmodome called the Waiting Room, with its Spartan décor—coke machines, card chairs, metal tables covered with bilious green plastic— and I in my angel-white space suit, my head under my arm (actually my helmet, but that's how you say it: your head's under your arm when you're ready to fly), and facing me, my loyal comrades, scientists, doctors, engineers. I think it was Castor who spoke first. That it wasn't their doing, it was the equation, the computer, because if you looked at the thing mathematically, abstractly, the solution to the problem of ensuring secrecy did not take into account any coefficient of ethics, and I was insulting them all by suggesting, at such a moment, that *they* were in on it.

"I've heard that before," I answered. "Blame it on the computer! Sure, sure. But forget ethics for the moment. I know, you're all saints and I'm one too. But didn't any of you, the computer included, think of *this?*"

"Of *what?*" asked a hangdog Cybbilkis.

"That I might suspect, and might confirm my suspicion, as I've done just now. Surely that will affect the equation of my loyalty . . ."

"Oh of course that was taken into account," said the other Cybbilkis. "It's the ABC of algomathematical statistics: I know that you know that I know that you know that I know. The infinite series of conflict theory."

"Very well," I said, getting interested in the scientific aspect of the thing. "Then how did it work out for you in the end? Does or doesn't the confirmed suspicion affect my loyalty?"

"It does," admitted Castor Cybbilkis reluctantly. "But the second derivative of the curve of your loyalty after a scene like *this one* (taking place as we speak) shows a leveling off to zero."

"Aha." I scratched my nose, shifting the helmet from my right arm to my left. "So that what is *now* happening *decreases* the mathematical expectation of reduction of my loyalty?"

"It decreases it," he said. And his brother added, looking at me both kindly and searchingly: "You yourself probably feel . . ."

"Exactly," I muttered, realizing, not without surprise, that they were right, they or the computer, in this psychological calculation: my indignation had noticeably diminished.

The green light went on over the exit to the launch pad and all the buzzers sounded, indicating that the problem had been corrected and I was to get in the rocket again. I turned without a word and walked, they in attendance, and as I walked I thought. I'm getting ahead of myself here, but I have to finish. After I left stationary earth orbit and they couldn't touch me, when they asked me how I felt, I answered fine, and that I was considering whether I shouldn't make friends with the "nation" of the moon in order to give a few people I knew on Earth a good kick in the pants. How hollow was their laughter in my earphones . . .

But that came later, after my trips to the simulated lunar testing range and the visit to Gynandroics. That corporation has greater earnings than IBM, even though it began as a small subsidiary of the company. I should explain here that Gynandroics, contrary to popular belief, doesn't manufacture robots or androids, if by those terms we mean humanlike machines endowed with human intelligence. It's practically impossible to put a human mind in a machine.

The computers of the eightieth generation and beyond are more intelligent than we, but their minds bear no resemblance to a human being's. Man is a highly illogical creature and therein lies his humanity. He has reason, yes, but it is heavily polluted with prejudices, emotions, and attitudes carried from childhood or the genes of the mother and father. That's why a robot passing for a person (over the telephone, for instance) is fairly easily unmasked. Nevertheless the porn industry put a limited line of S-dolls on the market, S for sex. These didn't catch on; they were too logical, too intelligent; a man going out with one would end up with an inferiority complex. And they were expensive. Why pay $90,000, not counting local taxes, when you could have a natural partner for much, much less? The real revolution in the sex market was caused by remotes, or "empties," dolls also fashioned in the image of humans but brainless, brainless not in a pejorative sense but literally: the remote woman and the remote man were empty shells operated at a distance by humans.

By putting on a suit that pressed hundreds of electrodes to the skin, anyone could link with a male or female remote. Little did people dream how this technology would change their lives, especially their sex lives. From marriage to the oldest profession in the world. The courts were faced with unprecedented problems, legal dilemmas. The law didn't recognize intimate relations with a doll as grounds for divorce. Whether stuffed or inflated by a bicycle pump, whether with automatic transmission or without, it didn't matter; that was no more adultery than if a person was cohabiting with a chest of drawers. But teleferic products forced judges to determine whether or not a married individual entering into a liaison with a male remote or a female remote was thereby committing adultery. The concept of "remote adultery" was the subject of heated debate not only in the legal journals but also in the daily press. And adultery was just the tip of the iceberg. Can you deceive your wife, for example, with her own self but younger? A certain Adlai Groutzer ordered from the Boston branch of Gynandroics a remote of his wife at age twenty-one, not fifty-nine, her actual age. A further complication was that when Mrs. Groutzer was twenty-one, she wasn't Mrs. Groutzer at all but the wife of James Brown, whom she divorced twenty years later to marry Adlai Groutzer. The case went all the way to the Supreme Court. A ruling also had to be made as to whether a wife who wouldn't operate the remote bought by her husband, for sex, was refusing him his conjugal rights. And whether remote incest was possible, and remote sadism and masochism. And remote sodomy. One company put out a line of dolls with modular private parts, so that you could quickly switch from male to female or even have it both ways. Among the customers of Gynandroics were quite a number of elderly prostitutes, no longer able to ply their trade; their years of experience made them masters, by remote, of the art of love. But the technology wasn't limited to the erotic in its application. Take for example the twelve-year-old schoolboy who, receiving a poor grade for spelling errors in composition, used his father's muscular remote to beat the English teacher to a pulp and break all his furniture. This remote, called Body Guard, sold like hotcakes. It was kept in the garden shed to protect the family from burglars. The boy's father wore electrode pajamas to bed, and when the alarm went off, signaling the presence of an intruder, he could deal with the culprit or even culprits without having to get out of bed, because the remote would hold them until the police arrived. The son borrowed his father's pajamas while his father was out. I had also seen picketing and street demonstrations against

Gynandroics and comparable Japanese companies. The protesters were mostly women. In the few states where homosexuality was still against the law, legislators were trying to decide whether a homosexual, in love with a man who was not, was breaking the law if he sent him a female remote which he, the homosexual, was operating. When the Supreme Court finally ruled that relations *per procura* (with the aid of a remote) lay within the lawful bounds of matrimony provided both parties consented, the Kuckerman case came up. Mr. Kuckerman was a traveling salesman; Mrs. Kuckerman ran a beauty salon. They spent little time together: she couldn't leave the salon, and he was on the road a lot. They agreed to intermediate their union, but couldn't agree whether it should be by remote-husband or remote-wife. The Kuckermans' neighbor brought down upon himself the wrath of both when he suggested, trying to be helpful, that they compromise and use a teleferic *pair:* a remote husband with a remote wife seemed to him a Solomonic solution to the problem. The Kuckermans considered it idiotic and insulting. They had no idea that their argument, after it appeared in the papers, would lead to a phenomenon called teleferic piggybacking—because a remote, too, can put on an electrode suit and operate another remote, and so on ad infinitum. The idea was received with enthusiasm by the underworld, because it is as easy to find the operator of a remote as it is to locate a radio transmitter. The police had no problem solving teleferic burglaries and murders. But if the perpetrator remote was operated by another remote, by the time you got to the second remote the criminal, the human, had broken radio contact with his "middleman" and left no clues.

The catalogs of Telemate and Sony offered remotes from Lillputians to King Kongs, as well as famous people-in-history remotes, uncanny re-creations of Nefertiti,

Cleopatra, and Queen Navarra, not to mention movie stars. In order to avoid lawsuits for "resemblance to persons living or dead," anyone wanting a copy of the First Lady in his closet, or his neighbor's wife, availed himself of a mail-order unassembled model. The customer, in the privacy of his own home, could put together the Playmate of his choice, following the instructions. Narcissists ordered their own likeness. The legal system could not handle the flood of new cases, moreover it became clear that one could not outlaw remotes as one outlawed the manufacture of drugs or atomic bombs by private individuals, because the remotes were already big business and indispensable, besides, in agriculture, technology, and science, including astronautics. It was only by remote, after all, that a man could land on such planets as Saturn or Jupiter. Remotes were also used, of course, for mining and for rescuing people in the mountains and during earthquakes and other natural disasters. The Lunar Agency had a special contract with Gynandroics for moon remotes. I would soon learn that they had indeed used them in project LEM, but with results as mystifying as they were catastrophic.

Chief Engineer Paridon Sawekahu showed me around the Gynandroics plant. Tottentanz and Blahouse were with me. Engineer Sawekahu complained about the new legal restrictions that hampered the firm's research and development of prototypes. And banks, he said, were now putting sensors at their entrances to detect remotes, but that was only the half of it. The banks, of course, feared remote robbery. But instead of using a simple alarm they employed thermoinduction. The remote, as soon as it is recognized, is blasted with high-frequency waves, which cause its wires to melt and turn it into scrap. And the customers complain not to the banks but to Gynandroics. Also, there have been attacks, with bombs even, on trucks carrying remotes, especially attractive females. Engineer Paridon said his firm suspected the women's liberation movement for these acts of terrorism but at the moment it had nothing that would hold up in court.

I was shown the whole production process, from the welding of the duraluminum skeletons to the covering of the "chassis" with fleshlike material. Most of the remotes are produced in eight sizes. A custom-made model costs twenty times more. Remotes don't have to resemble people, but the more different they are from a human build, the harder they are to control. A prehensile tail would be an excellent safety feature for remotes working at great heights, installing cables on suspension bridges for example, but a man has nothing with which to operate a tail. Then we drove in a small electric car (because of the size of the place) to the warehouses, and there I saw planetary and lunar remotes. The greater the gravity, the harder it is to build a remote, because a remote too small cannot accomplish much, and one too big, powered with big engines to make it move, will weigh too much.

We returned to the assembly hall. If Dr. Wahatan of the UN had been a diplomatic Asian, with a politely restrained smile, Engineer Paridon was an enthusiastic Asian: his bluish lips never closed, and when he smiled, he showed all his perfect teeth.

"Do you know, Ijon, what the team from General Pedipulatrics and its robots couldn't manage? Walking on two legs! They flopped because their prototype kept flopping over! Good, eh? Ha, ha, ha! Gyroscopes, counterweights, double feedback in the knees—nothing helped. Of course we have no problem there, a man balances his remote naturally!"

I watched the female remotes coming down the conveyor belt, their skin as rosy-white as a baby's. One after another they were taken by other belts to the packing area, so that we stood under a line of naked women moving steadily over our heads, inert but their long hair swinging as though it were alive. I asked Paridon if he was married.

"Ha, ha, ha! You make a joke, Ijon! I have a wife and children, of course. A shoemaker doesn't wear the shoes he makes. But we give our workers one a year as a bonus."

"What workers?" I asked. There were none in the hall. On the assembly line worked robots painted yellow, green, and blue, their articulated arms extending like geometric caterpillars.

"Ha, ha, ha! In the office we still have a few people. And in the sorting room, the control room, the packing department. Uh-oh, a reject! The legs are not quite right. Crooked! Would you like to try one, Ijon? No charge, you can have a week, and we deliver."

"No, thanks," I said. "I'm not the Pygmalion type."

"Pygmalion? Ah yes, of course, George Bernard Shaw! I see the allusion. True, some find it repugnant. But you must admit, it's better to make women than war! Eh?"

"There are still objections," I said. "I saw the picket line at the gate."

"Yes. An ordinary woman just can't compete with one who's remote. In life, beauty is the exception to the rule, but with us it is the norm! The marketplace, supply and demand, yes, that's the way of the world . . ."

We visited the dressing room, which was full of rustling skirts and lingerie and women busy with scissors and tape measures, not very attractive but then they were only live, and I said goodbye to Engineer Paridon, who accompanied me to the parking lot. Tottentanz and Blahouse were strangely quiet on the way back. I didn't feel like talking either. The day, however, was not finished.

On my return home I found a fat envelope in my mailbox. It contained a book with the title *The Unhumanization of Weapon Systems in the Twenty-first Century* or *Upside-down Evolution*. The author's name, Meslant, told me nothing. It was a heavy book, full of graphs and tables. Having nothing better to do, I sat down and began to read. On the first page, before the introduction, was an epigraph in German:

> *Aus Angst und Not*
> *Das Heer ward tot.*
> —Eugen von Wahnzenstein

The author presented himself as an expert in contemporary military history. His subject, the new pacifism at the close of the twentieth century: it was prosperity and cowardice that gave birth to the unhumanization of war. People were increasingly reluctant to be fired upon, and this loss of martial spirit was directly proportional to the standard of living. The youth of wealthy nations weren't interested in the noble motto *Dulce et decorum est pro patria mori.* And it was just at that time that prices began falling in the intellectronics industry. Microprocessing elements called *chips* were replaced by *corn,* the product of the genetic engineering of a culture of artificial microbes, mainly *Silicobacterium logicum wieneri,* named after the father of cybernetics. A handful of these elements cost no more than a handful of barley. Thus artificial intelligence grew cheap, yet the price of new weapons increased geometrically. In the first world war a plane cost as much as a car, in the second as much as twenty, and by the end of the century it was six hundred times more. It was calculated that in seventy years a superpower would be able to afford from eighteen to twenty-two planes. The falling curve of the cost of intelligence and the rising curve of the cost of weapons intersected, and at that point began the unhumanization of the armies. The military became unliving. At which juncture the world went through two crises. The first was when the price of oil soared, the second when shortly thereafter it plunged. The classic rules of economics went out the window, but few understood what was happening, or that the image of a soldier in uniform and helmet charging with bayonet was becoming as distant as the medieval knight in armor. Out of inertia the engineers continued to make big-gauge weapons for a while: tanks, cannon, carriers, and other fighting machines to be used by men, though already these could have gone into battle themselves, without them. Then followed a phase of accelerated miniaturization. Until now all weaponry had been fashioned to fit man: Tailored to his anatomy and physiology, so that he could kill and be killed.

As is usually the case in history, no one saw what lay ahead, for the discoveries which were to make possible the unhumanization of weapons took place in fields of science far from one another. Intellectronics produced microcomputers as cheap as grass, and neuroentomology finally solved the riddle of social insects who live and work together, communicating in their own language, even though bees, for example, have a nervous system 380,000 times smaller than a human brain. The intelligence of a bee is quite sufficient for a foot soldier, as military prowess and intelligence are two different things, at least on the battlefield. The major factor in the push for miniaturization was the atom bomb. The need to miniaturize came from simple facts, but facts that lay outside the military knowledge of the day. Seventy million years ago a huge meteor hit Earth and chilled its climate for centuries, making the dinosaurs defunct but hardly bothering insects and not even touching bacteria. The lesson of paleontology was clear: the greater the destructive force, the smaller the systems that escape it. The atom bomb required the *particularization* of both soldier and army. But in the twentieth century the idea of making soldiers the size of ants was only a fantasy. You could not reduce people in size or diffuse them. So thought was given to robot soldiers, humanoid, though even then that was a naive anachronism. Industry was un-humanizing itself, but the robots who replaced workers on the assembly line were not made in the likeness of men; they were, rather, human *parts* selected and enlarged: a brain with a big steel hand or a brain with eyes. But giant robots had no place on an atomic battlefield. So radioactive synsects (synthetic insects) were developed, and ceramic shellfish, and titanium worms able to burrow in the earth and come out after the blast. Flying synsects were airplane, pilot, and missiles all in one tiny entity. The operational unit became a *microarmy*, fighting only as a whole, much as a swarm of bees acts as a unit to survive while an individual bee is nothing. Thus microarmies of many kinds were made, on two opposing principles. An army based on the principle of independence proceeded like a column of ants or a cloud of germs or hornets. An army based on the principle of *teletopism*, however, was an enormous flying or crawling collection of self-assembling elements; according to need, tactical or strategic, it could reach its target in extreme attenuation only to condense there into its pro-grammed whole. The simplest example was the self-dis-persing atomic warhead. An ICBM could be tracked, from space by satellite or from Earth using radar; but it was im-possible to detect a cloud of infinitesimal particles of ura-nium or plutonium at very low density, which finally would converge and reach critical mass at its target, a factory or an enemy city.

For a while the old and new weapons coexisted, but the massive machines soon succumbed to the invisible micro. As germs secretly enter an animal organism and kill it from within, so did these unliving microbes penetrate cannon barrels, shell chambers, the engines of tanks and planes, and eat through metal, and detonate the ammunition inside. What could a brave, grenade-carrying soldier do against a microscopic, unliving adversary? He would be like a doctor trying to fight a virus with a hammer. Against an autonomous cloud programmed to destroy all things biological a man in uniform was as helpless as a Roman legionary standing with sword and shield before a rain of bullets.

Even in the twentieth century the tactic of fighting in closed ranks was replaced by the spreading out of troops, but there were still front lines. Now there were none. Microarmies easily penetrated all defenses. Nuclear weapons were ineffective combatting that viral contagion. The cost of a warhead, moreover, cannot be considerably greater than the value of its target. One doesn't use a destroyer to go after leeches.

The most vexing problem in this unhumanized stage of man's struggle with man turned out to be that of telling friend from foe. In the past it had been done by electronics, using the password principle. Challenged by radio waves, a plane or missile either transmitted back the correct answer or was attacked. This twentieth-century method became obsolete. Now the makers of arms borrowed from the plants and animals, from bacteria. For the recognition process they imitated the ways of living species: immune systems, the duel of antigen and antibody, tropism, mimicry, protective coloration, camouflage. A microweapon might pretend to be an innocent microorganism, or the fluff of a plant, a piece of pollen, but beneath that exterior lay corrosive death. The significance of informational combat also increased—not in the sense now of propaganda but as the invasion of enemy communications, to paralyze it or, as in the case of the atomic locust-cloud, to force premature condensation to critical mass before it reached its target. The author of the book discussed the cockroach, which was the prototype for one kind of micro-soldier. On its abdomen the cockroach has very fine hairs. When they are moved by the air, the insect flees, because these sensors are wired directly to its rear nerve ganglion, and they can distinguish between a draft and the distur-bance caused by a predator.

As I read, I felt pity for the champions of uniforms, flags, and medals for bravery: the new era of warfare must have been anathema to their high ideals. The author used the term *upside-down evolution,* because in the beginning of life there were microscopic systems which slowly changed into larger systems, while this military evolution proceeded the other way, microminiaturization, and the great human brain was replaced by mechanical insect ganglia. Microar-mies arose in two steps. First, the designers and builders were still human; then the unhumanized divisions were conceived, battle-tested, and put into mass production by computer systems that were equally nonhuman. People were eliminated from the military and then from the weap-ons industry by a phenomenon called "sociointegrational degeneration." The individual soldier underwent degener-ation: he became smaller and simpler. In the end he had the intelligence of an ant or termite. But the *collective* of these tiny warriors assumed a greater role. The nonliving army was far more complex than a beehive or ant hill; it was more like a biotope in nature, an ecosystem, a subtle equilibrium between competitive, antagonistic, and symbi-otic species. A sergeant or corporal in such an army obvi-ously had nothing to do. To grasp the whole picture, merely to inspect the troops, not even the brain power of an entire university would suffice. Thus officers as well as poor Third World countries did not fare well during the great military revolution of the twenty-first century. The irresistible momentum of army unhumanization destroyed the lofty traditions of maneuvers, marches, drills, changing the guard, and regalia. For a while but alas not for long, it was possible to preserve the highest ranks for people, but the strategy-computational superiority of the computerized echelons of command finally put even the most corpulent leaders, including four-star generals, out of work. A chest of ribbons and medals was no protection from early retirement. These officers, facing permanent unemployment— for they could do nothing else—revolted, forming an underground terrorist movement. The crushing of this revolt with the use of microspies and minipolice built on the abovementioned cockroach principle was a grim chapter in our history, because neither cover of dark nor mist nor any kind of camouflage could save those desperate traditionalists loyal to the ideas of Achilles and Clausewitz.

As for the poor countries, they could go on fighting as before, using live people, but only against opponents as anachronistic as themselves. Those who couldn't automate militarily had to sit quietly in the corner.

But it wasn't fun for the rich countries either. The old political games went out the window. The line separating war and peace, having long been blurry, was now completely erased. The twentieth century had dispensed with the formal declaration of war and introduced the fifth column, sabotage, cold war, and war by proxy, but that was only the beginning. Summit meetings for disarmament pursued mutual understanding and a balance of power but were also held to learn the strengths and weaknesses of the enemy. The world of the war-or-peace alternative became a world in which war was peace and peace war. First wide-range subversive activity was conducted under the mask of official peace: the infiltration of political, religious, and social movements, even such worthy movements as those to protect the environment; the infiltration also of the culture and mass media, taking advantage of the illusions of the young and the conservatism of the old. Then covert military activity intensified to the point of being overt, except that it was invisible. Acid rain had been known in the twentieth century; now rain fell that was so corrosive, it destroyed the roofs of houses and factories, roads, electrical lines, but no one knew whether this was pollution or the enemy sending poison clouds their way. It was thus with everything. Farm animals died in epidemics that could have been natural or intentional. A storm that flooded the coast might have been an act of God or the clever redirection of a hurricane at sea. A drought—a normal disaster, or one caused by the secret switching of heavy clouds with light. With seismic, meteorological, and epidemiological counterespionage and reconnaissance the scientists had their hands full. More and more of the scientific community became involved with intelligence work, yet the results of their research grew less and less clear. The tracking down of saboteurs was child's play in the days when they were human; but now, when the suspect was a hurricane or hailstorm, or a crop or cattle disease, or the rise in infant mortality or cancer rate, or even a meteor (the twentieth century had already considered the idea of aiming an asteroid at enemy territory), life became intolerable. Intolerable not only for the man on the street but also for heads of state, who were helpless and confused, and their advisors no less. The military academies added new courses such as cryptotactics, cryptocountering (that is, taking counterespionage to the nth power), crypto field theory, and finally cryptocryptics, the secret study of the secret use of secret weapons indistinguishable from natural phenomena.

To blacken the enemy, one could fake a natural disaster in one's own country—in a way that made it obvious it was not natural. Also it was proved that certain rich nations, helping those less fortunate, put a drug into the supplies of wheat, corn, and cocoa it sold (cheaply), which caused impotence. This was, then, a secret war of birth control. Although the catastrophic consequence of such escalation was obvious—wherein victory was equivalent to defeat for both sides—the politicians continued with business as usual, concerned more about the voters than the future, making fuzzy promises and being increasingly less able to affect the course of real events. War was peace, not from Orwell's totalitarian doublethink but because of a technology that erased the boundary between natural and artificial in every aspect of human life and its environment.

Where there is no difference, wrote the author, between natural and artificial protein or between natural and artificial intelligence, misfortunes caused deliberately cannot be distinguished from those caused by no one. Just as light that falls into a black hole cannot pull itself out of that gravitational trap, so humanity at war, reaching the secrets of matter, cannot leave the trap of technology. It wasn't the governments, heads of state, monopolies, generals, or pressure groups that made the decision to invest everything in the new arms, it was fear, fear that the Other Side would discover, invent, and develop first. Traditional politics were useless. Negotiators could negotiate nothing, because the offer to give up a new weapon only meant, for the other side, that you had a weapon that was even newer. I turned to a mathematical model of conflict theory which showed why further summit meetings were a waste of time. At such meetings, agreements were reached. But it took longer to reach an agreement than for a new development to change radically the situation on which that agreement was based, thus making it an immediate anachronism. The act of reaching an agreement, then, was an empty game of appearances. This was what compelled the world powers to accept the Geneva Agreement: an exodus of weapons to the moon. The world breathed a sigh of relief, but not for long, because fear returned—now as the specter of the nonhuman invasion of Earth by the moon. So there was no task more urgent than to pierce the mystery of the moon.

With these words the chapter ended. There were a few dozen pages left in the book, but they wouldn't turn. As if they were glued. Stuck together with bookbinder's glue, I thought. I couldn't separate them, so finally I took a knife and slid it carefully between the pages. The first page was blank, but where the knife touched it, letters formed. I rubbed the paper with the knife until I obtained the following message: "Are you ready to assume this burden? If not, put the book back in the envelope! If yes, turn the page!"

The next page was also blank. I ran the blade from top to bottom and eight numbers appeared, in groups of two with hyphens between them like a telephone number. I separated the remaining pages but there was nothing on them. "A curious way to recruit Savers of the World!" I thought. At the same time I began to suspect what lay in store. I closed the book but it opened again by itself at the page with the numbers. Nothing was left for me but to pick up the phone and dial.

In Hiding

It was a private loony bin for millionaires. Somehow you never hear about insane millionaires. A movie star or a statesman or even a king can go insane but not a millionaire. At least not judging from the newspapers which put revolutions and the fall of governments in small print buried in the middle of the paper but on the front page they tell you absolutely everything about the mental state of a practically naked young woman with big breasts, or a snake that crawled up a circus elephant's trunk, causing the animal to go on a rampage in a supermarket and crush three hundred cans of Campbell's tomato soup along with a register and one checkout girl. An insane millionaire would be welcome in a paper like that. But millionaires don't like publicity whether they're insane or not. Insanity might help a movie star's career but not a millionaire's. A movie star doesn't even have to have acting ability, or a voice, they can dub in another, and her real face can be totally unlike her posters and films, the main thing is to have "it," and she'll have "it" if she's getting divorced again or buys a convertible upholstered with ermine or poses nude for *Playboy* or has an affair with a pair of octogenarian Quaker Siamese twins. Today a politician too must have a great voice, a great smile, and a great body to win voters over the television. But millionaires can only be hurt by such things, not to mention the market. A millionaire has to be calm, predictable, and reserved. Any unpredictability better be hidden. And because it has become extraordinarily difficult to hide from the press these days, millionaire asylums serve as invisible fortresses, invisible because inconspicuous: there are no uniformed guards, no slavering dogs on leashes, no barbed wire, for that only whets a reporter's appetite. Such an asylum should look uninteresting, and above all it will never call itself an insane asylum. The asylum I found myself in was supposedly for people with ulcers and bad hearts. How then, you ask, did I know straight off that it was a loony bin?

We weren't allowed inside until Dr. House, a trusted colleague of Tarantoga's, came to get us. He asked if I wouldn't like to take a little walk in the park while he talked with Tarantoga. So I felt sure he assumed I was insane. Apparently the professor hadn't had time to fill him in, because we left Australia in such a hurry. House deposited me among flower beds, fountains, and hedges, and our bags were whisked away by two attractive women in elegant suits who didn't look at all like nurses, which also set me thinking, but the clincher was when a potbellied old man in pajamas, seeing me, moved over so I could sit beside him on the lawn swing, which I did, to be polite. We swung back and forth in silence for a while, then he asked if I wouldn't mind urinating on him, though he put it more crudely. I was so taken aback that instead of refusing I asked him why. This agitated him. He got up and walked away, limping on his left foot and muttering to himself, probably about me. I looked around the park, glancing now and then at my left hand and foot, as you might at a pure-bred dog that you've recently been given and that has already bitten a few people. The fact that they were behaving themselves now, swinging quietly with me, was not at all reassuring. I remembered the events of the last few days and thought that in my head another mind lurked side by side with mine, a mind also mine yet inaccessible, which was worse than schizophrenia because you can be cured of that, and worse than the disease of St. Vitus because there all that can happen is that you dance, while I was condemned to a life of mad antics within. Patients were walking along the paths, some followed at a distance by an electric golf cart, probably in case the patient got tired. Finally I hopped off the swing to see if Dr. House had finished talking with Tarantoga and that's how I met Kramer. He was riding piggyback on an elderly servant dripping with sweat and blue in the face because Kramer must have weighed two hundred and fifty pounds. I felt sorry for the servant but said nothing and stepped aside to let them pass, figuring that in my present situation I shouldn't involve myself. Kramer, however, slid off the old man and introduced himself. Evidently interested in a new face. I couldn't remember what my last name was supposed to be at the asylum though Tarantoga and I had agreed on one. All I could remember was the first name, Jonathan. Kramer liked my informality and asked me to call him Adelaide.

He grew talkative. He'd been terribly bored since his depression lifted. The anguish had kept him from being bored. His depression, he explained to me, resulted from his inability to fall asleep if he first didn't lie in bed and fantasize a while. In the beginning he pictured the stocks he bought going up and the ones he sold plummeting. Then he pictured having a million dollars. When he got a million, he pictured two, then three, but after five it lost its charm. He had to find new ground for his imagination. It was not easy, he said with a sigh. You can't fantasize about what you already have or can obtain right away. For a while he pictured getting rid of his third wife without paying a cent in alimony, but then he managed to do just that. House still didn't appear, and Kramer had got his hooks into me. For a while he used people he was mad at to fall asleep. But that was a mistake because such fantasizing fired up the hate inside him and then he had to take sleeping pills to fall asleep, but the doctors said he shouldn't on account of his enlarged liver, so the only way then to get rid of the hate was to get rid of the objects of it. No, of course he didn't hire some Mafia hit man, that kind of thing is strictly for the movies. He hired a real professional, and a hundred thousand dollars a throw was nothing. No, not killing, when you kill someone, you can't really do anything to him. Nor did he derive any particular satisfaction from physical torture. An enemy or a competitor should be ruined, shown pity, and that's the end of it. It's like a corporate raid on the personal level. Kramer had an intellectual side, too, which he concealed from his fellow millionaires, he read books, even de Sade. A sad case, that! Fantasizing about impalement, flaying, and disembowlment while he sat in a hovel with nothing to pick on but flies. The poor have it easy! Everything lures the poor man, everything appeals to him. Every beautiful woman is beyond his reach. Which is why the porn industry does so well. Pneumatic women with pouting fat-lipped mouths, detailed descriptions of orgies plus special oils and paraphernalia, it's all surrogate and silly. Orgies are so tiresome anyway, there's nothing to talk about, nothing left to fantasize about. Oh to have an unfulfillable longing! Adelaide shook his head and said that he had foolishly cut off the branch he sat on by settling those old scores. Now, having nothing to dream about, he suffered from chronic insomnia. He hired a professional fantasist, probably a writer or poet. The man did come up with a few passable ideas for him, but a good fantasy compels its realization and after that it's gone, so they had to be all but impossible. I interrupted to say that that shouldn't be so hard. Move a continent. Saw the moon into four equal parts. Eat the leg of the President of the United States in Chinese duck sauce (I pulled out all the stops, after all I was talking to a madman). Have intercourse with a firefly at the moment of its brightest light. Walk on water, become a national holiday, change places with God. Pay the terrorists to leave ministers, ambassadors, and company executives alone and go after the people who really deserve it.

Adelaide was looking at me now not only with fondness but also with admiration. "A pity we didn't meet sooner, Jonathan," he sighed. "You're on the right track, but, you see, with continents and moons and miracles there's no personal involvement. A true fantasist's emotions have to be engaged. And fireflies don't do anything for me. But a good fantasy isn't really a matter of lust or fury, it's like a rainbow, it's there and not there, and then you fall asleep. During the day I never had time for rainbows. My writer expert stated that the number of one's possible fantasies is inversely proportional to the amount of one's liquid assets. For him who has everything dreams are no longer possible. Change places with God? God forbid! But I would have hired you anyway."

On the broad leaf of a low needleless cactus was a large slug. An ugly thing, and that was no doubt why Adelaide nodded to his servant. "Eat that," he said, pointing. At the same time he pulled a checkbook and pen out of his pajama pocket.

"How much will he do it for?" I wondered. The servant put out his hand for the slug but I stopped him.

"I'll give you a thousand dollars more than Mr. Kramer if you *don't* eat it," I said, taking my notebook from my pocket. It was covered with the same green plastic as Adelaide's checkbook.

The servant froze. In the face of the millionaire was hesitation, and I didn't know whether or not we would start bidding now. My resources were certainly no match for Kramer's. So I had to change tactics.

"How much will *you* eat it for, Adelaide?" I asked, opening my notebook as though I were about to write a check. This delighted him. The servant was no longer in the picture.

"I'll give you a blank check if you swallow it without chewing and describe to me how it moves in your stomach," he said in a hoarse voice.

"Unfortunately I had breakfast already and I don't eat between meals," I said with a smile. "Anyway your bank account must be controlled by trustees."

"No, you're wrong! Chase Manhattan always honors my checks."

"Perhaps, but I'm not hungry. Let's return to fantasies." This conversation had so absorbed me that I forgot all about my left side but it reminded me. We were moving away from the slug of contention when I tripped the millionaire and at the same time chopped him in the neck so that he fell flat on the grass. I relate this in the first person though it was my left foot and left hand that did it.

"Forgive me," I said, thinking quickly, "but *that* was my fantasy." I helped him up. He was not so much offended as stunned. It was obvious no one had ever treated him like that, either here or before the asylum.

"A clever fellow," he said, brushing off the dirt. "But don't do that again, because I might slip a disk. And start fantasizing about *you*." He laughed an evil laugh. "So what is wrong with you?"

"Nothing."

"Yes, of course, but why are you here?"

"To get a little rest."

I saw Dr. House at the far end of the shady path. He lifted his hand, beckoned for me, then turned and went toward the pavilion.

"I have to go, Adelaide," I said, slapping him on the back. "We'll fantasize another time."

From the open door came the pleasant coolness of air conditioning. The walls were pale green and the place as quiet as pharaoh's tomb, with a thick carpet white like the fur of a polar bear. Dr. House was waiting for me in his office. Tarantoga was there too and seemed embarrassed. In his lap was a briefcase stuffed with papers which he sorted through while House pointed to an armchair. I sat down with a sinking feeling that I was getting into something I would not be able to get out of in one piece.

Dr. House sat at his desk reading a newspaper. Then Tarantoga finally found what he had been looking for.

"This is how it is, Ijon . . . I saw two attorneys, two of the best, to assess your situation from the legal point of view. I said nothing about your Mission, of course, and sketched your story only in the most general terms. A man gains access to certain highly secret information and must report it to a certain division of the government, but he is callotomized before he can do this, and part of what he learned is forgotten, residing no doubt in the right hemisphere of his brain. What is his duty now? What steps can the government take legally to retrieve the information? Both lawyers said it is a difficult case because it sets a precedent. If it is decided in court, expert witnesses will have to be called in, though their testimony might or might not be ignored. In any case without a subpoena you cannot be subjected to any examination or experiment, if that's the route the government wishes to take."

Dr. House raised his head from his paper.

"An amusing case," he said, taking a bag of ginger cookies from a drawer, sliding them onto a plate and pushing the plate in my direction. "I realize, Mr. Tichy, that you are not amused, but every paradox of the *circulus vitiosus* variety is amusing. Do you know what lateralization is?"

"Of course," I answered, frowning as my left hand reached for a cookie that I didn't want at all. But wanting even less to make a fool of myself, I bit into it. "I've read plenty about it. In the average man the left hemisphere is dominant because it governs speech. The right is generally silent though it understands simple sentences and sometimes can even read a little. If left lateralization is not strong, the right hemisphere may be more independent and also have more linguistic ability. In rare cases there is almost no lateralization and then the centers of speech are found in both hemispheres, which can cause stuttering and other problems . . ."

"Very good." House smiled at me approvingly. "From what I have been told I would conclude that your left brain, as we sometimes call it, is distinctly dominant, but that the right is unusually active. To be certain of this, though, I would need to examine you at length."

"Where is the paradox?" I asked, trying inconspicuously to avoid my left hand because it was putting more ginger cookies into my mouth.

"The value of questioning your right brain depends on

the degree of your right lateralization. We must first determine that degree, which means examining you, but to examine you we need your consent. In other words, the court experts could not go beyond what I am saying now: that the court's decision depends upon the extent of the lateralization of Ijon Tichy, but that cannot be determined without examination. One must examine you to decide whether you can be examined. Do you understand?"

"Yes. What do you advise me to do, doctor?"

"I cannot advise you to do anything, because I am in the same boat as the court and the experts. No one in the world, including you, knows what your right brain holds. Your idea to use sign language has been done before but without significant results, because the right lateralization in those cases was too weak."

"And that's really all you can tell me?"

"You might put your left arm in a sling or better yet a cast. It betrays you."

"What do you mean?"

Dr. House pointed at the plate of ginger cookies.

"The right brain usually likes sweets more than the left. There have been statistical studies. I wanted to show you how simply someone could establish your lateralization. As a right-handed person you would have reached for the cookies with your right hand—or not at all."

"But why should I keep my arm in a cast? What good would that do?"

Dr. House shrugged.

"Very well. I shouldn't say this but I will. You know about piranha?"

"The small carnivorous fish."

"As a rule they don't attack a man in the water. But if he has the least cut, one drop of blood is enough for them to attack. The language skills of the right brain are no greater than those of a three-year-old child, and usually less. With you, they are considerable. If that fact gets out, you are in serious trouble."

"Perhaps he should just go to the Lunar Agency," said Tarantoga, "and put himself in their hands. They owe him something, since he risked his neck for them . . ."

"That may not be the worst solution, but it is not a good one either. There is no good solution."

"Why?" Tarantoga and I asked.

"Because the more they extract from the right brain, the more they'll want, which could mean, to put it politely, a long isolation."

"A month? Two?"

"Or a year or more. Normally the right brain communicates with the world through the left, in speech and writing. It has never happened that the right has learned, and fluently, a whole language. But the stakes are so high in your case that they will put more effort into this area of research than all the specialists combined have done to date."

"Yet we must do something," muttered Tarantoga.

Dr. House rose. "True, but not necessarily today. At the moment there's no hurry. Mr. Tichy may stay here if he likes, for a couple of months. Perhaps in that time things will become clearer."

Too late I learned how right Dr. House was.

Since no one can help me better than I myself, I have written down everything that has happened, read it into a tape recorder, burned all the notes, and now will put the recorder and the cassette in a jar and bury them under the cactus where I met the slug. I am speaking now to use up the end of the tape. The expression "I met the slug" seems wrong somehow. You can meet a cow, or a monkey or an elephant, but hardly a slug. Could this be because you can meet only a party who is able to take notice of you? I doubt that the slug noticed me although it moved its little horns. It's not a question of size. No one says "I met a flea," on the other hand one can meet a very small child. Why am I using the end of the tape for such nonsense? I'll bury the jar and from now on write notes in a code I've thought up. I'll call my right hemisphere It or maybe Andi, which is *and I,* I and I, but maybe that's too transparent. The tape ends now and I'm reaching for the shovel.

JULY 8TH / An awful heat wave. Everyone's in pajamas or a bathing suit. Me too. Through Kramer I've met two other millionaires, Sturman and Padderhorn. Melancholiacs both. Sturman is about sixty, jowly, a big belly, bowlegs, and he whispers. Gives the impression that he's telling secrets. He says his is a hopeless case. His depression worsened recently because he can't remember why he got depressed in the first place. He has three daughters, all married and unfaithful, and photographers send him flagrante delicto photographs and he has to pay them off. Trying to be of help, I suggested that this might be the cause of his depression but he said no, he was used to it. I really don't know why I'm putting this down. It's not very interesting. Padderhorn doesn't talk. Supposedly he merged with a Japanese company and it soured. A dull group. Gagstein's the worst. He chuckles and drools. And exposes himself. I must avoid these characters. Dr. House tells me that tomorrow someone is coming whom I can trust as I trust him. A young intern, but in reality he's an ethnologist and writing a work on millionaires in the context of small-group dynamics or something like that.

JULY 9TH / Tarantoga has left and I am now alone with House, his assistant, and the millionaires who wander the park. House told me privately that he prefers not to learn the extent of my right lateralization because what is not known cannot be stolen. The assistant revealed to me after I swore I was no millionaire that he is doing field-work. He is studying the customs and attitudes of million-aires just as one might study the beliefs of a primitive tribe. The young ethnologist and I have had long evening con-versations over a bottle of Teachers in the small laboratory, using beakers for glasses. I've also met a few other Croe-suses. The most boring people in the world. The ethnolo-gist agrees with me. He begins to fear that he will not be able to gather enough data here.

"You know what?" I told him. "You could do a com-parative study: The Rich Then and Now. The state or foundations as patron of the arts is a recent phenomenon. In ancient Rome the patrons were private citizens. The protectors of art, muses, and so on. Rich men and princes took care of artists, sculptors, and painters. They took an interest. But these ones"—I pointed out the window with my thumb at the park, which was dark in the night—"are interested in nothing but market quotations. Take me, for example: I am fairly well known. Because of my travel books I've received a ton of letters, but among my millions of readers there has not been one millionaire. Why is that? Most millionaires, I'm told, live in Texas. We have three of them here. Even as lunatics they're boring. What is the reason? The Roman rich were intellectually alive, but these are not. What did this? The market? Money? And how?"

"No, it's something else. The rich of old were believ-ers. They wanted to serve God, but without mortifying the flesh. Building a cathedral or supporting a painter, making a *Last Supper* possible or a *Moses*, or something big and splendid with a spire, in that they saw a dividend, Mr. Ti-chy, for they saw Him in it," and he pointed to the ceiling, the sky. "And others followed their example. It became the thing to do. A prince, doge, or magnate surrounded himself with gardeners and coachmen, scribblers and painters. Louis XV hired Boucher to do portraits of naked women. Boucher's third-rate, of course, but his work has survived, while the coachmen and gardeners have left nothing."

"The gardeners produced Versailles."

"The point is that those rich didn't understand art but thought it was in their interest. Today, in the age of specialization, they couldn't care less . . . What's wrong? A chest pain?"

"No. I think I've been robbed."

My hand was in fact on my heart, because the inside pocket of my jacket was empty.

"Impossible. There are no kleptomaniacs here. You must have left your wallet in your room."

"No. I had it in my pocket when I came in. I know because I was going to show you a picture of me with a beard."

"But there's no one else here, and I haven't even come near you . . ."

I had the glimmer of an idea.

"Please tell me exactly what I did from the time we entered."

"You sat down, and I took the bottle from the cupboard. What were we talking about then? Kramer. You told me about the slug, but I wasn't watching you, I was looking for clean beakers. When I turned, you were sitting . . . no, standing. Next to the tachistoscope. Over here. You were looking into it when I gave you your whiskey . . . We drank, and you went back to where you are sitting now."

I got up and looked at the apparatus. A chair, a console, a black partition with a pair of eyepieces, side lamps, a screen, and the box of a projector. I turned on a switch and the screen lit up. I looked behind the partition: oxidized black plates. Between the partition and a black plate was a space no wider than a letterbox slot. I tried to get my hand in but it was too narrow.

"Any tweezers around here?" I asked. "As long as possible . . ."

"I don't know. I don't see any. Here's a piece of wire."

"Let's have it."

I twisted it into a hook, let it down into the crack, and touched something soft. After a few unsuccessful tries, a black leather corner appeared. I needed my other hand to grab it, but the hand refused. The young ethnologist helped me retrieve my wallet.

"It's It," I said, lifting my left hand.

"But how? Didn't you feel anything? And for what reason?"

"No, I didn't notice. And it wasn't easy, either, because the pocket is on the left side. It was done nimbly, delicately, like a professional thief. But that's the speciality of the right brain, coordination, in games, in sports. For what reason? I can only guess. It's a nonverbal intelligence, logical but a bit childish. Perhaps in order that I lose my identity. With no identifying papers or cards a man is nameless to those who do not know him."

"Ah . . . to make you disappear? But that is magical thinking."

"Yes. And it's not good."

"But It only wants to help you. Which is not surprising, after all It is *also* you. Though a little isolated."

"This is not good because Its wanting to help me means that It believes something is threatening me in this situation. We can laugh now, but the next time . . ."

House came to see me later that evening. I was sitting

on the bed in my pajamas inspecting my left calf, which had a bad bruise.

"How are you feeling?"

"Fine, but . . ."

And I told him about the wallet.

"Curious. You really felt nothing?"

Then I saw the bruise and remembered. As I had looked into the tachistoscope, my left leg hit against something hard. It hurt, but I paid no attention. That's when the pocket must have been picked.

"Most interesting," said Dr. House. "The left hand cannot perform complicated movements without alerting the muscles on the right side of the body. Therefore it was necessary to distract you."

"With this?" I indicated the bruise.

"Precisely. The left hand and left foot worked together. When you felt the pain, you felt nothing else in that moment, and a moment was enough."

"Does this sort of thing happen often?"

"It is extremely rare."

"But what if someone wanted to get at me—could he use the same trick? For instance, stab me on the right so the right wouldn't interrupt while the left was being interrogated?"

"A professional would do it differently. An injection of Amytal in the left carotid artery, and the left brain goes to sleep while the right is awake. It lasts a few minutes."

"And that's sufficient?"

"If not, you insert a little tube into the artery and give the Amytal in drops. After a while the right hemisphere falls asleep too, because the brain arteries are connected by the so-called collaterals. Then you have to wait a while before you can begin again."

I rolled down my pajama leg.

"I don't know how long I can sit here waiting for I don't know what. A little knowledge is better than none. Why don't you handle it, doctor?"

"But can't you do this yourself? You've found a way to communicate between one hand and the other. Have you learned anything by that method?"

"Very little."

"Does It refuse to answer questions?"

"Rather, Its answers are incomprehensible. I know only this: It remembers in a different way. Perhaps in whole pictures, whole scenes. But when It tries to put it in words, riddles result. Possibly everything should be recorded in order and treated as a kind of symbolic shorthand."

"More a task for a cryptographer than a doctor. Suppose you took such notes. What would that give you?"

"I don't know."

"Neither do I. And on that note I'll say good night."

He left. I turned out the light and lay down but couldn't sleep. I lay on my back. After a while my left hand raised itself and several times, slowly, patted my cheek. Evidently it felt sorry for me. I got up, took a Seconal, and with both Ijon Tichys extinguished I sank into oblivion.

My situation was not only bad, it was idiotic. Hiding in an insane asylum without knowing from whom. Waiting without knowing for what. I tried talking to myself by hand but although It answered more willingly than before, I couldn't understand It. I rooted through the asylum library and filled my room with textbooks, monographs, and piles of professional journals to find out once and for all who or what I was on my right hemisphere's side. My hand answered, making a clear effort to be cooperative, and it even learned new words and expressions which encouraged me to question further and at the same time made me uneasy. What if It became my equal or even passed me? Then I would not only have to take It into account but listen to It or maybe it would even come to a tug of war where I would not remain in the middle but be torn in two forever and struggle like a stepped-on beetle, some of whose legs pull forward while others pull back. At night I dreamed about escaping and wandering among dark crags and didn't even know which half of me was dreaming it. What I found out from the pile of books is true: the left brain, deprived of contact with the right, grows colorless, its language becomes dry which you can tell by the infrequency of adjectives. Reading over some of my notes, I saw that that was happening to me. But aside from such details I learned nothing from the publications of the experts. There were a lot of hypotheses but none of them fit me, and I got furious with these scientists who claimed to know better than I did what it was like to be me doubled. One day, I was ready to abandon all caution and go to New York, to the Lunar Agency, but the next morning that seemed to be the last thing I should do. I hadn't heard from Tarantoga and even though I'd asked him to wait for a sign from me, his silence too began to irritate me.

Finally I decided to pull myself together like the old, whole Ijon Tichy. I would go to Berlin, a small town about two miles from the asylum, to buy a typewriter so I could cross-examine my left hand and type its answers until I had enough of them to see if there was any sense there. It was possible of course that I was a right-sided moron and it was only my personal vanity that kept me from seeing this. Blair, Goddeck, Shapiro, Rosenkrantz, Bombardino, and McCloskey held that in the muteness of the right hemisphere lay an unplumbed depth of talent, intuition, instinct, perhaps even a kind of genius, for this region contained all the wonders that left-handed rationalism refused to acknowledge: telepathy, clairvoyance, the traveling of the spirit to other planes, and visions, and states of mystic transport and enlightenment. But Kleist, Zuckerkandel, Pinotti, Veehold, Meyer, Ottitchkin, Nüerlö, and eighty other experts said nonsense. Yes, a sounding board, an organizer of emotions, an associative system, an echo chamber of thought, and perhaps some memory, but nothing that could be put in words, for the right brain was a nonlogical freak, an eccentric, a dreamer, a boaster, a hermit, a soul but in the raw state, it was flour and yeast but only the left brain could bake the bread. And a third opinion ran thus: the right was the engine, the left the steering mechanism. The right was therefore at a distance from the world and so had to be led, translated into human speech, commented upon, disciplined, and made into a person by the left brain.

House offered me the use of his car. He was not surprised by my plan and did not try to dissuade me. On a scrap of paper he drew a map of the main street and made a cross where the department store was. But I wouldn't make it today, he said, because it was Saturday and the store closed at 1:00. I spent all Sunday in the park avoiding Adelaide. On Monday I couldn't find House anywhere so I took the bus that left every hour. It was nearly empty: the black driver, and two children licking ice-cream cones. The town, a few miles from the asylum, was an old-fashioned American town. One wide street, houses with low hedges, gardens, fences, mailboxes, telephone poles, and a couple of larger buildings at the corner. A mailman stood talking to a fat, sweaty man in a flowery shirt whose dog, a big shaggy mongrel, was lifting its leg on a lamp post. I got out not far from them, and when the bus drove off in a cloud of foul smoke, I looked for the department store Dr. House had told me of. It was on the other side of the

street, large and with big windows. Two employees in uniform were loading boxes by motor cart onto a truck. The
sun beat down. The truck driver, sitting with his door
open, drank beer from a can, not his first because there
were empty cans at his feet. He was a black man completely white-haired though his face was not old. On the
sunny side of the street walked two women, the younger
pushing a baby carriage with the top up, the older peering
into the carriage and saying something. Despite the heat
she wore a black wool shawl over her head and shoulders.
The women passed a car repair shop with its doors open
and a couple of shining cars inside, you could hear the
whoosh of water and hiss of air. I noted all this as I stepped
from the curb to cross the street to the department store.
I stopped because a long dark-green Lincoln that was
parked about fifty feet away suddenly moved in my direction. The front windshield was so tinted I couldn't see the
driver. I got back up on the curb to let him pass but he
braked sharply in front of me. I thought he wanted to ask
me something, but someone grabbed me from behind and
covered my mouth with his hand. I was so surprised that I
didn't even try to defend myself. A man sitting in the back
seat opened the car door, and I started to struggle but I
couldn't make a sound. The mailman dived at us and
grabbed me by the legs. Then there was a sharp crack and
in an instant the whole scene changed.

The old woman dropped her shawl on the sidewalk
and turned to us. She held a short machine gun with both
hands and fired a volley at the car, putting holes in the
radiator and tires. The white-haired black man, not drinking beer now, was behind the wheel and with one sharp
turn his truck blocked the Lincoln's way. The shaggy mongrel sprang at the old woman but fell writhing to the as-
phalt, meanwhile the mailman let go of me, jumped back,

took from his bag something round and black, and hurled it at the women. There was a boom and white smoke and the young woman fell to her knees behind the baby carriage which opened up and started shooting a column of foamy liquid like a huge fire extinguisher at the driver of the Lincoln who had jumped out onto the sidewalk. Before the foam covered him I saw that he was not a black man but only wore a black mask and held a revolver. The stream hit the windshield of the limousine with such force that the glass shattered and some of it hit the mailman. The fat man who gripped me from behind all this time retreated, protecting himself with my body. From the garage several people in overalls ran out and pulled him off me. All this took no more than five seconds.

One of the cars inside the garage backed out and two men in smocks threw a net over the driver of the Lincoln, taking care not to touch him as he was covered with gluey foam. The fat man and the mailman, now handcuffed, were pushed into this car. I stood staring as the man who had opened the rear door of the Lincoln got out slowly with his hands up and walked obediently to the truck where the white-haired black man put handcuffs on him. No one even spoke to me. The car drove away. The truck holding the driver who'd been shot and his accomplice also pulled away, and the woman picked up the black shawl, brushed it off, put the machine gun back into the carriage, raised its hood, and walked on as if nothing had happened. The street was again quiet and empty. Only the large limousine with flat tires and broken headlights plus the dead dog were proof that I hadn't dreamed this.

Next to the department store was a low wooden house with a porch and a garden full of sunflowers. A sunburned gentleman, his hair so blond it was almost white, stood in the open window with his elbows comfortably on the windowsill and a pipe in his hand. He gave me a quiet but eloquent look that seemed to say: "You see?" Only then did I become aware of something that was even stranger than the kidnapping attempt: though my ears still rang with the shots, the screams, and the explosions, not a single window had opened and no one was looking out into the street—as if I was on an empty movie set. I stood there for a good while, not sure what to do. Buying a typewriter no longer seemed important.

The Lunar Agency

"Mr. Tichy," said the director, "our people will fill you in on the details of the Mission. I would just like to give you the general picture—so you don't miss the forest for the trees. The Geneva Agreement made four impossibilities possible. A continuing arms race at the same time as universal disarmament—that's one. Arming at maximum speed and at no cost—that's two. Full protection of each nation against surprise attack while each reserves the right to wage war—that's three. And finally the liquidation of all armies despite their continued existence. No troops, but the staffs stay on and can think up anything they like. In a nutshell, we've instituted *pacem in terris*."

"True," I remarked. "But I read the papers. They say we've gone from the frying pan into the fire. That the moon is silent and swallowing all probes because Someone has been able to enter into a secret understanding with the robots there. That an unnamed nation is behind everything that's now happening on the moon. And that the Agency knows this."

"Pure drivel," said the director. We were sitting in his enormous office. On a platform at one end stood a huge globe of the moon covered with its smallpox of craters. The sectors of the different nations, colored green, rose, yellow, and red like a political map, went from pole to pole, making the sphere look like a child's toy or illuminated glass orange without its peel. On the wall behind the director hung the flag of the United Nations.

"There's a lot of that now," he said with a pitying smile on his swarthy face. "The press prints it all, and it's all nonsense."

"But that movement, those neopacifists, the lunarians, don't they exist?"

"Oh yes. Have you read their statement? Their program?"

"I have. They call for negotiation with the moon . . ."

" 'Negotiation!' " the director snorted with contempt. "Not negotiation, capitulation! And nobody knows to whom! Those muddled heads think the moon has become a party, that it can enter into agreements and pacts, that it's intelligent and powerful. That up there now is some giant computer that has devoured all the sectors. Fear not only has big eyes, Mr. Tichy, it has a small brain."

"Yes, but can we really rule out the possibility of some sort of unification of all those weapons up there—of those armies, if they are armies? How can we be sure this hasn't happened, if we are in the dark . . . ?"

"Because even in the dark we know that certain things are impossible. The sector of each country was installed as a self-evolving testing range. Take a look." He held a small flat box. The different sectors of the moon lit up, until the globe was as bright as a Chinese lantern. "The larger areas belong to the superpowers. Of course we know what we put there: the Agency acted as transporter, after all. We also dug the foundations for the simulators. Each sector has two simulators surrounded by a production compound. The sectors cannot fight each other; it's impossible. One simulator designs new weapons and the other works to counter them. Both are computers programmed on the sword-and-shield principle. It's as if each nation put on the moon a computer that played chess with itself. Except that the game is played with weapons instead of chess pieces and everything can change: the moves, the pieces, the board, everything."

"You mean," I asked, surprised, "there's nothing up there but computers simulating an arms race? Then how is this a threat to Earth? Surely the simulation of a weapon no more dangerous than a piece of paper . . ."

"Oh no! The weapons that survive selection go into real production. The whole problem is *when*. You see, the simulators design not just a new weapon but a whole new system of warfare. These are, of course, nonhuman systems. The soldier becomes one with the weapon. Think of natural evolution, the struggle for existence, Darwin. One simulator designs, say, a kind of predator, and the other finds its weakness in order to destroy it. Then the first simulator thinks up something new, and the second parries that too. In principle a contest like this, with endless improvements, could go on for a million years—but each sector after a certain time must begin actual production of the weapons. The time—and the effectiveness required of the prototypes—was determined in advance by the programmers of each nation. Because each nation wanted to have an arsenal of real weapons on the moon, not just simulations like blueprints on paper. Therein lies the rub, the contradiction. Do you understand?"

"Not entirely. What contradiction?"

"Simulated evolution proceeds much more swiftly than natural evolution. He who waits longer obtains the better weapon. But for as long as he waits, he is defenseless. While the one who accepts a shorter simulation run will obtain his weapon sooner. We call this the coefficient of risk. Every nation, placing its military might on the moon, had to decide first whether it wanted better weapons later or poorer weapons sooner."

"Curious," I said. "And what happens when sooner or later production begins? The weapons are stockpiled?"

"Some of them, perhaps. But only some. Because then an actual, not a simulated, battle begins—of course only within the given sector."

"Something like maneuvers?"

"No. On maneuvers the fighting is an exercise, soldiers don't die, whereas there"—the director pointed to the colorful moon—"genuine combat is taking place. But always within the borders of each sector. Neighbor cannot attack neighbor . . ."

"So the weapons attack and destroy each other in the computer first, and then for real. And what then?"

"Good question! No one knows. There are basically two possibilities. Either the arms race reaches a limit or it doesn't. If it does, this means 'an ultimate weapon' exists and that the simulated arms race has finally arrived at it. The weapon cannot defeat itself, and thus ensues a state of permanent equilibrium. An end to progress. The lunar arsenals fill with that weapon, which has passed the final test, and nothing more happens. This is what we would like."

"But it isn't so?"

"Most likely not. In the first place, natural evolution has no end. It hasn't because no 'ultimate' organism exists, that is, one which is perfect in survivability. Every species contains a weakness. Secondly, the evolution on the moon is artificial, not natural. And it's certain that each sector monitors what is happening in the others and reacts to that in its own way. Military equilibrium is different from biological equilibrium. A living species must not be too successful in its struggle against competitors. Why? Germs that are too virulent kill all their hosts and so perish with them. Therefore in Nature equilibrium is set at a point *below* annihilation. Otherwise evolution would be suicidal. But research and development in weapons seeks to crush the enemy. Weapons have no instinct of self-preservation."

"Just a minute," I said, taken by a sudden thought. "Each nation could in secret build for itself the exact same computer complex on Earth as the one it put on the moon, and by watching the copy, it would know what the original was doing . . ."

"Ah, no," said the director with a sad smile. "That is not possible. The course of evolution cannot be foreseen. We learned this the hard way."

"How?"

"As you said. We used identical computers in our research lab and identical programs and let them go. Plenty of evolution, but divergent. It's as if you wanted to predict the outcome of a chess tournament in Moscow between a hundred grand-master computers by simulating the games on a hundred identical computers in New York. What would you learn about the Moscow games? Absolutely nothing. Because no player, man or computer, always makes the same moves. Of course the politicians wanted us to provide them with such simulators, but it didn't give them anything."

"But if nothing so far has helped and all your probes

disappeared like stones in water, how can I hope to succeed?"

"You will have devices no one has had before. My assistants will give you the details. Good luck . . ."

For three months I wore myself out on the training instruments at the Lunar Agency and I can tell you that at the end of it I knew telematics like the palm of my hand. It's the art of operating by remote. You have to strip completely and pull on an elastic suit a little like a wet suit but thinner and shining like mercury because it's made of wires lighter than a spider's web. They're the electrodes. They cling to the body, transmitting the electrical changes in your muscles to the remote which uses them to repeat exactly your every movement. That's not odd, the odd part is that you not only see with the eyes of the remote but you feel what you would feel if you were in its place. If it picks up a stone, you feel the shape and weight as if you had it in your own hand. You feel every step, every stumble, and when the remote bumps into something too hard, you feel pain. I thought that was a malfunction, but the chief of my training program, Dr. Lopez, told me it has to be that way. Otherwise the remote will be constantly damaged. If the pain is great, you can disconnect the channel, but it's better to lower the intensity with the modulator instead so you don't lose contact with the remote. A person in an artificial skin loses all sense of himself and identifies entirely with the remote. I trained on different models. A remote doesn't need to be man-sized or -shaped; it can be smaller than an elf or larger than a Goliath but that causes certain problems. If instead of legs it has, say, a tractor tread, you lose the feeling of direct contact with the ground, a little like driving a car or a tank. When the remote is enormous, you have to move very slowly because its limbs might weigh several tons each and possess no less inertia on the moon than on Earth. I experienced this with a two-hundred-ton remote and it was like walking underwater. But such a remote presents a target the size of a tower. I also used tiny remotes resembling insects. It was quite amusing, but from that vantagepoint every pebble is a mountain and it's hard to get your bearings. The heavier moon remotes were grotesque. Squat, with short legs to keep the center of gravity as low as possible. My LEM maintained its balance better than a man in a spacesuit because it didn't totter, and the arms were long like an orangutan's. Those arms turned out to be useful in twenty-meter leaps. I particularly wanted to hear which models had been used in the previous reconnaissance attempts and how they had functioned. To brief me on those unsuccessful expeditions my tutors had to get special permission from the director because all this was top-secret. The whole Mission was top-secret and so was the fact that the earlier ones had failed. The point was not to fan the flames of panic which was spread by the press with its speculations. Central Control gave me the cover of adviser to the Lunar Agency and I had to avoid journalists like the plague. I was finally able to interview the two reconnaissance pilots who had returned in one piece but I never laid eyes on them, talking with them by telephone. Each had changed not only his name but also his face so that his own mother wouldn't recognize him.

The first pilot reached the zone of Radio Silence with no difficulty and went into stationary orbit some two thousand miles above the Mare Nubium, sending down an armored remote that landed in a completely deserted region. It was attacked before it took a hundred steps. I tried to get some details out of him, but he just repeated the same thing. The remote was walking alone on the flat plain of the Mare Nubium, having first checked the area in a radius of several hundred kilometers and detecting nothing suspicious, when an enormous robot, at least twice the size of the LEM, appeared to one side, very close, and opened fire. There was a blinding, silent flash and that was all. The pilot photographed the place from orbit afterwards, and there beside a small crater lay the remains of the remote, melted into a lump of metallic slag.

Around it was nothing but the empty plain.

The second pilot had two remotes but one began somersaulting after it left the ship and broke up on the rocks. The other one was a double, called twins. Twins are a pair of telemates operated by one person. They do everything in tandem, one staying a hundred meters behind the other to see what attacks it. Both were protected moreover by micropes, which are microscopic cyclops, a sort of television camera made of a swarm of sensors no bigger than flies and each equipped with a minuscule lens. The whole cloud of micropes accompanied the twin remotes at an altitude of a mile above the surface of the moon in order to keep them and their surroundings too in sight. The pilot operates the remote but the micropes send their pictures directly to Central Control on Earth. The result of all this careful planning was miserable. Both remotes were destroyed in the same moment, with hardly time for them to stand straight in the lunar dust. The pilot told me they were attacked by two robots of singular build, low to the ground, humpbacked, and extremely pudgy. These appeared out of thin air and took immediate aim. He lifted his gun but didn't have time to pull the trigger. He saw a blue-white flash, laser for sure, and found himself back on the ship. He photographed the remains of the remotes, and Control confirmed his report. The remotes had become incandescent as they were hit by a laser of great power, but the source of the beam could not be determined. I watched the film of what the micropes recorded and also examined pictures of the last moment, magnified to the maximum. The computer analyzed the image of every stone in a radius of two kilometers which is the lunar horizon because you can only go in a straight line with a laser. It was mystifying. The two remotes landed well, not even staggering, and began marching one after the other in slow motion, when suddenly they lifted their guns as one man, though the camera showed nothing, and opened fire, and were hit, one in the chest, the other a little lower. The bolts of light blew them apart in a cloud of dust and burning metal. Although the pictures were analyzed from every angle, it was impossible to find the place from which the lasers were fired. The desolation in the pictures was greater than the Sahara, and both the attackers and their weapons remained invisible. But the pilot insisted that at the moment of the attack he saw two grotesquely humpbacked robots where a second earlier there was nothing. They came out of nowhere, took aim, fired, and vanished. He didn't see them vanish, of course, because the eyes of his remotes were vaporized, but from the ship he observed the settling cloud of dust and glowing cinders in the place of his defeat.

I had learned little, yet something of significance: that one could return from the Mission in one piece. Regarding these mysterious attacks, there were a number of hypotheses, including one that said that on the moon *something* had taken control of both remotes, making them destroy themselves with mutual fire. The enlarged pictures, however, showed that they hadn't aimed at each other but to the side, and that the laser response to their shots—the measurement made was very precise—was practically simultaneous, one tenth of one millionth of a second after. Spectroscopic analysis of the burning metal of the remotes showed that the lasers used by the moon robots had the same power as that of the twins but a different frequency.

It's impossible to simulate the weaker gravity of the moon on Earth, so after a few exercises at the lab I flew a couple of times a week to the Agency's orbital station where a special platform had been set up with a gravity six times weaker than Earth's. When I was able to move comfortably in the skin of the remote, the next stage of my training followed, highly realistic though not at all dangerous. But it wasn't pleasant. I had to walk on an imitation moon among large and small craters and have things jump out at me.

Since my predecessors had not benefited from their weapons, the Mission staff decided it would be better if I went unarmed. I was to keep with the remote as long as possible because every second meant a mass of data recorded by the micropes following me like a swarm of bees. There was no point trying to defend myself, Tottentanz persuaded me, because I would be entering a waste bristling with death and inevitably fall and the whole hope was that we would learn something from my death. The first reconnaissance pilots insisted on guns for psychological reasons not hard to understand. In a tight spot it always feels better to have your finger on a trigger. Among my mentors (tormentors) there were also psychologists. Their task was to prepare me for every kind of unpleasant surprise. Although I knew I was not in any real danger, I walked on that imitation moon as on a hot plate, looking in all directions. It's one thing to seek an enemy whose face you know, quite another to have no idea because a nearby boulder, as lifeless as a corpse, might suddenly split open and belch flame at you. It was a simulation, but the moment of every such shock was a nasty thing. Automatic circuit breakers would disconnect me from the remote when there was a hit, but they weren't instantaneous and many times I experienced an indescribable sensation: like being blown to bits and seeing, with the dimming eyes of the severed head, intestines flying from my ruptured belly. The fact that they were made of porcelain and silicon did provide some comfort. I went through several dozen deaths like this and so had some idea what awaited me on the moon. I went to the chief teletronicist, Seltzer, and put my doubts on the table. I might return from the moon in one piece leaving behind the remains of broken LEMs, but what good would that do? What can one learn about an unknown weapon system in a few fractions of a second? What was the point of sending a man there if he couldn't land anyway?

"Surely you know the reason, Mr. Tichy," he said, offering me a glass of sherry. He was small, thin, and hairless as a knee. "We can't do it from Earth. A quarter of a million miles means a three-second round-trip delay in transmission. You'll descend as much as possible, to a thousand miles, the lower ceiling of the zone of Silence."

"That's not what I mean. If we know in advance that the remote won't last a minute, we could send it from here with micropes to record its end."

"We've done that."

"And?"

"And nothing."

"And the micropes?"

"They showed a little dust."

"Can't we send, instead of a remote, something with real armor?"

"What do you consider real armor?"

"I don't know, perhaps a sphere like the kind once

used in deep-sea exploration. With windows, sensors, and so on."

"That was also done. Not exactly as you've described but near enough."

"And?"

"Nothing."

"What happened to it?"

"It's still there. We lost communication with it."

"Why?"

"That's the big question, isn't it? If we knew the answer, we wouldn't have to put you to all this trouble."

There were other conversations along the same lines. After completion of the second phase of my training, I was given a little leave. I'd been living three months now on the carefully guarded base and wanted to get away for one evening at least. So I went to the security director for a pass. He was a pallid, melancholy civilian in a short-sleeved shirt who listened sympathetically and said:

"I'm awfully sorry, but I can't let you go."

"What? Why not?"

"Those are my orders. Officially that's all I know."

"And unofficially?"

"Unofficially also. I imagine they're afraid for you."

"On the moon, I understand, but *here?*"

"Here even more."

"Does that mean I can't leave here until the launch?"

"Unfortunately."

"In that case," I said very quietly, very politely, which I do when I'm furious, "I'm not flying anywhere. There was no talk of this. I agreed to risk my neck but not to sit in prison. This is a volunteer flight. Well, I hereby unvolunteer. Or do you intend to put me in the rocket kicking and screaming?"

"What are you saying?"

I stuck to my guns and finally got the pass. I wanted to feel like an ordinary person, walk in a city crowd, perhaps go to the movies, but most of all eat in a decent restaurant instead of a canteen with people discussing second by second Ijon Tichy's last moments in a remote that bursts like fireworks. Dr. Lopez gave me his car and I left the base at dusk. As I turned onto the highway I saw in my headlights someone standing, hand raised, by a small car with its blinkers on. I stopped. It was a young woman in white slacks and white sweater, a blonde, with grease on her face. She said her motor was dead, it wouldn't turn over, so I offered to take her to town. As she got her coat out of the car, I noticed a large man in the front seat. He was motionless, as if made of wood. I looked at him more closely.

"That's my remote," she explained. "He's broken. Everything breaks on me. I was taking him to be fixed."

She had a husky voice and spoke almost like a child. I had heard that voice before somewhere. I opened the door to let her in, and before the car light went out I saw her face. She was incredibly like Marilyn Monroe, a movie star of the last century. The same face, the same innocence in the eyes and mouth. She asked if we could stop at some restaurant so she could wash. I moved to the slow lane, and we passed bright signs.

"There's a small Italian restaurant up ahead, really quite good," she said.

And indeed, neon flashed: RISTORANTE. I parked, and we entered a dark room. On a few small tables there were candles. The young woman went to the ladies' room. I stood for a moment undecided, then finally sat down in a corner booth. The place was nearly empty. Against the usual background of colored bottles a red-headed bartender wiped glasses, and near him brass-covered swinging doors led to the kitchen. In the next booth a man was bent over a notebook beside his plate, writing something. The woman came back.

"I'm starved," she said. "I stood outside for over an hour. No one would stop. Can we eat something? My treat."

"All right," I replied.

A fat man sitting at the bar with his back to us stared at his glass. He held a big black umbrella between his knees. The waiter appeared, took our order while balancing a tray of dirty dishes, and, kicking open the swinging doors, went into the kitchen. The blonde said nothing; she took a crumpled pack of cigarettes from her pocket, lit one from the candle, and held the pack out to me. I shook my head no. I tried not to stare at her. She did not differ from Marilyn Monroe in any way. Strange, since so many women have tried and failed. Monroe was inimitable though hers was neither a great nor an exotic beauty. Many books were written about her but none ever captured that mixture of child and woman which made her different from the rest. Looking at pictures of her once when I was still in Europe, I thought that this was more than a girlish woman, with her constant surprise and joy of a capricious child and the hidden despair or fear, like someone who has no one to confess her sins to. My companion inhaled from her cigarette deeply and blew the smoke slowly at the candle flickering between us. No, it was not a similarity, it was an exact replica. All kinds of suspicions came to me because I wasn't born yesterday, for example why did she keep her cigarettes in her pocket: women never do that. She had a purse after all, and a big one, bulging, which she had hung on the arm of her chair. The waiter brought the pizza but forgot the Chianti, he apologized and rushed away. Another waiter brought it. Although the restaurant was run tavern-style and the waiters wore large napkins to their knees like aprons, this waiter held his napkin in the crook of his arm. He didn't leave after he filled our glasses but only stepped back and stood just behind the partition. I could see him there because the brass doors acted like a mirror. The blonde couldn't see him from where she sat. The pizza was all right but the crust was hard. We ate in silence. Pushing aside her plate, she reached for another Camel.

"What is your name?" I asked. I wanted to hear another name, to weaken the impression that this was *she*.

"Let's drink first," she said in her hoarse voice. And took both our glasses and switched them.

"What does that mean?" I asked.

"A superstition I have."

She didn't smile.

"To our health!"

With these words she raised the glass to her lips. I also. The pizza had been peppery and I would have emptied the glass in one draught, but with a crack and a whirl something knocked it out of my hand. The wine spilled on the woman, staining her white sweater like blood. It was the waiter who did this. I wanted to jump up but couldn't, my legs were too far under the table, and by the time I got free, a lot was happening. The waiter without the apron seized the blonde by the arm. She pulled away and took her purse in both hands as if to shield her face with it. The bartender ran out from behind the counter. The sleepy, bald fat man tripped him, and he fell with a crash. The woman did something with her purse, and a stream of white foam shot from it as from a fire extinguisher. The waiter jumped back and clutched his face covered with white that dripped down his vest. The blonde aimed a white stream at the other waiter, who fell screaming through the swinging doors, hit. Both desperately rubbed their foamy eyes like slapstick actors who had taken cream pies in the face. We were now in a white fog because the foam gave off an acrid gas that filled the room. The blonde, with a quick glance left and right at the two waiters put out of action, turned her purse at me. I was next. To this day I don't know why I didn't try to cover myself. Something large and black appeared before me and boomed like a drum. It was the fat man shielding me with the open umbrella. The purse went sailing to the center of the room and ignited, thick dark smoke pouring from it and mixing with the white fog. The bartender sprang from the floor and ran along the counter toward the kitchen doors, which were still swinging. The blonde had disappeared through them. The fat man threw the open umbrella at the feet of the bartender, who jumped over it, lost his balance, careened into the glass behind the bar, which fell with a great crash as he dove into the kitchen. I looked at the battlefield. The charred purse smoldered between the tables. The white fog thinned out, still stinging my eyes. Around the open umbrella on the floor lay pieces of glass, broken plates, cups, and pizza, all covered with sticky foam and spilled wine. This all happened so fast that the Chianti bottle was still rolling in its basket, until it hit the wall. From the next booth someone rose—the man who had been writing in his notebook and drinking beer. I recognized him at once. It was the pallid civilian I'd quarreled with at the base a couple of hours ago. He lifted his melancholy eyebrows and said:

"Was it worth fighting for that pass, Mr. Tichy?"

"A tightly rolled cloth napkin at close range can stop a bullet," said Leon Grün thoughtfully. He was the security chief and known as Lohengrin. "The French *flics* knew this when they were still in long capes. And neither a Parabellum nor a Beretta would fit into a handbag. She could have had a larger bag, but the bigger the piece, the longer it takes to get it out. Nevertheless I advised Truffles to take an umbrella. And I was right, as you saw. Sodium pectate, wasn't it, doctor?" The chemist he turned to scratched behind his ear. We were back at the base, in a smoky room full of people, well after midnight.

"Who knows? Sodium pectate or another salt in aerosol form with free radicals. Radicals of ammonia plus an emulsifier and an additive to reduce surface tension. At high pressure—a minimum of fifty atmospheres. A lot of it could fit in that purse. They obviously have experts."

"Who?" I asked, but no one seemed to hear me.

"What was the purpose? Why did they do it?" I asked, louder this time.

"To put you out of commission. To blind you," said Lohengrin pleasantly. He lit a cigarette but immediately ground it out in the ashtray with disgust. "Give me something to drink. I've smoked too much. You've cost us a lot of trouble, Tichy. To put together protection like that in half an hour wasn't easy."

"I was to be blinded? Temporarily or permanently?"

"Hard to say. It's extremely caustic stuff, you know. Possibly a cornea transplant could have saved you."

"And those two? The waiters?"

"Our man managed to close his eyes in time. A good reflex. But the purse was a bit of a novelty."

"But why did that . . . false waiter knock the glass out of my hand?"

"I haven't spoken with him. He's not able to talk yet. I assume it was because she changed glasses."

"There was something in my glass?"

"A ninety-five percent likelihood. Why else would she have done it?"

"But she drank the wine too—I saw her."

"Not the wine, the glass. Wasn't she playing with the glass before the waiter came?"

"I'm not sure. Wait, yes, she was. She turned it around in her fingers."

"Well, there you are. We're waiting for the lab test results. Only chromatography or mass spectrometry will work because there is so little material left."

"Poison?"

"I'd say so. You were to have been put out of the picture: neutralized, but not necessarily killed. Probably not killed. Put yourself in their place. A corpse means news coverage, theories, an autopsy, talk. But a psychosis, that's a different story. Gives more elegant results. There are plenty of such drugs today. States of depression, dementia, hallucinations. I think that if you had drunk the wine, you wouldn't have felt a thing then. Only tomorrow, or later. The more delayed the effect, the more it looks like a real psychosis. Who can't go insane these days? Anybody can. Starting with me, Mr. Tichy."

"And the foam? The spray?"

"The spray was the last resort. The spare tire in the trunk. She used it because she had to."

"Who are the *they* we're talking about?"

Lohengrin smiled. He wiped the sweat from his forehead with a handkerchief that was not the cleanest, looked at it with a grimace, put it back in his pocket, and said:

"You are naive. Not everyone is as thrilled about your nomination as we, Mr. Tichy."

"Do I have an alternate? I never asked . . . Do you have someone in reserve? Through him, we might be able to learn who . . ."

"No. There is *not one* alternate now. There are many with similar scores, but we'd have to start a whole new selection process."

"One more thing," I said, a little embarrassed. "Where did that woman come from?"

"About that we know something," Lohengrin said evenly. "Your European apartment was gone through a couple of weeks ago. Nothing taken but everything examined. That's where they got it."

"I don't understand."

"Your library. You have a biography of Marilyn Monroe and two picture albums of her. The proclivity is obvious."

"You searched my apartment and didn't tell me?"

"Everything was put back in place, even dusted, and as for searching, we weren't the first. You can see it was a good thing our men learned about the books. We didn't tell you so as not to upset you. You have enough on your mind as it is. Maximum concentration is essential. We are collectively, you see, your nursemaid," and he swept his arm to include everyone present: the fat man now without an umbrella, the chemist, and three silent men leaning against the wall.

"So when you demanded the pass, I thought it best not to tell you about your apartment, because that wouldn't have stopped you. Would it have?"

"I guess not."

"So you see."

"All right. But the uncanny resemblance. Was she — human?"

"Yes and no. Not directly. Do you want to see her? She's lying in that room." He pointed to the door behind him. For a second I had the mad thought that Marilyn Monroe had died a second death.

"A product of Gynandroics?" I asked slowly.

"A different company. There are others. Would you like to see her?"

"No," I said. "But someone must have been . . . steering her?"

"Of course. Probably a woman, and one with great acting ability. The way she moved—did you notice?—was perfect. An amateur couldn't have done it. To render her so well, to capture the spirit, must have taken a lot of study. Practice. Going over the old movies . . ." He shrugged.

"They went to all that trouble . . ." I said. "For what?"

"Would you have picked up an old lady?"

"Yes."

"But you wouldn't have stayed for the pizza. Anyway, not for sure, and they had to be sure. And you couldn't refuse a Marilyn Monroe, could you? But enough said."

"What did you . . . do to her?"

"Nothing. A disconnected remote is a puppet with the strings cut. A doll."

"But then why did she run?"

"Because the product can tell you things. They didn't want to leave any evidence, any prints. It's almost three. You must take care of yourself, Mr. Tichy. You have, if you will forgive me, old-fashioned tastes in women. I wish you a good night and pleasant dreams."

The next day was a Sunday. We didn't work on Sundays. I was shaving when a messenger arrived with a letter. Professor Lax-Gugliborc wanted to see me. I had heard of him. His field was communications and telematics. He had his own laboratory at the base. I dressed and at ten o'clock went to his place. He had drawn me a little map on the other side of the letter. Among some low buildings stood a long pavilion surrounded by a garden and a high wire

fence. I pushed the bell once, twice. A sign lit up above it:
I'M NOT AT HOME TO ANYONE. Then the lock buzzed and
the gate opened. A narrow gravel path led to a metal door.
It was closed and had no knob or handle. I knocked. Not
a sound inside. I knocked again. I was about to leave when
the door opened a little and a man peered out, tall, thin,
in a blue smock covered with spots and splatters. What was
left of his white hair was cut very short, and he wore thick
glasses that gave him the look of a startled fish. A long
sniffy nose, a massive forehead.

He stepped back without a word to let me in, then
locked the door and not with just one lock either. The
hallway was very dark. He went first and I followed, my
hand on the wall. This was strange, conspiratorial. The
stink of chemicals hung in the hot, dry air. The next door
was a sliding door. He had me go first.

I found myself in a large lab that was incredibly clut-
tered. Metal apparatuses, oxidized black, were piled one
on top of the other and connected with wires that lay tangled on the floor. In the middle of the lab was a table
heaped with more equipment, papers, tools, and a cage
stood next to it, a birdcage large enough to hold a gorilla.
The most curious thing was the dolls lying in a row along
three of the walls. Naked, resembling store mannequins,
with open skulls or with no heads at all, and their chests
parted like doors, containing a jumble of connectors and
circuit boards, and under the table was a pile of arms and
legs. There was not one window in the room. The professor threw on the floor a coil of cable and electronic parts
occupying a chair, and with an agility I wouldn't have expected of him he crawled under the table, pulled out a tape
recorder, and turned it on. Looking up at me, he put a
finger to his lips, and at the same time his strident voice
came from the machine:

"I have invited you here, Tichy, to instruct you in a few things you must know about communications. Please have a seat and listen. You may not take notes . . ."

While his voice went on, the professor gestured for me to get in the cage. I hesitated. Without ceremony he pushed me in, climbed in after me, and pulled my arm to make me sit. He sat opposite me on the floor, crossing his legs, his sharp knees jutting from his smock. The whole thing was like a scene out of a bad movie about a mad scientist. In the cage too there were wires going every-where, and he brought two together, which made a quiet, monotonous buzz. Meanwhile his voice spoke on the ma-chine by the chair. Lax-Gugliborc reached behind him for two thick black collars. One of these he pulled over his head and around his neck, and gave me the other and in-dicated that I do likewise. Then he took a wire with an olive-shaped plug and put the plug in his ear, and again in pantomime told me to do the same. The tape recorder went on speaking, but in my ear I heard what he said to me.

"Now we can talk. You may ask questions but only in-telligent ones. No one will hear us. We are shielded. You are surprised? No need to be. Even the trusted are not trusted, and that's as it should be."

"Can I talk?" I asked. We sat in the cage so close that our knees touched. The tape recorder jabbered on.

"Go ahead. For every electronic device there is another electronic device. I know you from your books. The clutter here is just for decoration. You've been promoted to hero. The moon reconnaissance mission. You're going."

"I'm going," I said. He hardly moved his lips when he spoke, but I could hear him perfectly through the micro-phone.

"Everyone knows that. A thousand people will assist

you from Earth. The never-failing Lunar Agency. Except that it's divided."

"The Agency?"

"Yes. They'll provide you with a series of remotes. But only one is worth anything. Mine. A completely new approach. Dust thou art, unto dust shalt thou return, then rise again. I'll show it to you later. A demonstration. But first you'll get a viaticum from me, tips for the traveler."

He raised a finger. His eyes, small and round behind the thick glasses, smiled at me with kindly cunning.

"You'll hear what they want you to hear, but I will tell you first what they don't want you to hear. I'm a man of old-world principles. Now listen. The Agency is an international institution but it can't hire angels. On the far perimeter, on Mars, say, you would have to act alone. One against Thebes. But on the moon you will be only the tip of the strategic pyramid, the Earth team supporting you beneath. Do you know who will be on that team?"

"I know most of them. The Cybbilkis brothers, Tottentanz, Dr. Lopez. And Seltzer and the rest—what? What's wrong?"

He shook his head sadly. We must have looked pretty funny inside that big wire cage, with the constant insect buzz from the outside, from the tape, mixing with his voice.

"Those people represent different interests. It can't be otherwise."

"Whom can I trust?" I asked, understanding.

"No one, going by what you will hear from me. Myself included. Yet you must confide in *someone.* That whole idea of the change of venue," and he pointed at the ceiling, "and the doctrine of ignorance—it was stupid, of course. It had to end this way. If this is the end. They made their bed. The director told you about the four impossibilities made possible?"

"He did."

"There's a fifth. They want to learn the truth and don't want to learn the truth. That is, not every truth. Each a different truth. Do you understand?"

"No."

We sat opposite each other on the floor but I heard him as if over the phone. And he me. The current buzzed, the machine kept talking, and he said, blinking often and with his hands on his knees:

"I set this up to block the bugs. It doesn't matter whose bugs or for whom. I want to do what I can because I believe I should. Common decency. Don't bother to thank me. They will defend you—but it would be healthier to keep certain facts to yourself. You won't be in a confessional. We don't know what has happened on the moon. Sibelius and others like him believe that evolution up there has taken a step backward. The development of instinct instead of intelligence. An intelligent weapon is not an optimal weapon. It can become frightened, for example. Or stop wanting to be a weapon. It can get ideas. A soldier, living or nonliving, shouldn't get ideas. Intelligence is the multidimensionality of action, and that means freedom. But *there* it's completely different. The level of human intelligence has been surpassed."

"How do you know?"

"Because he who sows evolution reaps mind. And mind does not wish to serve anyone. Unless it must. And there is no must there. But I should not speak about what is or isn't there because I do not know. What matters is what is here."

"Which is . . . ?"

"The Lunar Agency was supposed to have made it impossible to obtain information from the moon. Now it will do that once and for all. Which is why you are going. You return either with nothing or with news more destructive than the atom bomb. Which do you prefer?"

"Hold on. Speak more plainly. Are you saying your colleagues represent other intelligence agencies? That they're spies?"

"No. But you could bring that about."

"I could?"

"Yes. The balance of power since the Geneva Agreement has been shaky. When you return, you may replace the old threats with new ones. You cannot play the savior of the world, the messenger of peace."

"Why not?"

"The scheme of moving Earth's conflicts to the moon was doomed in its inception. For how could it be otherwise? Arms control had been made impossible by microminiaturization. One can count missiles and satellites but not artificial bacteria. Or keep track of natural disasters that are not natural, or what is causing the decline in the population rate of the Third World. Which decline was necessary. Though it was impossible to do properly. You can take a couple of people aside and explain what's good for them and what isn't. But you can't take all humanity aside and explain things, can you?"

"What does this have to do with the moon?"

"Just this, that destruction hasn't been ended, only moved in space and time. And that cannot last forever. I have created a new technology which can be used in telematics. For the building of dispersants. Remotes capable of reversible dispersion. I didn't want the Agency to have it, but what's done is done." He put up both hands in resignation.

"One of my assistants showed it to them. I'm not sure which one, and it doesn't really matter. When the pressure is great, there's invariably a leak. Any loyalty has its limits."

He ran a hand over his shiny pate. The tape recorder was still talking. "I can do one thing: I can show that dispersion telematics isn't ready yet. That I can do. For a year, let's say. Eventually they'll find out that I tricked them. Would you like me to do this?"

"I have to decide? Why me?"

"If you return with nothing, no one will be interested in you."

"True."

"But if you return with information, the consequences will be incalculable."

"For me personally? You want to save me? Out of kindness?"

"No. To play for time."

"To put off learning about the moon? Then you don't believe the moon will ever invade Earth? You think that's just mass hysteria?"

"Mass hysteria, or rumors intentionally spread by certain nations."

"To what purpose?"

"To break the doctrine of ignorance and return to the old Clausewitz-style politics."

I was silent, not knowing what to say—or even what to think.

"But that is only one man's assumption," I said finally.

"Yes. The letter Einstein wrote to Roosevelt also was based on an assumption, that an atom bomb could be built. He regretted it to the end of his life."

"I understand—you don't want to have such regrets?"

"The atom bomb would have been developed with or without Einstein. My technology too. But the later, the better."

"*Après nous le déluge?*"

"No, something else. This fear of the moon was created intentionally. Of that I'm certain. Returning from a successful mission, you'll only be exchanging one fear for another. That other could be worse: more realistic."

"I see now. You want me to fail?"

"Yes. But only if you agree to it."

"Why?"

The nastiness suddenly left his little squirrel eyes. He was laughing, open-mouthed, soundlessly.

"I told you why. I'm a man of old-world principles, and that means Fair Play. Please answer now, because my legs are starting to hurt."

"You could have put in a couple of cushions," I said. "And as for that . . . dispersion technology, please give it to me."

"You don't believe what I've said?"

"I believe you, and that's why I want it."

"To be a Herostrates?"

"I'll try not to burn the temple. Could we get out of this cage now?"

The Mission

Take-off was aborted eight times. Something went wrong at every countdown. It was the air conditioning, or a backup computer reporting a short circuit that wasn't real, or a short circuit that was real but not reported by the main computer, and on the ninth countdown, when it looked like I'd be on my way at last, the Number 7 LEM balked. There I lay, swaddled and wrapped in tape that held a thousand sensors, like a mummy in a sarcophagus, my helmet shut, the laryngophone at my throat, and the tube of the orange juice container in my mouth. With one hand on the emergency ejector switch and the other on the steering wheel, I was trying to think of things pleasant and far away, so my heart wouldn't pound, because it was being watched on screens by eight people along with my blood pressure, muscle tension, sweat level, eye movements, and galvanic skin response, all revealing the fear felt by the intrepid astronaut as he waits for the ritual *zero* and the thunder that will thrust him upward. But each time what I heard was profanity, in chief coordinator Wivitch's voice, and the words "Stop! Stop! Stop!" I don't know whether it was my ears or the microphones but his voice echoed as in an empty barrel; I said nothing, however, knowing that if I mentioned this, they'd examine the helmet and call in resonance experts and there would be no end to it.

This last problem, called LEM's Mutiny by the technicians, was really quite peculiar: from the diagnostic signals intended only to check out its systems the unit began moving, and when it was turned off, instead of stopping it shuddered and tried to get up. Like a mindless idol it struggled against its straps and nearly tore apart the harness, though they disconnected all the lines to it one by one and couldn't figure out where the power was coming from. It must have been a leak of some sort in the current. Impedance, capacitance, resistance, susceptibility. When engineers don't know what's happening, their vocabulary takes on the richness of physicians discussing a hopeless case. As is well known, whatever can go wrong eventually will and in a unit of 298,000 circuits and chips no amount of redundancy can provide a hundred-percent certainty. A hundred-percent certainty, says Halevala, the oldest repairman, is provided only by a dead body, in that it won't rise up. Halevala liked to say that God, creating the world, didn't take statistics into account, and when problems started in Paradise He resorted to miracles but by then it was too late. Wivitch said that Halevala brought bad luck and asked the director to dismiss him. The director believed in bad luck but the Council didn't, so the Finn, appealing the dismissal, kept his job. Such was the atmosphere in which I prepared myself for the Mission.

I had no doubt that in lunar orbit too something would go wrong, though the simulations and inspections had been repeated ad nauseam. But of course I didn't know when that would happen or into what sort of mess it would put me. At the next countdown everything went fine, but this time *I* pulled the plug, because my left leg fell asleep, too tightly wrapped, and I argued on the phone with Wivitch who said the pins and needles would pass and the tape shouldn't be any looser. But I insisted, and they had to spend an hour and a half unwinding me from my cocoon. It turned out that someone—but of course no one confessed—had used a pipe-cleaning utensil to help pull the tape and it had been forgotten under the wrapping around my shin. I asked them to let the matter drop even though I could guess who had done it, since only one of them smoked a pipe. In heroic tales of space such things never happen. An astronaut does not get the runs, nor do the amenities malfunction so that his spacesuit fills with piss. Which actually happened to the first American astronaut in his suborbital flight but out of natural historical-patriotic delicacy NASA didn't mention it to the press.

The more care they take for your comfort, the more likely it is that some tangled bit of wire will dig under your arm or a buckle pinch in the worst possible place, driving you up the wall. When I once suggested they put remote scratchers inside the suit, they all thought it was a joke and laughed, except the seasoned astronauts who knew what I was talking about. It was I who discovered Tichy's Law which says that the first itch occurs in a place on the body you can't possibly reach. The itching stops only when something serious happens, because then your hair stands on end, your flesh crawls, and breaking into a cold sweat does the rest. True as this is, the authorities don't want to hear it because it doesn't rhyme well with One Giant Leap for Mankind. Can you imagine Armstrong climbing down the rungs of that first LEM and saying instead that his underwear was riding up? I've always thought that the people at Central Control who sit back in their chairs with a can of beer and give advice to the astronaut-turned-mummy, with their words of encouragement and support, should first put themselves in his shoes.

The last two weeks I spent at the base were not pleasant. There were new attempts to remove Ijon Tichy. Even after the incident with the false Marilyn Monroe they didn't tell me that my mail was being scanned by a special machine. The technology of epistolary terrorism is so developed that a charge able to blow the addressee to pieces can be placed inside a Christmas or birthday card wishing him health and happiness. It was only after a deadly letter from Professor Tarantoga almost put me out of the picture and I raised holy hell that they showed me the machine, an armored container with slanted steel slabs to absorb explosions. Each letter is opened by pincers and examined by x ray and ultrasound to trigger the detonator if there is one. The letter in question didn't explode and Tarantoga had actually written it, so they brought it to me and I was saved thanks to my sense of smell. The envelope reeked of mignonette or lavender, which seemed strange to me, suspicious, because Tarantoga is the last person to use perfumed stationery. No sooner did I read the words "Dear Ijon" than I began to laugh and instantly realized that although I was laughing I was not amused, and since one does not laugh for no reason, I concluded, putting two and two together, that this laughter was not natural. I did a very prudent thing then, slipping the letter under the glass that covered my desk, to read it that way. And thank God I also had a runny nose, which I blew. The Council afterward debated whether I blew my nose automatically or from an instant insight, and I myself wasn't sure. In any case this was why I inhaled only a very small amount of the drug with which the letter had been impregnated. It was a completely new drug. The laughter it produced was the overture to hiccups so persistent that they could be stopped only by a strong narcotic. I immediately phoned Lohengrin, who at first thought I was playing some joke because while I spoke, I roared with laughter. From the neurological standpoint laughter is the first stage of a hiccup. Finally the matter became clear, the letter was taken to the laboratory by two men in masks, and Dr. Lopez and his colleagues came and gave me oxygen. When I had subsided to a chuckle, they made me read all the lead articles in the newspapers of that day and the day before.

I didn't realize that during my absence the press as well as television had split in two. There are papers and programs that give all the news and those that give only the good news. Until now they had been feeding me the second kind, which is why at the base I had the impression that the world had truly improved after the signing of the Geneva Agreement. You would have thought that at least the pacifists were happy, but no. A book Dr. Lopez loaned me tells the story of our new society. The author shows that Jesus was a subversive sent to undermine Jewish unity with that love thy neighbor business, on the principle of divide and conquer, which worked, and which a little later brought down the Roman Empire. Jesus himself had no idea he was a subversive, and the apostles too were in the dark, having only the best intentions although everyone knows what is paved with good intentions. The author, whose name I have unfortunately forgotten, says that anyone who proclaims brotherly love and peace on earth should be immediately arrested and interrogated to see what his agenda really is. So it's not surprising that the pacifists have changed their tactics. Some have taken up the cause of delicious animals. There has nevertheless been no decline in the consumption of pork chops. Others urge solidarity with all living things, and in the German Bundestag eighteen seats were won by the Probacteria Party which says that microbes have as much right to live as we so instead of killing them with medicine we should alter them genetically to live not on humans but on something else. There is a real groundswell of good will, with disagreement only about who is standing in its way. But there is no disagreement that the enemies of brotherly love should be exterminated root and branch.

At Tarantoga's I saw an interesting new encyclopedia entitled *The Lexicon of Fear*. It used to be, says the book, that fear had its roots in the supernatural: in spells, witches, demons, heretics, atheists, black magic, ghosts, Bohemians, and abstract art, but in the industrial age fear shifted to things more concrete. There was fear of tomatoes (carcinogenic), aspirin (stomach bleeding), coffee (birth defects), butter (saturated fat), sugar, cars, television, discotheques, pornography, birth control pills, science, cigarettes, nuclear power plants, and higher education. I wasn't surprised by the popularity of this encyclopedia. Professor Tarantoga is of the opinion that people need two things. First, an answer to the question "Who is responsible?" and second, to the question "What is the secret?" The first answer should be brief, obvious, and unambiguous. As for the second, scientists have been annoying everyone for two hundred years with their superior knowledge. How nice to see them baffled by the Bermuda Triangle, flying saucers, and the emotions of plants, and how satisfying it is when a simple middle-aged woman of Paris can see the whole future of the world while on that subject the professors are as ignorant as spoons.

People, says Tarantoga, believe what they want to believe. Take astrology for instance. Astronomers, who after all should know more than anyone about the stars, tell us that they are giant balls of incandescent gas spinning since the world began and that their influence on our fate is considerably less than the influence of a banana peel, on which you can slip and break your leg. But there is no interest in banana peels, whereas serious periodicals include horoscopes and there are even pocket computers you can consult before you invest in the stock market to find out if the stars are favorable. Anyone who says that the skin of a fruit can have more effect on a person's future than all the planets and stars combined won't be listened to. An individual comes into the world because his father, say, didn't withdraw in time, thereby becoming a father. The mother-to-be, seeing what happened, took quinine and jumped from the top of the dresser to the floor but that didn't help. So the individual is born and he finishes school and works in a store selling suspenders, or in a post office. Then suddenly he learns that that's not the way it was at all. The planets came into conjunction, the signs of the zodiac arranged themselves carefully into a special pattern, half the sky cooperated with the other half so that he could come into being and stand behind this counter or sit behind this desk. It lifts his spirits. The whole universe revolves around him, and even if things aren't going well, even if the stars are lined up in such a way that the suspenders manufacturer loses his shirt and the individual consequently loses his job, it's still more comforting than to know that the stars don't really give a damn. Knock astrology out of his head, and the belief too that the cactus on his windowsill cares about him, and what is left? Barefoot, naked despair. So says Professor Tarantoga, but I see I am digressing.

They shot me into orbit on the 27th of October, wrapped in sensor tape like an infant in swaddling clothes.

From a height of four hundred miles I observed Mother Earth and could hear the engineers at the base cheering that this time it worked. My first stage, the main booster, separated as it was supposed to, above the Atlantic, on the dot, but the second got stuck and I had to help it. I think it fell in the Andes. After the traditional good lucks and safe trips I took over the controls myself and proceeded through the most hazardous zone on the way to the moon. You have no idea how many old satellites, civilian and military, are circling Earth. Something like eighteen thousand not counting the ones that have come apart, particularly dangerous because the pieces are almost too small for radar. And then there's a lot of ordinary garbage in space, all kinds of waste products, especially radioactive, deposited here by jet. So I flew with extreme caution until space was properly empty. Only then did I unbuckle all the belts and start checking my LEMs.

I turned on one after the other, seeing how each felt, seeing the interior of the bay through its crystal eyes. I had nineteen remotes, but the last one was by itself in a crate marked FRUIT JUICE to fool unauthorized persons. Inside the crate was a hermetically sealed cylinder, light blue, which housed a powdered remote, Professor Lax-Gugliborc's top-secret creation, and I was to use it only as a last resort. I knew the principle of its operation but still don't know whether I should reveal that yet. Nor do I want to turn this account into a Gynandroics catalog or a product list of the Lunar Agency's teleferic division. LEM 5 started shivering when I turned it on. Since it was feedback-connected to me, I shivered too, as in a fever, teeth chattering. I was supposed to inform the base at once about such defects, but I didn't because I knew from experience what would happen. They would immediately call in a whole army of mechanics, designers, engineers, and specialists in electronic pathology, who would be angry with me for making such a big deal out of light convulsions that might go away by themselves, and they would give me contradictory instructions, connect this, disconnect that, and how many amps to zap the poor thing with because electroshock can help machines as well as people. And that would produce some new, unpredicted response, and they would tell me to wait patiently while they ran simulations of the LEM, analog and digital, and of me too, as they argued with each other constantly and now and then told me to stay calm. The team would split into two or three camps like distinguished doctors in consultation. Perhaps they would have me climb into the bay with tools and open the LEM's belly and train the hand camera on it since all the circuitry is there and not in the head which hasn't room. So I'd be following the baton of the experts, and if it worked, they'd take the credit, and if it didn't, I'd get the blame.

But I was 100,000 miles from Earth now and increasingly glad I had kept quiet about the problem, because soon there would be more than a second's delay in communicating with the base and I'd be sure to bust something, precise movements are difficult when you're weightless, a spark would tell them I'd caused a short, and then there would be a chorus of sour remarks. Tichy's screwed it up, they'd say, there's nothing we can do. So I had spared both them and myself that aggravation.

The nearer I got to the moon, the more unnecessary the advice and cautions I was receiving over the radio, until finally I said that if they didn't stop bothering me, I'd turn the damned thing off. I knew the moon like the palm of my hand from the days when they were considering turning it into a Disneyland. I circled it three times in high orbit and over the Oceanus Procellarum began a slow descent.

On one side I could see the Mare Imbrium and on the other the crater Eratosthenes, then Murchison and the Sinus Medi all the way to the Mare Nubium. I was now so low that the continuation of the moon's pock-marked surface was hidden from me. I was at the lower boundary of the Zone of Silence. So far nothing unexpected had happened if you don't count the two empty beer cans that came to life during my maneuvers. When I braked, the cans—as usual discarded in haste by our technicians—manifested themselves and began flying around the cabin, hitting the walls and my head. A greenhorn would have tried to catch them. I changed orbit and flew above the Taurus mountains. When the great Sea of Serenity stretched out before me, I was hit in the back of my helmet so sharply that I jumped. It was a tin of salted crackers that probably had gone with the beer. The base heard the noise and immediately there were questions, but I lied, explaining that I had tried to scratch my head and forgot both helmet and bulky glove. No point in getting the technicians in trouble. They *always* leave stuff in rockets. It's like a law of nature.

I flew through the zone of internal control without difficulty, because its satellites had been told by Earth to let me pass. It wasn't in the program, but I braked hard a few times to dislodge any other mementos from the assembly-and-inspection crews. A comic book stuffed in the reserve selenography drawer fluttered out like an enormous moth. Taking a quick inventory—two beer cans, a cracker tin, a comic book—I concluded that there would be more surprises in store and I would have to stay alert.

I surveyed the moonscape through twenty-power binoculars, but it looked lifeless, uninhabited, empty. I knew that the computer arsenals in the different sectors were a good hundred feet below sea level, sea level meaning those great plains created long ago by lava flows. The arsenals had been set so deep to protect them from meteors. Nevertheless I looked with particular care at the Mare Vaporum, the Mare Tranquillitatis, and the Mare Fecunditatus (the old astronomers who named these plains of stone had some imagination), then circled the Mare Crisium and the Mare Frigoris, thinking I might see a little movement there. I had excellent binoculars and could count the gravel on the slopes of the craters, or at least rocks the size of a person's head, but nothing stirred and that was what intrigued me. Where were those legions of armed robots, hosts of intelligent tanks, steel giants and equally death-dealing Lilliputians which had been constantly spawning for years beneath the surface? I saw nothing but stones and craters ranging from very large to small as a plate, trenches in the shiny ancient magma radiating out from Copernicus, the Huygens fault, the pole, Archimedes toward Cassini, Plato on the horizon, and everywhere the same incomprehensible desolation. Along the meridian marked by Flamsteed, Herodotus, and Rümker and through the Sinus Roris ran the widest strip of the no man's land, and that was where I was supposed to land the first remote after putting the ship into selenosynchronous orbit. They hadn't given me an exact spot; I was to decide that myself, choosing the safest place. Though there was no indication here, none whatever, of safety or danger. To go into selenosynchronous orbit I had to ascend, and maneuvered and maneuvered until the whole enormous sunlit moon below me stopped moving, at which point I was directly over Flamsteed, a very old crater, shallow and almost filled with volcanic tuff. I hung there a while, maybe half an hour, looking down at the rubble and deliberating.

The remotes didn't need rockets to land. They had little braking nozzles on their legs, and gyroscopes. I could take one down at any speed I liked, using the leg jets, which could be kicked off easily after touching down, the jets and the empty fuel tank. From that moment on the remote was forever moonbound, unable to return. It was neither robot nor android, having not a thought in its head; it was, rather, a tool, an extension of me, incapable of the least initiative. And yet I was uncomfortable thinking that no matter what the outcome of my reconnaissance it was doomed, because I would have to leave it behind in this dead wilderness. It even occurred to me that maybe LEM 7 had faked its malfunction to get out of this in one piece. A ridiculous thought, because I knew perfectly well that Number 7, like all the other LEMs, was but a man-shaped shell. But this gives you some idea of my state of mind.

There was no reason to wait any longer. I examined carefully one more time the gray plateau I'd chosen for the landing, roughly estimating its distance from the northern edge of Flamsteed, then put the ship on automatic and pushed button number one. The leap of all my senses, though expected and indeed experienced so many times before, was violent. I was no longer sitting in a deep chair in front of the blinking lights of the computers and holding my binoculars, but lying on my back in a bunk as cramped as a coffin and open on only one side. I worked my way out, looked down and saw dull-gray armor, a trunk, thighs, and shins of steel, the retrojets strapped to them like holsters. I straightened slowly, feeling my magnetic shoes cling to the metal floor. Around me, in stacked bunks like the one in which I had been lying, lay the other remotes, all motionless. I could hear my own breathing but did not feel my chest moving. With difficulty I pulled first my left, then my right foot from the floor of the bay and walked to the handrail at the hatch, stood with my arms in so they wouldn't hit an edge when I was pushed down by the ejector and went hurtling, and waited for the countdown. After a few seconds I heard the lifeless voice of the timer: "Twenty . . . nineteen . . ." I counted with it, calm now because there was no turning back. But I couldn't help tensing a little when we reached "zero" and something soft but powerful shoved me into the open well so that I went flying like a stone. Lifting my head, I was able to see for a moment the dark shape of the ship against the darker background of the sky with its myriad dots of dimly glowing stars. As the ship disappeared in the black horizon, I felt a strong push at my feet and was wrapped in pale flame. With the retros firing, I fell much slower, but the moon still increased in size, as if trying to pull me in and devour me. Feeling the heat of the flame in uneven waves through my thick steel, I kept my arms in and, craning my neck, watched the fields of rubble, now gray-green, and the sandy slopes of Flamsteed grow before my eyes. When no more than three hundred feet separated me from the crater, I reached for the control stick at my belt and applied thrust carefully to brake more and shift direction, avoiding a great jagged rock. I aimed in order to land in sand, with both feet, but something flashed above me. I saw it out of the corner of my eye, looked up, and was dumbfounded.

White against the black sky and no more than thirty feet above me, a man in a heavy spacesuit descended, wrapped from feet to waist in the pale flame of retrojets and with his hand on the control stick at his belt. He fell, slowing, his body straight, until he was even with me, and hit the ground at the exact moment I felt it under my own feet. We stood five or six steps apart, like two statues, as though he too was astounded not to be alone. He was exactly my height. Gray smoke from the nozzles by his knees curled around his large moon boots. I sensed he was staring at me, though I couldn't see his face behind the shaded glass of his white helmet. My head was in a whirl. At first I thought this must be remote Number 2 which had been pushed from the ship after me by mistake, a malfunction, but then I saw the large black #1 on its chest. But that was my number, and I was pretty sure there were no other Number 1s on board. I stepped forward to see his face through the glass, and at the same time he stepped toward me. When we were quite close, I froze and my hair stood on end because I could see through the glass now and there was no one inside. In the helmet, two small black bars pointing at me, nothing more. I shrank back and lost my balance and almost fell, forgetting that one has to move slowly in low gravity, and he did exactly the same. I began to understand. I held my control stick in my right hand; he held his in his left. When I raised my hand slowly, so did he, and when I moved my leg, so did he, therefore it was clear (although nothing really was clear) that this was my mirror image. To make sure, I forced myself to approach him, and he approached me, until our suits practically met. Slowly, as if reaching to touch a hot iron, I put my hand on his chest and he did likewise to me, I with my right and he with his left. My large five-fingered glove went through him, disappearing, and his hand disappeared in me up to the wrist. I had no doubt now that I was alone and standing in front of a reflection, though there was no trace of a mirror to be seen. We stood there, and I began to look not at him but at his surroundings and noticed, behind him and to the side, a jagged rock jutting from the gray sand, the same rock I had avoided a minute ago while landing. But the rock was behind me, of that I was absolutely certain, thus I faced not only my own image but the image of everything around me. Now I looked for the place where the mirroring ended, because it had to end somewhere and merge with the shallow dunes, but I could not find the boundary, the seam. Not knowing what to do next, I retreated, and he too went backward like a crab, until we were so far apart that he seemed a little smaller. Then, I don't know why, I turned and walked toward the low sun which blinded me in spite of my antiglare glass. Taking thirty or forty steps with that uncertain ducklike waddle one can't avoid on the moon, I stopped and looked back at myself. He stood at the top of a small dune and, sure enough, had turned to face me.

Further experiments were unnecessary. I may have stood there like an idiot but my brain was working feverishly. It dawned on me, only now, that the reconnaissance probes sent by the Lunar Agency to the moon had been armed. No one ever said anything specific about that, and I stupidly didn't inquire further. But of course: If the probes were armed with lasers, their sudden silence after landing might have a simple explanation. I had to find out what kind of lasers, but how? There was no direct communication between me and the base on Earth, only via the ship that hung high above me in stationary orbit. I was indeed on that ship in my physical person, but standing in the Flamsteed crater here as a remote. To talk to Control, I had to turn my transmitter back on, having deliberately switched it off just before leaving the ship so they wouldn't ruin my concentration during the descent with their advice which no doubt would have come thick and fast had I remained in radio contact with them according to instructions. So I turned the volume knob on my chest and called Earth. The response would come with a three-second delay, I knew, and those seconds seemed like ages. At last I heard the voice of Wivitch. He had a million questions but I told him to be quiet, saying only that I had landed without mishap and was at the target 000 and nothing was attacking me. On the subject of the other remote I was silent.

"Please answer one question, it's very important," I said, trying to sound phlegmatic. "The remotes that were sent here before me carried lasers. What kind? Neodymium?"

"You found their remains? Are they burned? Where are they?"

"Please don't answer a question with questions," I said, interrupting. "Since it's my first communication from the moon, this is obviously important. What kind of lasers did the two recon pilots have? Were they the same?"

A moment of silence. Standing stockstill, under the heavy black sky and beside the shallow crater filled with sand, I saw the line of my footprints across three sloping dunes to the fourth, where my reflection stood. I kept him in sight while listening to the indistinct voices in my helmet. Wivitch came back with the information.

"The automata had the same lasers as the pilots," his voice suddenly rang in my ear, making me jump. "Model E-M-9. Nine percent emission in the x-ray and gamma range, the rest in blue."

"Visible light? Ultraviolet too?"

"Yes. The E-M series all have continuous spectra. Why?"

"Just a minute. Maximum emission in the bands above visible light?"

"Yes."

"What percent?"

Again silence. I waited patiently, feeling the left side of my suit, where the sun was, slowly warm up.

"Ninety-one percent. Tichy, what's going on?"

"Wait."

This information puzzled me at first because I remembered that the emission spectrum of the lasers that destroyed our probes was different. More in the red. Could the device have been a mirror even so? Then I remembered that with nonlinear optics a reflected ray need not have the same frequency as the one incident. Even in the case of ordinary glass. Though this wasn't glass here, of course. Whatever reflected laser beams could also move them in the spectrum toward the red. I couldn't ask to talk to physicists now—later maybe—so I racked my brain for what I remembered of optics. To turn high-energy radiation into visible light didn't require additional energy, it just needed some energy absorption. It was therefore easier. I could stay with the mirror hypothesis without looking for miracles. I felt better. I started to figure out where I was by the stars. The French sector was about five miles to the east, and less than a mile behind me was the American sector.

"Wivitch? Do you read me? Moon here."

"Yes. Tichy! There have been no flashes. Why did you ask about lasers?"

"Are you recording me?"

"Of course. Every word."

I could hear the exasperation in his voice.

"Listen. What I'm about to say is important. I am standing in the Flamsteed crater. I am looking east, in the direction of the French sector. There is a mirror in front of me. I repeat: a mirror. Not an ordinary mirror but something that reflects only me and my surroundings. I don't know what it is. I see myself exactly, that is I see remote Number 1 at a distance of approximately two hundred and forty paces. The image landed with me. I don't know how high this reflecting area extends, because while landing I was looking downward, at my feet. I first saw the double right above the crater, very close. It was a little higher than me, also larger. But when it stood in front of me, it was exactly my size. The mirror may be able to enlarge the images. I think that's why the moon robots that destroyed those remotes seemed so incredibly squat. I tried touching my double. My hand went right through, there was no resistance. If I'd had a laser and shot at it, that would have been the end of me, I'd have received the whole reflected charge. I don't know what happens next. I can't see where the mirror ends. That's it for now. I've told you all I know. If you're quiet, I'll keep the radio on, but if there's a lot of talking, off it goes, because I don't want distractions. Which is it to be?"

"Keep it on, keep it on . . ."

"Then be quiet."

I could hear Wivitch breathing heavily, each huff with a three-second delay, two hundred and forty thousand miles above me, because Earth stood high in the black sky, almost at the zenith, a gentle blue among the stars. The sun, on the other hand, was low, and as I watched my double in the white spacesuit I could see the long shadow from me stretching across the dunes. A little crackling in the earphones, but there was silence. I could hear my own breathing, realizing it was me on the ship, yet I heard it as if I were standing in my own body here in Flamsteed. We had expected surprises but not in the no man's land. Apparently they used this mirror trick to make every intruder, living or nonliving, self-destruct upon landing, before he could start sniffing around. Clever. More, intelligent. But inauspicious for me. No doubt much more was in store. I wouldn't have minded returning to the ship to think over the situation and discuss it with Control—it was easy to leave the remote, just break the safety glass on my chest and turn a knob—but I wasn't about to do that. Besides, I was in no greater danger here than on the ship. What then, look for the source of the mirror? And if I found it? The image would disappear, that was all.

They say you get your best ideas when you're taking a walk. I started moving, not exactly the way one strolls but with that slightly drunken moon stride, first one foot forward as on Earth but then both feet together, hopping like a sparrow. Or rather like an oversized ball that bounces and between bounces sails for a while above the sandy ground. Having covered some distance in this manner from where I had landed, I stopped to look back at myself. I saw a small figure on the horizon and was dumbfounded for the second time. Even far away I could see that it was no longer myself in white but someone else. Someone slender, graceful, the head shining brightly in the sun. A human figure on the moon without a spacesuit! And completely naked. Robinson Crusoe seeing Friday couldn't have been more astounded than I. I quickly raised both arms but the creature did not follow suit. It was not my reflection. It had golden hair that fell over its shoulders, a white body, long legs, and it came toward me without haste and as if without any particular purpose, and not waddling and halting either but smoothly, as one walks on the beach. Thinking "beach," I realized it was a woman. A young woman, and with not a stitch on her. In her hands she held something large and multicolored, and it covered her breasts. She approached not directly but at an angle, as if to pass me at a modest distance. I almost called Wivitch but bit my tongue. He wouldn't believe me. He'd think I was hallucinating. I didn't move, searching her face, wishing desperately I knew what to do but I didn't. The only thing I was sure of was that my eyes weren't deceiving me, nor my brain. I don't know why but it seemed to me that everything depended on her face. If it was Marilyn Monroe again, as at that Italian restaurant, then I would have to doubt the evidence of my senses, because how could any wave or force get into my memory and obtain precisely that image? I wasn't even standing here on this lifeless ground in my own person, I was sitting in the ship, strapped to the armchair at the controls, but even if I were here myself, what could enter my head with such perfect accuracy? Apparently, I thought, there were different kinds of impossibility, some greater and some lesser.

She was the siren of the islands that Odysseus passed. Luring men to their death. I don't know what made me think of that. I stood, and she kept coming, now and then lowering her face framed by flowing hair to sniff the flowers she held, though on the moon one can't smell anything. She paid no attention to me. But no matter what her appearance or actions, the mechanism inside her had to function logically, following logical programs. That had to be my point of departure. The invisible mirror was to put every armed intruder out of action. Seeing an opponent, the intruder would pull its gun to defend itself, though not to attack, its purpose being only reconnaissance. But when the other also drew its gun, the intruder would shoot, because if it allowed itself to be destroyed, it would not be carrying out its information-gathering program. But I did not produce a weapon. Instead I called Earth and told Wivitch what I saw. Were my words overheard? Almost certainly. An enormous, truly criminal oversight on the part of the whole project was that no one had thought to shield Tichy's communication with the base, which wouldn't have been that hard to do. A device built into my radio could have converted what was said into an unintelligible code. The underground military computers knew human speech, and even if they weren't given it to begin with, it was child's play for them to learn it, all they had to do was listen to Earth's tens of thousands of radio stations. Not to mention television programs, which is no doubt where the naked woman came from like Venus riding the sea foam.

All very logical. If it's not a robot because it doesn't shoot and doesn't even inspect its double, which surely would be the first thing a robot would do upon landing, then it's a man. And if it's a man, then it must be a male because people wouldn't send a female first on such a mission. And the Achilles heel of every male has been revealed ad nauseam on television, to wit, the opposite sex. Whatever I did, therefore, I shouldn't approach the siren. How dearly I would pay if I did I didn't need to determine by experiment. Her face couldn't be Marilyn Monroe's, also, because no one knew about that episode, which was top-secret. Unless some of the moon-weapon makers had spies inside the Lunar Agency . . . No, inconceivable.

She walked slowly and that is why I had time for all this thought, but now only a few dozen steps separated us. Not once did she look in my direction. I wondered if her bare feet left prints in the sand, but couldn't tell. If she left prints, that would be worse, for it would indicate an awesome level of technology for this mirage. When I saw her face, I breathed a sigh of relief. It was not Marilyn Monroe, though her features did seem familiar, probably taken from a movie because she was not only young but beautiful. She walked even slower, as if undecided whether or not to stop and lie down in the sun as on the beach. The flowers no longer hid her breasts; she held them lower. She looked around until she found a large, slanted rock with a smooth surface, sat on it, and let the flowers fall. They looked strange, red, yellow, and blue in that lifeless, gray-white moonscape. She sat sideways, and I thought furiously, trying to answer the question of what her creators or operators expected of me now, as a man, because whatever it was I should be very careful not to do it. Had I told Wivitch about this meeting, that would have served *their* purpose, because he wouldn't have believed me, not he or anyone else at Control, though of course they wouldn't have said that. Convinced that I was raving, they would have ordered me to abandon remote Number 1 like an empty shell and return to the ship, and to proceed to target 002 or 003 on the moon's other hemisphere and repeat the whole landing procedure from the beginning, meanwhile they would have held an emergency psychiatric meeting to decide which pills the deranged Ijon Tichy should take from the ship's medicine cabinet. It was well stocked but I hadn't opened it yet. Having lost credibility with the earthly powers that be, I would have thereby had ninety percent less chance of succeeding in my mission, which would have suited the creators of the mirage, for this hid their activity from Earth as effectively as their earlier destruction of the lunar spy satellites. Therefore I should not consult with Control. Nor did sex enter into it. Surely they knew enough about humans not to expect a live scout to make advances to a naked woman in a moon crater. But he would definitely want to have a closer look, to see if she was maybe a physical manifestation and not just a holograph. Obviously we were not talking about a real woman. If I touched her, I might not survive that touch. A mine for humans, built on the principle of sexual attraction. I was in a quandary. Telling Control was no good, not telling Control was bad too, and personally investigating this moon siren was risky to say the least. So I had to do what no man would do, on Earth or the moon, when he encountered a gorgeous naked blonde. I had to do something the program of this trap could not foresee.

Looking around, I saw a boulder split in half about a dozen steps away, large enough for me to hide behind. Gazing passionately at the woman and as if not knowing where I was going, I went toward the boulder, and when I was behind it, I moved quickly. I picked up a sizable stone,

one that on Earth would have weighed ten pounds, and hefted it. It was hard and light, like a petrified sponge. To throw or not to throw, that is the question, I thought as I watched the seated siren. Half recumbent on her boulder, she seemed to be sunbathing. I could see her rosy nipples and that her breasts were whiter than her belly, as with women who wear two-piece suits to the beach. I threw. The stone sailed slowly, endlessly, hit her shoulder, passed through her, and embedded itself in the sand at her bare feet. I expected an explosion but there was none. I blinked, and in that blink she vanished. One second she was sitting with her elbow on her knee and twisting a lock of golden hair around a finger, and the next second she was gone without a trace. The stone I had thrown wobbled a little before it stopped, and a small cloud of kicked-up sand settled on the gray rock. I was alone again. I rose from my crouch, and Wivitch spoke. Apparently he couldn't take my silence any longer.

"Tichy! We have no picture! What happened?"

"No *picture* . . . ?" I asked.

But of course—they must have observed this whole episode on the video. I had forgotten there was a cloud of micropes somewhere above me.

"We had static for forty seconds. The engineers thought it was our equipment but that's been checked and everything here is working. Look hard, you should see them."

He meant the micropes. They're as small as flies but in the sun you can see them at a considerable distance, like sparks. I looked up at the black sky but saw not one spark. What I did see was different and quite strange. It was raining. Here and there little dark droplets fell into the sand. One of them hit my helmet, and I was able to catch it before it rolled off. It was a microbe, but blackened, melted into a tiny lump of metal. The drizzle grew lighter as I told this to Wivitch. After three seconds I heard him curse.

"Melted?"

"That's what it looks like."

Which was logical. If the naked woman ploy was to succeed in undermining my credibility, Earth should see nothing.

"What about the backups?" I asked.

The micropes were operated by the teletronics people and not under my control. Four additional batches of them were on the ship.

"The second cloud was sent. Wait!"

Wivitch turned to speak to someone. I could hear another voice.

"It was sent two minutes ago," Wivitch said. He was breathing heavily.

"Have you reestablished video?"

"Yes. Hey, Jack—how much on the telemeters? We can see Flamsteed now, Tichy, they're descending. We'll have you too in a second . . . what's that?"

The question was not addressed to me, but I could have answered it, because again it began to rain melted micropes.

"Radar!" cried Wivitch, not to me but I could hear him, he was so loud. "What? Not enough resolution? Ah . . . Listen, Tichy. We saw you for about eleven seconds. Again there's no picture. You say they're melted?"

"Yes. And black as if fried to a cinder."

"We'll try once more, this time with a tail."

Which meant that the third cloud of micropes would be followed and observed by the fourth. I didn't expect anything from this. *They* knew the micropes from previous reconnaissance attempts and knew how to deal with them. Heating by induction, a zone in which any piece of metal would melt from eddying Foucault currents. At least as far as I could remember from high-school physics. But the particular device was not important. The micropes were worthless no matter how radar-proof and state-of-the-art they were. Built on the model of an insect's eye, where in flight each ommatidium-prism could take in more than 2,400 square feet. The resultant picture was holographic, three-dimensional, in full color, and sharp even if three quarters of the cloud was blinded. The moon obviously knew all about the micropes. Not encouraging, though to have been expected. The main thing that puzzled me was why I was still standing in one piece. If they could dispose of the micropes so easily, why wasn't I disposed of when the mirror trick didn't work? Why hadn't they disconnected me from my remote? The teletronicists said that that was virtually impossible because the control channel was in the band of the hardest cosmic rays, an invisible needle that reached from ship to remote and was so high-energy that it could be significantly affected probably only by the gravitational pull of a black hole. Only a million-tesla magnetic field would be able to bend that needle, and to generate such a field would require on the order of trillions of megajoules. In other words they'd have to pump gigatons of energy into space between the remote and the ship, and maintain something like an open umbrella over the moon, a shield of thermonuclear plasma. Either they couldn't, or they chose not to do so at this moment.

Such restraint, perhaps, came not from insufficient power but from a strategy. So far nothing on the moon had really attacked the reconnoiterers, whether robots or people. They had destroyed themselves, being the first to shoot. As if the nonliving inhabitants of the moon, had decided to remain on the defensive. And true, an adversary on the attack is in less clear a position than the adversary who knows an attack is coming. And so the doctrine of ignorance as a guarantee of peace, devised with so much trouble, had been turned with mockery and menace against its inventors.

Wivitch was speaking: the third group of micropes had arrived safely and I was on their screens again. So maybe *they* had only wanted to blind Control during the nude-woman mirage. I was plunged into thought. The moon, listening to the radio, had to know about the growing anxiety on Earth. The fear stirred by the press had infected not only the people but the governments. Though everyone realized that a nuclear strike against the moon would spell the end of peace on Earth. Therefore either a preemptive attack against the human race was imminent, or something very strange was taking place on the moon. Wivitch called me again to tell me that *all* the micropes would be deployed. They would come in successive clouds, wave after wave, not only from my ship but from all four corners of the world, as it were, because it had been decided to activate the reserves stockpiled under the zone of silence. I hadn't even known they were there. I sat down in that lifeless desert and leaned back a little to take in the black sky. I couldn't see the ship but saw the micropes, sparkling clouds descending and also approaching from all horizons. Some hung over me, swelling and billowing and glittering like a swarm of golden gnats playing in the sun. Others, the reinforcements, I could make out only now and then, when one of the stars winked out for a moment, obscured by a cloud of my microscopic guardians. They had me in their screens now at all angles. I should have got up and continued on but I was suddenly reluctant. Slow and ungainly in my heavy spacesuit, quite the opposite of the micropes, I made a good target even for someone with bad cataracts. Why did I have to be at the front of this mission

131

anyway? Why couldn't the swift micropes go instead, scouting ahead for me? Control agreed. A change of tactics. Swarms of golden mosquitoes sailed above me in a wide swath toward the lunar Urals.

I walked, looking carefully in all directions, until I came to a gently rolling plain pitted with small craters filled with sand. In the sand of one crater was something that looked like a thick dead branch. I grabbed it and tugged, as if pulling a deep root from the ground. Then I used a small folding shovel that I carried strapped to my side. From the sand and dust emerged a piece of iron, burnt, perhaps a fragment of one of the countless primitive rockets that crashed here in the early days of lunar exploration. I didn't call Control, who through the micropes could see my discovery for themselves. I pulled at the strangely bent bars until a thicker part appeared, and under that was a shinier metal. It didn't look particularly promising, but having begun this scavenging, I pulled harder, not afraid that one of the sharp pieces might puncture my suit, because I had no need of air. But something changed. At first I didn't understand why it was hard for me to keep my balance, then realized that my left boot was caught, gripped by flattened, curved prongs. I tried to free it, thinking I'd walked right into this one, but the foot was held fast and even the blade of my shovel didn't help, unable to pry the prongs apart.

"Is Wivitch there?" I asked, and waited three seconds for him to respond.

"They have me in some kind of bear trap," I said.

How incredibly stupid, getting taken by something like this! I couldn't get loose. The micropes surrounded me like excited flies as I struggled with the clamps that had closed on my boot like a vise.

"Return to the ship," Wivitch suggested. Or it might

have been one of his assistants, because the voice sounded different.

"I don't want to lose the remote," I said. "I need to cut this!"

"You have a Carborundum saw."

I unhooked the flat holster at my thigh, and in fact it contained a nice little saw. I plugged its cord into the generator in my suit and bent over. Sparks flew from the spinning edge. The pincers holding my boot at the ankle began to give, practically cut all the way through, when I felt a growing heat in the boot. With all my strength I wrenched my leg away, then saw that the metal bulb from which the bars protruded like roots from a great potato was glowing red-hot. The white plastic of the boot had blackened and was cracking from the heat. I made one last effort and, suddenly released, fell backward. Blinded by forked lightning, I felt a violent blow in my chest, heard the sound of the suit torn open, and was plunged into impenetrable darkness. I didn't lose consciousness, I was simply in darkness. After a moment I heard Wivitch:

"Tichy, you're on the ship. Say something! The first remote was taken out."

I blinked. I was sitting in the chair, my head on the headrest, my legs curiously bent, and holding my chest where a moment ago I had taken the blow. A painful blow, I realized only now.

"Was it a mine . . . ?" I asked. "A mine connected to a bear trap? Was that the best they could think up?"

I heard voices, but they weren't talking to me. Someone asked about the micropes.

"There's no video," said someone else.

"What? They were all destroyed by that one explosion?"

"Impossible."

"Impossible or not, we have no video."

I was still breathing as if after a long run, regarding the face of the moon. With the tip of my finger I could cover the entire crater of Flamsteed and the plain on which I had so stupidly lost the remote.

"What's wrong with the micropes?" I asked at last.

"We don't know."

I looked at my watch and was surprised: I had spent almost four hours on the moon. It was after midnight, by ship time.

"I don't know about you," I said with a yawn, "but I've had enough for today. I'm going to sleep."

Round Two

I awoke rested and immediately went over the events of the day before. You always think better after a good shower, which is why I had insisted on a bathroom with running water instead of those wet towels which are no substitute for a tub. Of course there couldn't be a tub, with the wash area no bigger than a barrel. Water rushed in on one side and was sucked out by a strong current of air on the other. In order not to drown, because water in zero gravity covers the body and face in a growing layer, I had to put on an oxygen mask before showering, which was a nuisance but better that than no shower. As we all know, even after the engineers could build rockets in their sleep, astronauts were still plagued by toilet accidents, and technology wrestled with that problem for a long time. Human anatomy is horribly unsuited for outer space. The astroengineers lost sleep over this but not the science fiction writers, who being artists simply didn't mention it. Urinating (for men, that is) wasn't too bad, but defecating was solved only with the offices of a special computer, which was fine, but when that broke down you found yourself in extremity and had to improvise. In my lunar module, this computer—about the only one—worked throughout like a Swiss timepiece, thank God. Washed and refreshed, I drank my coffee from a plastic bulb and ate a raisin cake under a funnel with its suction set on high so the crumbs wouldn't stick to my fingers or choke me. I don't like to give up my habits. Having breakfasted properly, I took a seat at the selenograph and, gazing at the globe of the simulated moon, smiled, since they wouldn't be inflicting advice on me for a while. I hadn't informed Control that I was awake; they thought I was still sleeping.

The mirror phenomenon and the naked blonde had clearly been two tests to determine who or what had landed, and apparently I had passed those tests, being allowed to wander through Flamsteed unenticed and unattacked. But the trap that turned out to be a mine didn't fit this picture. On one hand they go to great trouble to produce a mirage in the no man's land, all done at a distance because it is a no man's land, and on the other they plant mines—as if I was facing an army equipped with both early-warning radar and clubs. But the mine could have been there from earlier days, though neither I nor anyone else had any idea what had taken place on the moon during all those years of hermetic isolation. Not solving this mystery, I began preparing for the next reconnaissance.

LEM 2, in perfect working order, was the product of General Teletronics and a different model from the one I had lost so unexpectedly, poor thing. I crawled into the bay to have a look at it before I became it. It was exceptionally strong judging from the girth of its legs and arms, its broad back, the triple plates of armor that made a dull boom when I tapped with my finger. Apart from the apertures in the helmet it had six additional eyes, on its shoulders, hips, and knees. To outdo their competitor who designed the first LEM, General Teletronics had given their model two personal rocket systems: besides the retros ejected after landing this athlete of steel had jets fastened to its heels, shins, and even one in its behind, which was for balance — as I read in the self-congratulatory instructions — and for the execution of fifty-foot leaps. Its armor moreover gleamed like pure mercury, so that the ray of any laser would be deflected. This LEM may have been marvelous but I can't say I was thrilled as I inspected it, because the more eyes and dials and jets and auxiliary devices there are, the more the attention they take, and being a standard-model person myself I have no more limbs and senses than anyone else. Returning to the cabin, I hooked into the remote and stood in it, acquainting myself with the complicated controls. The switch that activated the great jumps was a wired wafer you took between your teeth. But how was I to talk to Control with a switch in my mouth? Well, it was elastic and could be molded like clay and tucked inside your cheek, and you could move it between your molars when necessary. In difficult situations, warned the instructions, you should take care not to bite down too hard. There was nothing about teeth chattering from excitement. The switch tasted awful; I immediately spat it out. Possibly they had smeared it with something at the proving ground on Earth, orange or mint toothpaste. I disconnected from the remote, went into a higher orbit, and flew around the moon to target 002 between Mare Spumans and Mare Smythii while conversing with the base as politely as I could.

I was flying as peacefully as a fed baby in its cradle when something happened to the selenography. It's an excellent instrument when it's working. There's no reason to travel with an actual globe of the moon; you can use a hologram, which is like having the entire satellite hanging in the air not three feet from you, rotating slowly, and you can see both its sculpted surface and the boundary lines of the sectors, the nations indicated by the kind of letters that appear on cars: US, G, I, F, R, S, N. But something had gone wrong, because the sectors began changing color, all the colors of the rainbow, then the pockmarks of the craters blurred, the image shuddered, and when I frantically turned knobs, it returned as a smooth white sphere. I tried adjusting the focus, size, contrast, but the moon for a second appeared upside down then disappeared altogether and the selenograph couldn't bring it back. I told Wivitch, and of course he said I had pushed a wrong button. After I assured him ten times that we had "a serious problem here," because since Armstrong that's how you put it, the experts finally got to work on the selenograph, and that took half a day. First they told me to go into an orbit above the Zone of Silence in order to rule out any interference from unknown forces or waves directed at me from the moon. When that didn't help, they checked directly from Earth all the circuits, integrated and not, in the holograph, meanwhile I fixed myself lunch then dinner. Since it's not easy to make a good omelette in zero gravity, I took off my helmet and earphones so the disagreements between the information scientists and the teletronicists, not to mention an ad hoc team of professors, wouldn't distract me. After all the debating they came to the conclusion that the selenograph *was* broken. They also established which microcomponent had blown, but it happened to be the only one I didn't have a spare for. They told me therefore to take my ordinary moon maps, the ones printed on paper, and tape them to the screen and use that to navigate. I found the maps but unfortunately I had four copies of the first quarter of the moon, where I'd been, and that was all. Great consternation. They told me to look again, more carefully. I searched the ship with a fine-tooth comb but found only a small comic book, pornographic, left by one of the technicians during the final preparations before takeoff.

Control now split into two camps. One said that under such conditions I couldn't continue the mission and should return; the other wanted to leave that decision to me. I agreed with the second camp and decided to land as planned. They could always transmit to me a television picture of the moon. Not a bad idea, except that this couldn't be synchronized with my trajectory; they'd either show me the surface of the moon whizzing past or hardly moving at all. On top of that I would be landing at the very edge of the face visible to Earth and then proceeding to the far side, which presented another problem. They wouldn't be able to send me a television picture directly when the ship was parked above the far hemisphere, which should have been child's play because the picture could be relayed to me by the monitoring satellites but they refused. They refused because somehow no one had foreseen this eventuality and the satellites were programmed according to the doctrine of ignorance and therefore weren't allowed to transmit anything to Earth or from Earth. Not anything. True, to maintain contact with me and my micropes, so-called Trojan satellites had been put into high equatorial orbit, but these were not for relaying television signals. That is, they were, but only via the micropes. There was an awful lot of discussion about this, then someone suggested they brainstorm the problem, and for the next four hours the scientists talked. They talked so much, I couldn't stand it, and then they drifted off the subject and were talking not about how to help me but who was to blame for not having provided redundancy in the selenographic system. As usual when people work collectively, shoulder to shoulder, the blame was not individual, but the accusations flew back and forth like tennis, until finally I told them I'd handle it myself. The risk was already so tremendous that a little additional risk, it seemed to me, wouldn't make any difference. Besides, the question of which sector I landed in, US, R, F, G, I, C, or any other letter of the alphabet, was purely academic.

The whole idea of the nationality of the robots inhabiting the moon, who knows in what generation now, was absurd. As you know—or may not—the most difficult task of military automation programming turned out to be the identification of the enemy. On Earth this was not a big problem; that's what uniforms were for, flags, colorful insignia on the wings of airplanes, helmet styles, and it wasn't all that hard to tell if a prisoner of war spoke Dutch or Chinese. With machines it was a different story. Therefore two strategies emerged: the Friend strategy and the Foe strategy. The first advocated the use of a multitude of sensors, analytical filters, differential selectors, and other such recognition devices; whereas the second was simplicity itself—the enemy was whoever or whatever didn't know the password and so had to be destroyed. But nobody knew what course the autoevolution of weapons on the moon had taken, or what kind of tactical programs had developed to distinguish friend from foe. Though of course friend and foe are highly relative terms. You can dig through public records and other documents to find out if a certain person had an Aryan grandmother, but there's no way to tell if that grandmother's Eocene ancestor was a sinanthropus or a pithecanthropus. Moreover, the automation of the armies eliminated ideology. An attacking robot follows its program, acting in accordance with focalization and optimization algorithms, differential diagnostics, and game theory—not patriotism. Military mathematics and weapons automation, moreover, if they had their apostles, they also had their apostates. The former maintained there were programs that could ensure perfect loyalty in a war robot so that nothing could turn it to treason; the latter said nonsense, because there is no code that can't be cracked and no security system that can't be subverted, just look at the history of computer crime. A hundred and fourteen programmers protected Chase Manhattan Bank's information centers from entry by unauthorized persons, and a bright young kid armed with nothing but a hand calculator and an ordinary telephone broke into that inner sanctum as a joke and left a calling card: auditors wanting to check a balance, before each CREDIT and DEBIT command had to type PEEKABOO. Of course the experts immediately devised a different, much more complicated, unbreakable program. I don't remember now who broke that one. But this has no bearing on round two of my mad mission.

I don't know the name of the crater I landed in. From the north it resembled Helvetius but not from the south. I had examined this second landing site from orbit although not that carefully. It didn't matter to me whether or not it had been a no man's land once. I could have determined the coordinates, playing at the astrograph and doing declinations from this star and that, but I decided to save that for later. LEM 2 was a lot better than I thought it would be, but it did have one problem, the temperature control worked in only two positions, so I had to keep turning the switch, jumping back and forth between oven and icebox which made my nose run. But why was I still sitting in the ship, putting off the landing? It wasn't fear, I suddenly understood, but the fact that I didn't know the name of the crater where I would be landing. As if a name had special significance. Which no doubt explains the zeal with which astronomers christened every surface feature of the moon and Mars, and why they fell into despair when they discovered on other planets so many mountains and valleys and had no more names left that sounded good.

The area was flat except for the northern horizon where a line of ash-gray vertical rocks stood against the black sky. I slogged with difficulty through abundant sand, checking from time to time to see if the micropes were still with me. They hovered so high above that only occasionally could I see them sparkle, distinguished from the stars by their movement. I was near the terminator, the night side of the moon about two miles ahead of me. The sun, very low, touching the horizon at my back, cut the plain with long parallel shadows. Every depression in the ground, even small ones, was filled with such darkness that it was like stepping into water. Hot and cold by turns, I walked stubbornly on, in the direction of my own giant shadow. I could talk with Control but had nothing to say. Every few minutes Wivitch asked me how I was doing and what I saw, and I answered: all right, and nothing. On a sloping dune lay a stack of large flat stones, and I went toward them, seeing a glint of something metallic there. It was the shell of an old rocket, clearly from the days of the first moon shots. I lifted it, looked at it, dropped it, and walked on.

At the top of a rise where there was hardly any of that fine sand that clings to your boots, was a stone the shape of a badly baked loaf of bread, and I don't know why but I kicked it. Maybe out of boredom or because it was lying so apart. The stone broke instead of rolling downhill, and a piece the size of a fist flew off, leaving a surface that gleamed like quartz. Of course I knew plenty, from my briefing, about the chemical composition of the moon's crust but couldn't remember if it included quartz, so I picked up the fragment. It was surprisingly heavy. I held it and looked at it, and not knowing what more to do with it, tossed it away and moved on, but didn't move on because at the last moment, as it left my hand, it glittered in the sun very curiously, as if something tiny was trembling in the concave broken place. I didn't pick it up again, but bent over it and watched for quite a while, blinking because I thought my eyes were playing tricks on me unless something really strange was taking place in that stone piece. The surface of the break was quickly losing its shine, in a few seconds was dull, and then it began to fill out as if drawing substance impossibly from within. The stone seemed to exude a viscous sap like a cut tree. Carefully I touched it with a finger, but it was not sticky; gummy, rather, like plaster before it sets. I looked at the other, larger piece and was even more surprised. It had not only dulled but swelled out a little at the place of the break. I didn't say anything to Wivitch, just stood there, legs apart, feeling the sun at my back, a hot pressure, it hung not far above the gently curved, white-and-black striped plain, but I didn't take my eyes from the stone.

It was growing or, more precisely, healing. After a few minutes the two parts, the stone and the fragment I had held in my hand, no longer fit, they had both swelled until each was a lump that had no flat side from the fracture. I waited to see what would happen next but nothing more happened, as if the wound had been sealed in both places by a scar. Absurd yet true. Remembering how easily the stone had broken, because I hadn't kicked it very hard, I looked around for more. A few, smaller, lay on the sunny slope, so I took out my folding shovel, went over and hit them, one by one, with its sharp blade. They split like overripe chestnuts and shimmered inside, until I came to an ordinary rock, because the shovel bounced off it leaving only a white line on its surface. I returned to those that had fallen in two. They were healing, there was no doubt about it. I had a little Geiger counter in a pocket on my right thigh. It registered nothing when held near the stones. This was an important find because stones don't heal, therefore these were probably the product of some local technology and I should collect them. I was reaching for one when I remembered that I couldn't return to the ship because that wasn't in the Mission. Nor could I do an in-the-field chemical analysis, having no reagents. If I told Wivitch about this phenomenon, a lengthy conference would ensue, full of expert opinions, and excited scientists would forbid me to leave the spot and ask me to break as many of the stones as I could, like eggs, and observe what happened while they theorized more and more boldly, but I felt in my bones that nothing would come of it, because you have to have some idea in your head before you start experimenting. Then I heard from Wivitch, who had seen me hitting something with the shovel but apparently the picture transmitted by the micropes was not sharp enough for him to see what. I answered that it was nothing and quickly continued on my way, full of thoughts.

The ability of those injured in battle to repair themselves might be useful to warrior robots but hardly to stones. Could this mean that the computers in this locality were building weapons from the ground up, as it were? But even so, why would stone projectiles need to heal? Then the thought occurred to me that I was here, after all, not as a living being but as a nonliving remote. Could it be that the evolution of the moon weapons had proceeded along two independent lines: as the production of weapons that would attack what was nonliving, and separately, what was

living? Let us assume that. Let us assume—I thought—
that a device designed to destroy a nonliving weapon could
not with the same efficaciousness destroy a living enemy,
and that I had encountered the second type of device, one
set for the landing of a man. Since I was not a man, these
mines—if they were mines—failing to detect a living body
inside my suit, did nothing to harm me, and only sealed
themselves up. A robot scout from Earth, happening upon
them, would pay no attention to healing rocks, not programmed to notice so bizarre and unforeseen a phenomenon. But I, neither man nor robot, had noticed. What then?
I did not know, but if there was any truth at all in my
theory, I could expect other mines, mines not for humans
but for automata. I walked more slowly, placing my feet
with great care, passing dune after dune, the unmoving sun
behind me. The stones I came to, some larger, some
smaller, I didn't hit with the shovel or kick in case there
were indeed two kinds of mines. I went on like this for a
good three miles or maybe more but didn't take out my
pedometer, which was in a shin pocket so deep and narrow
it was murder getting my glove in. Then, looking to the
south, I saw ruins.

It didn't make much of an impression on me because
there are so many piles of rock on the moon that from a
distance look like the ruins of buildings. Still, I changed
direction and waded through deeper sand, expecting that
grouping of rocks to reveal its true, random nature, but it
didn't. On the contrary, the closer I got, the more definitely it looked like the half-broken façade of a low building, and the black places weren't shadows but holes, maybe
not as regular as windows but on the moon no one had
ever come across such large holes in rock and certainly not
in a row. The sand stopped giving way beneath me, and
my boots hit something rough, pitted, and glassy, like lava

except it wasn't lava but perhaps sand that had been raised to an extremely high temperature then cooled. I wasn't mistaken because this surface was dazzling in the sun and covered the entire slope that led to the ruins. A high dune lay in front of them, and when I reached the top of it I had a perfect view and understood why I hadn't seen them from orbit. The ruins were deep in rubble. If these were truly houses, then the rubble came up to the windows. From a distance of about three hundred yards they resembled something familiar from photographs: stone foundations after an earthquake, for example in Iran. From orbit you would see them only near the terminator, the low sun shining through the window openings, which were misshapen as if from an explosion. But I still hadn't ruled out the possibility that this was merely a peculiar rock formation. I went closer. Feeling very uneasy, I took out my Geiger counter and plugged it into my suit so I could hear if the ground was radioactive. It was plenty radioactive but not until halfway down the dune. When I stepped onto the rubble that surrounded the squat houses with jagged walls and no roofs (now quite positive this was not the product of natural forces), I heard the counter's rapid clatter. The rubble didn't move under my feet as normal rubble would, it was as if all fused by the intense heat of an explosion. I was at the first house now but couldn't inspect it properly because I had to watch every step, placing my heavy boots carefully among the pointy ledges of that great heap so I wouldn't slip and become stuck between two boulders, which wouldn't have been difficult. Higher up, on a level with a nearby ruin, the rubble changed to a glaze covered with black streaks like soot. It was easier to walk, and I went to a window, an irregular opening with hanging stones at the top. I looked inside and saw—though not at once, because it was so dark—long objects lying haphazardly. Reluctant to crawl through the broken window because my remote, a massive thing, might get wedged, I looked for a door. If there were windows here, why not a door. But I didn't find one. Walking around the house, which was grotesquely squashed as if by some tremendous force, I discovered a crack in a side wall, wide enough to let me in if I hunkered down. On the moon, where sun and shadow coexist without intermediaries, the contrast is too much for the human eye even when relayed by a remote. I crawled groping into a corner of the room, pressed my back against the wall, and closed my eyes until they grew accustomed to the dark. I counted to a hundred, then looked around.

The interior was like a cave without a ceiling, which didn't mean light from above because the lunar sky is as black as night. And the sunlight through the window was not visible as a shaft because there was no air or dust to diffuse it. The sun remained outside, present only as a blazing white patch on the wall opposite the corner where I stood. In its reflection, at my feet, lay three corpses. That's what I thought in the first moment, because although blackened and distorted they had legs, arms, and one even had a head. Blinking and shielding my eyes from the patch of sun, I knelt over the nearest one. It was not a human body, nor any kind of mortal remains, for what has never been alive cannot die. The form sprawled before me was a manikin but probably not a robot, because its torn-open trunk was completely empty. There were only a few bits of rubble and sand inside. Cautiously I pulled at the thing's shoulder. It was surprisingly light, as if made of styrofoam, and black as coal, and headless, but then I saw the head by the wall—it was upright on its severed neck and regarded me with its three empty eyesockets. Naturally I wondered: why three and not two? The third eye was a round cavity positioned where on a man you would have the bridge of the nose, but this curious manikin surely never had a nose because on the moon there would have been no point. The other manikins were also only roughly humanoid. Although the destruction of the house had greatly deformed them, you could see that even to begin with they had been only approximations to the human shape. Their legs were too long, about one and a half times the length of the torso, and their arms were too thin and attached not to the shoulders but oddly, one to the chest, the other to the back. Which must have been by design because the explosion, shock wave, and cave-in could have contorted the limbs of one like that but not all of them in the same way. Having an arm in front and an arm in back might be, who knows, advantageous in certain situations.

Squatting opposite the sharp patch of sun and in the darkness with three manikin corpses, I realized that aside from the rapid clicking of the Geiger counter I was hearing nothing—that for at least a few minutes the voice of Wivitch had not reached me. The last time I spoke to him was from the top of the dune that overlooked the ruins, and I had said nothing about my discovery, wanting to make sure first that it wasn't an illusion. I called Control, but heard only the alarm-rattle of my counter. The radiation level was high, but I didn't bother to take a reading because as a remote I didn't have to worry, then suddenly it occurred to me that it was some ionized gas given off by these irradiated broken stones which had cut off my radio communication, and that at any moment resonant absorption could cut my contact with my ship. A stab of fear that I would be stranded here forever, which was stupid because if I lost contact with my ship, only the remote would remain in this rubble and ruins while I found myself back on board. But so far I felt no lessening whatever of control over the remote. My ship must have been hovering right over the house, maintaining the orbit that kept it near the zenith above me. No one of course had foreseen such a discovery or such a situation, but the zenith position is optimal for maneuvering a remote, since the distance between it and its operator is smallest and thus so is the response time. Without an atmosphere the concentration of ionized gas (perhaps from vaporization after the explosion) could not be great. Was it also interfering with communication between the base and the micropes? I didn't know and wasn't concerned about that at the moment; what intrigued me was what had happened here and why.

I dragged the biggest corpse, the one with the head, backward through the crack in the wall. Outside, the radio still didn't work, but I was more interested in this poor thing that had never lived, true, but for all its ghastliness made a most pathetic impression. He must have been nine feet tall, or maybe a little less, was thin, and the head was elongated, it had three eyes, no nose or mouth, a narrow neck, and the hands were prehensile, but I couldn't count the fingers because the material from which he was made had melted the most there. He was covered with tarry cinders. It must have been hot, I thought, and only then did it occur to me that this could have been a group of buildings like those they once set up on Earth to study the effects of nuclear explosions, it was in Nevada and someplace else too, with houses, courtyards, stores, and streets, but animals were used for people, sheep and goats I think, and especially pigs because like us they don't have fur and therefore suffer the same kind of burns we do. Had this been such a test site? If I knew the force of the blast that turned these buildings into rubble, I could determine from the present level of radioactivity how long ago that happened, but the physicists could also probably calculate it from the mix of isotopes here, so I put a little gravel into the thigh pocket of my suit, then remembered angrily, again, that I wouldn't be returning to the ship. But it was necessary to date the explosion, even if only approximately. I decided to leave the contaminated area, reestablish contact with Control, and tell them about this, letting the physicists solve the problem of how to analyze the specimen I'd taken.

I don't know exactly why, but I picked up the corpse and threw it over my shoulder, it didn't weigh more than ten or fifteen pounds here, and beat a rather awkward tactical retreat, its long legs dragging on the ground and catching on stones. I had to go very slowly to keep from falling. The slope was not that steep but I wasn't sure whether it would be better to walk on the slippery glassrock or over the rubble which rolled and shifted at every step. Because of this difficulty I went in the wrong direction and found myself not on the dune again but about a quarter of a mile to the west of it, between large round rocks that looked like monoliths. I put the corpse down on a flat place and sat to catch my breath before I tried raising Wivitch. I looked for the micropes but the glittering cloud of them was nowhere to be seen. And still I heard no voices though I should have by now. The clatter of the Geiger counter in my helmet slowed until it was like individual grains of sand falling on a drum. Then I heard a muffled voice and went numb, because it wasn't the base. Incoherent and hoarse, yet I caught two words: "My brother ... my brother ..." A moment of silence, and again: "My brother ..."

"Who is that?" I wanted to shout but didn't dare. I sat hunched, feeling the sweat break out on my forehead, and the voice again was in my helmet. "Come, my brother. Come to me. Without fear. I do not wish you harm, my brother. Come. We will not fight. Do not fear. I do not wish to fight. Come. Let us be brothers. Let us help each other, my brother." A snapping sound, and the same voice but in a completely different tone, sharp, barking: "Put down your weapon! Put down your weapon! Or I'll fire! Don't try to run! Turn around! Hands up! Both hands! And don't move! Don't move!"

Something snapped again and the first voice returned, weak and hesitant: "My brother, come. Let us be brothers. Help me. We will not fight." It was the corpse talking, that was clear. It lay where I had dropped it, and looked like a stepped-on spider with its abdomen split and its legs tangled and its empty eyesockets staring at the sun. It didn't move but something inside it was addressing me in a loop. A song in two keys, first come my brother and then the barking. That's its program, I thought. Whether manikin or robot, it was designed first to lure a man, a soldier, then take him prisoner or kill him. It couldn't do anything now, all that was left in it was an unburned scrap of the program playing in a loop. But why by radio? If it was built to fight on Earth, surely it would speak in a regular voice. I didn't understand the radio. There were no live soldiers on the moon, and a robot wouldn't be taken in by this. Or would it? It just didn't make sense. I looked at the blackened skull, the twisted hands and melted fingers, the torso ripped open, but now without the instinctive pity of a moment ago. With disgust, rather, with ill will, even though the thing was not to blame, it had been programmed this way. How can one be indignant with a bunch of circuits?

When it began its my-brother routine again, I spoke to it, but it didn't hear me. Or gave no sign of hearing me. I stood, my shadow fell on its head, and it stopped in the middle of a word. I stepped back, and it continued. So it was activated by the sun. I wondered what to do next. This manikin-trap was of little interest, too primitive to be much of a "war machine." And even the lunar armorers must consider these long-legged figures obsolete and worthless, seeing as they used them to test the effects of a nuclear hit. Because its lifeless refrain made it hard for me to concentrate, but to tell the truth it may have been for another reason, I picked up some larger pieces of rubble and threw them at the thing's head and then its torso, as if to bury it. It fell silent, and all I heard was a thin squeaking. At first I thought the squeaking was from the corpse, and looked around for more rocks, but then I realized it was Morse code. —t-i-c-h-y—l-i-s-t-e-n—t-h-i-s—i-s—c-o-n-t-r-o-l—s-a-t-e-l-l-i-t-e—m-a-l-f-u-n-c-t-i-o-n—s-o-u-n-d—w-i-l-l—r-e-t-u-r-n—s-o-o-n—w-a-i-t—t-i-c-h-y.

So one of the Trojan satellites between us had gone on the fritz. They would fix it soon, sure, I thought sarcastically. I couldn't reply, there was no way. For the last time I looked at the charred remains, and at the ruins white in the sun on the other side of the dune, and I ran my eyes over the black sky trying in vain to find the micropes. I walked toward a large convex wall of rock that rose from the sand like the gray hulk of a whale. I made for a break in the rock, which was black as tar in shadow, like the mouth of a cave. I blinked. Someone was standing there. A human figure, almost. Short, broad-shouldered, in a gray-green spacesuit. I raised an arm, thinking it was again my reflection and that the color of the suit was only from a shadow, but the figure did not move an inch. I hesitated, perhaps from fear or some premonition. But I hadn't come here to run, besides where would I run to? I stepped forward. He looked just like a squat man.

"Hello," came his voice. "Hello . . . Can you hear me?"

"I hear you," I said without much enthusiasm.

"Come over here . . . I have a radio too!"

That sounded pretty idiotic, but I went to him. There was something military in the style of his suit. Shining metal bands across his chest. His hands held nothing. Well, that was something, I thought, approaching but more slowly. He came toward me and lifted his arms in a simple gesture of greeting an old friend.

"Welcome! Welcome! How good of you to come at last! We can talk . . . you and I together . . . about bringing peace to the world . . ."

He spoke in an effusive, vibrant, strangely penetrating voice as he came toward me through the deep sand, arms held out, and his whole bearing expressed such cordiality that I didn't know what to think. He was now only a few steps from me, the dark glass of his helmet blazing with the sun. He embraced me, hugged me, and we stood that way on the gray slope. I tried to see his face but saw nothing, even as close as a hand's breadth, because the glass was opaque. It wasn't even glass, more a mask covered with glass. How could he see me then?

"You'll feel at home here with us, old friend . . ." He bumped my helmet with his as if trying to kiss me on both cheeks. "At home . . . we don't want war, we are peace-loving, meek, you'll see . . ." And with that he kicked me so hard that I fell on my back, and jumped on me, both knees in my stomach. I saw stars, literally, the stars of the black lunar sky, while my "friend" held my head down with his left hand and with his right pulled off his metal bands which themselves twisted into horseshoe hoops. I said nothing, dazed, as he fastened my arms to the ground one at a time with the hoops, driving them in with powerful, unhurried blows of his fist, and continued:

"At home, old friend . . . We're simple folk, kind, I like you and you like me, old friend . . ."

"And not 'my brother'?" I asked, now unable to move either arms or legs.

"Brother?" he said thoughtfully, as if trying out the word. "So be it, brother! I'm good, you're good, brother for brother!"

He stood, quickly and expertly tapped my sides, legs, found my pockets, took out everything I had, the flat box of tools, the Geiger counter, the folding shovel, and frisked me again, harder this time, especially under the arms, and tried to work his fingers into the top of my boots, and during this careful search of my person not for a moment did he stop talking.

"My brother, you said. Maybe yes, maybe no. Did one mother give birth to us? Ah, mother. Motherhood. Mother is a saint, and you're a saint too, brother, no weapon on you, none. A clever brother . . . just taking a little stroll, to pick mushrooms. Lots of boletus here, but the forest is hard to see. Yes, old friend . . . I'll make it better for you soon, all better. We're simple folk, meek, and we will inherit the earth."

He took a kind of flat knapsack off his back and opened it. Sharp instruments gleamed. He hefted one in his hand, put it back, selected another, powerful shears like the cutters used by soldiers in battle to get through barbed wire, and turned to me, the blades sparkling in the sun. He sat on my stomach, lifted the tool, and with the words "To your health" thrust it into my chest. It hurt but not much. Evidently my remote had pain dampers. I knew that this lunar friend of mine would open me like a fish and that I should return to the ship and leave him the body to cut up, but I was so fascinated by the contrast between his words and his actions that I lay as if mesmerized.

"Why don't you speak?" he said, slicing through my

suit with a crackling sound. Excellent shears, made of incredibly hard steel.

"I can say something?" I asked.

"Go ahead!"

"Hyena."

"What?"

"Jackal."

"You insult me, my friend? Not nice. Not friend but enemy. Treacherous. You came here unarmed to confuse me. I wished you well, but an enemy must be searched. My duty. That's the rule. I was attacked. With no declaration of war you stepped upon this sacred ground. Your own fault. My brother, hah. Brother of a dog! Worse than a dog, and you'll regret calling me hyena and jackal, but not for long, because memory ends with life."

The last of my chest welds gave way, and he began to break and pry apart things. He looked inside and hmmed.

"Interesting little gadgets," he said, getting up. "Fancy stuff. Our experts will figure it out. You wait here. But where can you go? Nowhere. You're ours now, my friend!"

The ground shook. Turning my head to the side as far as I could, I saw others like him. They marched in formation, goose-stepping the dust up. My executioner stood at attention, preparing to make his report, I supposed.

"Tichy, answer, where are you?" roared in my ears. "The sound is back. Wivitch here. Control. Can you hear me?"

"I hear you," I said.

Some of this must have been overheard by the soldiers, because they broke into a run.

"Do you know what sector you're in?" Wivitch asked.

"Yes. I've just realized. They've taken me prisoner! I'm cut open!"

"Which country?" Wivitch began, but my executioner drowned him out.

"Emergency!" he shouted. "Seize him!"

"Tichy!" cried Wivitch from far away. "Don't let them take you!"

I understood. Letting Earth's latest technology fall into robot hands was to be avoided at all cost. I couldn't move even a finger, but there was still a way. I bit down as hard as I could, heard a snap like an overwound spring, and was plunged into total darkness. Instead of sand under my back was the soft upholstery of my chair. I was on the ship. A little dizzy, I couldn't find the right button immediately, but then saw it. I broke the plastic cover and hit the red button with my fist so the remote would not be examined by them. Below, a pound of ecrasite blew it to smithereens. I felt sorry for the LEM but I had to do it. And so ended the second reconnaissance.

Carnage

Of the next ten landings I have memories as fragmentary as they are unpleasant. The third reconnaissance lasted the longest, three hours, even though I came down in the middle of a pitched battle between robots that looked like prehistoric lizards. They were so busy fighting, they didn't notice me when I descended on the battlefield in a halo of fire, white as an angel though without wings. Still aloft, I understood why this region had seemed empty from the ship. The robots were camouflaged; on their backs they had a knobby design that was like scattered stones in sand. They slithered with terrible speed. At first I didn't know what to do; there were no bullets whizzing past, no explosives, but the laser flashes were blinding. I lumbered quickly to some large white rocks, because this was the only cover in reach. Peering out from behind a boulder, I watched the battle.

I couldn't tell who was fighting whom. The lizard robots, which resembled caimans, were attacking up a shallow slope in my direction, hopping. But the enemy seemed to be among them, in their ranks, perhaps the enemy had parachuted in, because I saw some lizards struggling with others and they looked exactly the same. At one point three that were pursuing one came quite close. They caught it but couldn't hold it because it shook off all its legs and escaped, writhing like a snake. I hadn't expected such primitive combat, with tails and legs being torn off, and I waited for them to get around to me, but somehow in the heat of battle I was ignored. A line of soldiers advanced on the slope, spitting laser fire from mouths funnel-shaped like blunderbusses. But something odd was happening higher up on the slope. The robots in front, covered by the fire of those behind, slowed about halfway up and began to change color. Their sandy backs darkened, then were covered with gray smoke as though from an invisible flame, and then they ignited. But there were no flashes from the other side, so it could hardly have been lasers. The slope was now strewn with charred and melted machines, but new troops came and went rushing to their doom.

It was only when I turned on my telesights that I saw what they were attacking. At the top of the hill was something huge and unmoving like a fortress, but a peculiar fortress because it was all mirrors. Or maybe not mirrors but screens of some kind, which in the top half showed the black sky with stars and in the bottom the sandy slope strewn with debris. Unless they were both mirrors and screens at the same time. The lasers had no effect on the fortress, were deflected, meanwhile lower, where the biggest pile of robot corpses lay, the temperature of the rock was over three and a half thousand degrees according to the bolometer in my helmet. A force field heating by induction or something like that, I thought, pressing tight to the boulder that was my shield. The lizards attacked, and the mirror-screen thing surrounded itself with an invisible wall of heat, fine, meanwhile what was I supposed to do, defenseless as an infant caught in a wave of charging tanks? I didn't have to report all this to Control because my third remote was followed by a special rocket that looked like an ordinary rock. It impersonated a meteor, except that this meteor didn't fall but hung two miles above me.

Something touched my thigh. I looked down and froze. It was one of the legs of the robot that a moment ago had turned into a snake. The leg had inched its way to the boulder where I was hiding and had come upon me. In this blindly twitching thing with three sharp claws and sandy camouflage there was something both repulsive and pathetic. It tried to attach itself to my thigh but of course couldn't, finding no purchase. I picked it up with disgust and threw it as far from me as I could. It came back. So instead of observing the battle I had to fight with that leg, because it was trying to climb up me again, ineffectually, as if it was drunk. And now the others will come, I thought, and the situation will be really ridiculous. I threw it. At least Control was silent, because any conversation might be overheard, which would be bad for me. Crouching in the shadow of my boulder, I gripped my shovel and waited for the leg, and thought darkly that all I needed was for the damned thing to have some radio transmitter too. Contracting and lengthening in turn, it reached my knees because I was kneeling, and I held it down with one hand and with the other started chopping with the shovel. Instead of taking notes on robot warfare Ijon Tichy sits on the moon making lizard-leg hamburger. Wonderful. Finally I must have hit a sensitive spot because it rolled over and stiffened. I got up then and peered around the boulder.

The laser-shooters had fallen, and I could hardly distinguish the individual robots, their gray blending into the surroundings. But now up the slope came, from where I don't know, a spider as big as a shack and listing like a ship at sea. Flat as a turtle on top, it wavered on its many widespread legs, the knees higher than itself on both sides, but it proceeded methodically, heavily, carefully placing those many-jointed stilts, and approached the wall of heat. I was curious to see what would happen. Under its belly something long and dark, almost black, came into view, probably a weapon of some kind. The spider stopped at the wall of heat and stood awhile, as if thinking. All action stopped. The only thing I could hear was high squeaking in my helmet, a signal in some incomprehensible code. A strange battle, for it was primitive, resembling the struggle of Mesozoic dinosaurs on Earth millions of years ago, but at the same time it was sophisticated, because these lizards had not hatched from reptilian eggs but were robots armed with lasers and packed with electronics. The giant spider now hunkered down, its belly touching the ground, and seemed to close in upon itself. I heard nothing, but of course even if the very moon were to split open you would hear no sound, however the ground shook once, twice, three times. The tremors became continuous, till everything around me, and myself, shook with an increasingly intense vibration. The dunes in the distance strewn with the bodies of gray lizards, the slope facing me, and the black sky above it, I saw everything as through trembling glass. The outlines of objects blurred, even the stars on the horizon winked as on Earth, and I shook feverishly, like a tuning fork, and so did the boulder I clutched. I shook in every bone and finger, more and more violently, as if every part of my being were quivering jelly. The vibration was painful now, like a thousand microscopic drills at once. I tried pushing away from the boulder, to stand separate, because then it would reach me only through the soles of my boots, but I couldn't move, my hands were paralyzed, I only watched, half-blind, as the giant spider drew itself into a dark bristling ball like a real spider dying under a magnifying glass that focuses the sun. Then everything went black and I was falling into an abyss, until I opened my eyes, covered with sweat, my throat tight, and saw the bright, friendly colors of the control panel. I had returned to the ship. Apparently a safety mechanism disconnected me at a certain level of discomfort. I rested a minute, then decided to go back, although with the hideous feeling that I might be entering a corpse. Carefully I pushed the lever, as if it could burn me, and found myself again on the moon and in the all-consuming vibration. Before the safety mechanism threw me on the ship again I saw, though not that clearly, a great mound of black fragments that were slowly tumbling down. The fortress fell, I thought, and again was back in my own body. But the fact that the remote hadn't come apart gave me the courage to try it one more time.

Nothing shook now. All was deathly still. Among the charred lizards lay the ruins of the mysterious fortress that had blocked the way to the top of the hill. The spider that had destroyed it using resonance lay in a ball of twitching legs which straightened and bent, straightened and bent, movements that grew slower until they stopped completely. A Pyrrhic victory? I waited for another advance but nothing moved. If I hadn't seen what I had seen, I might not even have noticed the burnt debris that littered the whole field, it blended in so with the sand. I tried to rise but couldn't.

I was not even able to move a hand. At most I managed to tilt my head in the helmet so I could see myself.

It was not a pretty sight. The boulder that had served me as a shield was split into large pieces and those were covered with a network of hairline cracks. My legs or rather what remained of them were stuck in rubble. The poor remote was an armless, legless torso. I had the eerie sensation that my head was on the moon and my body was on the ship, because even as I saw the battlefield under the black sky, I felt the seat and shoulder belts of my chair. The chair was with me yet not with me because I couldn't see it. It wasn't hard to figure out the reason: the remote's sensors, without incoming data, shut down so I remained in contact only with the head which, protected by the helmet, had survived the murderous moonquake caused by the spider. Nothing more for me to do here, I thought. But I stayed, half in half out of the rubble, and looked over the sunlit field.

In the distance something was flapping in the sand, sluggishly, like a fish on a beach. One of the lizard robots. Sand rolled off its back as it hauled itself into a sitting position like a kangaroo or dinosaur, and it sat there, the last witness of a battle that no one won. The robot turned toward me and suddenly began to spin, and spun so fast, the centrifugal force made its long tail fly off. I watched, amazed, while it whirled now like a top, until pieces flew in all directions and it fell flat, flopped over a few times, and with a final somersault landed on the other bodies and was still. Although I had attended no lecture on the theory of electronic expiring, I knew that this was what I had just seen, it was so like the death spasms of a crushed beetle or caterpillar. We know how their death looks but cannot know if those last spasms signify suffering. I had had enough of this. I felt, in a way difficult to describe, that I was involved in it, even responsible. But because I hadn't come to the moon to philosophize on moral questions, I bit down hard to disconnect myself from the pitiful remnant of LEM 3 and in the blink of an eye was back on board to tell Control what had happened this time.

Invisible

Tarantoga, to whom I showed these notes, said that I describe all who worked on my mission and kept watch over me as either idiots or bunglers. Whereas the General Theory of Systems proves mathematically that there exists no element or part that is infallible, and even if you reduce fallibility to one in a million, in other words provide that a given part will break down only once in a million times, a system containing a million parts *must* fail because one of the million will fail. But the lunar system I belonged to was made up of not one but eighteen million components, therefore the idiot bungler responsible for the majority of my problems was *the world*, because if all the experts stood on their heads and were geniuses every one, the situation could only be worse, never better. Probably true. On the other hand, I was the one who suffered as a result of all those unavoidable breakdowns, and anyway psychologically, when you're in a fix, you don't curse the atoms or electrons

164

but specific individuals so my radio tantrums were also unavoidable.

Control pinned their hopes on the last LEM because
it was a miracle of technology and guaranteed the maximum safety. It was a remote in powdered form. Instead of
a steel athlete you had a container filled with microscopic
grains, each grain of such concentrated intelligence it ri-
valed a supercomputer. In the presence of certain impulses
these particles came together to form a LEM. I could land
as a thin cloud of molecules, could coalesce if necessary in
the form of a robot of human shape, but I could just as
easily become one of forty-nine other programmed things,
and even if eighty-five percent of the grains were destroyed, the rest would be enough to carry on. The science
behind such a remote, called a dispersant, was so advanced
that Einstein, von Neumann, the entire physics department
of M.I.T., and Rabindranath Tagore working together
would have had a problem with it, so I didn't even try to
figure it out. All I knew was that they'd embodied me in
thirty billion separate particles, particles more versatile
than the cells of a living organism, and there was unimag-
inable redundancy for joining these in various combinations which could all be turned back to dust at the push of
a button, dust so scattered you couldn't see it, and each
particle incorporating stealth technology, making it unde-
tectable by radar or laser or anything except gamma rays.
If I was ambushed I could disperse myself, retreat, and
reform in whatever way I liked. What one experiences as a
cloud spread over several thousand cubic feet is impossible
to put into words. To know it, you have to be such a cloud.
If I lost my vision, or to be more precise my optical sensors, I could replace them with any other organ, and the
same for arms, legs, tentacles, tools. I just had to be careful
not to become lost in the wealth of possibilities. This time,

I would have only myself to blame if I failed. The scientists thus washed their hands of responsibility if the remote malfunctioned. I can't say this made me happy.

I landed at the equator on the other side of the moon, smack in the middle of the Japanese sector, as a centaur, that is as a being with four extremities plus two arms attached to the upper trunk, with an additional device that surrounded me like an intelligent gas, so actually there was not much resemblance to the mythological creature. Even though I had familiarized myself with this powdered remote too at the Lunar Agency's testing range, I first crawled into the bay to check it out. It was indeed fascinating to watch that pile of glittering powder begin to move when you turned on a program, and flow, and connect, and mold itself to make the given shape, and how when you turned off the field (electromagnetic or possibly something else), it flew apart like a kicked sand castle. This ability to fly apart at any moment was supposed to make me feel secure. The sensation was quite unpleasant, like a strong vertigo combined with the shakes, but there was nothing I could do about that. At least it only lasted until I assumed a new form. The one thing that could destroy me was a thermonuclear explosion and even that had to be up close. I asked if it was possible for me to disperse completely due to a malfunction but they never gave me a straight answer. As an experiment I tried to run two programs at once, becoming at the same time a humanoid giant and a nine-foot caterpillar with a flattened head and enormous pincers, but it didn't work because the selector worked on an either/or principle.

This time I stood on lunar soil without the rear guard of the micropes, because I was myself in a sense a multitude of eyes, pulling after me a flowing gauzy train of transmitters. Possessing an inquiring mind, I had asked what would happen if it turned out that similar protean robots had been developed on the moon. They couldn't answer that though on the testing range they had pitted two, even three such robots against each other, which mixed like clouds going in different directions. The clouds preserved ninety percent of their identity. Ninety percent of an identity is probably also something you have to experience to understand. This reconnaissance, at any rate, started without any trouble. I trotted forward, not even having to turn my head because I could see on all sides at once, the rear included, like a bee, which has round eyes and sees out of thousands of ommatidia at the same time.

The way that the individual nations programmed their weapon factories was known only to them, but from the Japanese particularly, famous for their ingenuity, I expected unpleasant surprises. Professor Hakagawa, a member of our team at Control, had no more idea than any of us what monsters the Japanese computers might hatch, but he warned me to stay on my toes and not be taken in by appearances. Not knowing how to tell appearance from reality, I cantered across the monotonous, flat terrain. At the horizon rose the embankment of a large crater, and Wivitch, Hakagawa, and the rest of them were delighted with the picture relayed to Earth by the Trojan satellites because it was razor-sharp. After an hour I observed some low shoots among the rocks and in the sand, and they turned in my direction. They looked like the withered leaves of potato plants. I asked if I should pull up a clump, but nobody wanted to make the decision for me, some said I definitely should and others said I'd better not. I leaned my centaur's body over one of the larger plants and tried to pick a pliant stem. Nothing happened, so I lifted it to my eyes. It began writhing like a snake and coiled itself tight around my wrist, but after trying a couple of things I discovered that if you stroked it lightly, like tickling with a finger, it let go. I felt stupid addressing potato leaves though I knew this had nothing to do with the vegetable kingdom, but I gave it a try anyway. There was no answer, not that I expected one. I shook off the tendrils, which squirmed like worms, and galloped on. The area looked like a poorly kept garden, a bucolic scene, but I was prepared for an attack at any moment and even provoked those pseudoplants, stepping on them with my hooves (which are what my boots looked like; had I wanted, I could have made them cloven hooves). Then I came to a patch of another dead vegetable, in long rows, and before each row stood a large sign with the words STOP! HALT! ARRÊTE! and so on in some twenty tongues including Malay and Hebrew. Despite this I plunged ahead into the field. Farther on, tiny pale-blue flies swarmed in circles near the ground, and when they saw me they arranged themselves into the letters DANGER! ОПАСНОСТЬ! GEFAHR! PERÌCOLO! YOU ARE ENTERING JAPANESE PINTELOU! I called Control, but no one, not even Hakagawa, knew what PINTELOU meant. I encountered my first problem, because when I pushed through these trembling letters they stuck to me and began crawling over my body like ants. They did me no harm, however. I flicked them off with my tail (showing its usefulness for the first time) and ran down a furrow between two patches until I came to the edge of the crater. The plants continued into a gully and on, deeper, into a wide ravine, its bottom hidden in moon shadow as black as coal.

Suddenly a large tank came at me out of that darkness, squat, huge, its wide treads grinding and rumbling, which was odd because one can't hear on the moon, there's no air to carry the sound waves. Nevertheless I heard the noise, heard even the gravel crunching under the steel tracks. The tank bore down on me. Behind it appeared a long column of other tanks. I would gladly have stepped aside to let them pass, but it was too narrow where I stood. I was going to disperse but when the first tank reached me, it went through like fog, making everything a little darker for a couple of seconds. More phantoms, I thought, and let the next tanks roll through me. After them came a line of soldiers, ordinary soldiers, with almond eyes, bayonets fixed on short rifles, and among them walked an officer with a saber and a flag that displayed the rising sun. They all went through me like smoke, and I was alone again. It grew darker in the deepening ravine so I turned on my lights, which bordered all my eyes, and proceeding more slowly I came to the mouth of a cave behind a rampart of scrap iron. The opening was too low for me, so in order not to have to keep stooping I changed into a dachshund-centaur, which sounds stupid but is descriptive because my legs shortened and my belly brushed stones as I entered the moon's interior, going where no human being had ever set foot though my feet weren't exactly human either. I stumbled more and more, my hooves slipping on gravel, when I remembered what I was capable of and turned them into padded paws that held the floor like a lion's or tiger's. I felt more at home in my new body but didn't have time to play games. Lighting up the irregularly cut walls of the cave, I reached a grating that filled the entire passage-way, and I thought how polite these Japanese weapons were to intruders because on the ceiling above the grating glowed the large sign: NOT ENTERING! NOT TO TRESPASS THIS BARRIER! YOU HAVE WARNING TO KEEP OUT! and beyond the bars floated a phosphorescent skull and cross-bones with the words DEATH IS VERY PERMANENT CONDITION. That didn't deter me. I went to powder, passed through the grating, and pulled myself together on the other side. The natural stone of the corridor gave way to an oval tunnel, its walls bright and smooth like ceramic. I tapped it with a finger, and from the place I touched a small root emerged and flattened into a plaque that read MENE MENE TEKEL UPHARSIN. It was clear they weren't joking but I hadn't come this far to retreat now, so I proceeded on quiet paws, feeling my tail following softly, ready to come to my assistance at any moment. It didn't bother me that Control couldn't see me. The radio had fallen silent, and I could hear only a low, plaintive sound, like keening. I came to a wider place where the tunnel forked. Above the left passage glowed a neon THIS IS LAST WARNING but over the right there was no sign so I went left of course and saw white: a wall, and an enormous armored door with a row of locks and keyholes, like a door to a sultan's treasure. I clouded my right hand and slipped it through one of the keyholes. It was darker than midnight inside. I felt around, then slipped my whole body through in the form of a mist or aerosol, hoping that intruders flowing through keyholes was something the Japanese or rather their machines hadn't foreseen. I had difficulty breathing but only figuratively because I didn't breathe. I lit up the place not only with the lights around all my eyes but also with my whole self, like a glowworm, remembering the versatility of this LEM. So much light blinded me at first, but I soon grew accustomed to it.

The tunnel kept descending, straight as an arrow, until it was blocked by a curtain of what seemed ordinary straw. I pushed it aside and entered a large room lit with ceiling lights. The scene was one of complete chaos. In the center lay a ruin among large shiny pieces of porcelain; it looked like a supercomputer taken apart by a bomb. Broken curling cables went in and out between these fragments covered with crushed glass and the glittering flakes of integrated chips. Someone had been here before me and wreaked havoc in the heart of the Japanese weapons complex. The strangest part was that the giant computer, several stories high, had been smashed by a force acting from within and probably from the bottom up, since its thick armor-plated walls had buckled and split outward. Some of the sections were like library shelves or cabinets, filled with tight coils of wire, banks of switches, and circuit boards. As if an unbelievable hand had struck up into this colossus and ripped and shattered, but in that case I should have been able to see that hand in the center of the destruction. So I began climbing the rubble, which was as dead and empty as a plundered pyramid, and reached the top and looked down.

Someone lay there as if in a deep and well-earned sleep. At first I thought this was the same robot who had greeted me so warmly during my second reconnaissance, calling me brother only to knock me flat and open me like a can of sardines. I looked at him lying at the bottom of the uneven funnel of debris from the smashed computer. He was man-shaped though larger than a man. There is no hurry to wake him up, I thought. Better to figure out first what happened here. Obviously the Japanese weapons factory had not wished this attack upon itself. I dismissed the hara-kiri possibility as unlikely. Seeing as the borders between sectors were so well guarded, the invasion may have been carried out below them, by burrowing through the rock. In that way the unknown attacker could have made it to the very heart of the computer arsenal to demolish it. I should question this robot who slept so soundly after completing his murderous mission. The prospect didn't fill me with enthusiasm. In my head I went through all the different forms I could assume, to choose the one that would be safest for our conversation, because this character, awakened, might prove hostile. I couldn't speak as a cloud but could as a partial cloud, a cloud with a voice box inside it. That seemed the most prudent. To wake the giant I didn't bother with niceties but pushed a chunk of computer so it would roll down on him, and changed myself as quickly as I could. It hit his head, which made the whole mountain of rubble tremble, and other pieces of electronic debris began to sift down. He got to his feet immediately, stood at attention, and barked:

"Mission a success! Enemy position taken, for the fatherland! Reporting for further instructions!"

"At ease," I said.

He probably hadn't expected a command like that but he relaxed, stood with his legs apart, and only then noticed me. Something inside him whirred.

"Hello," he said. "How are you? You're a little hazy, my friend. But it's good that you've finally come. Come closer, we'll have a chat, sing a song, put our heads together. You'll like it with us. We're meek, peaceful, we don't want war, we hate war. Which sector are you from exactly . . ." he added in a different tone, as if suddenly suspicious, or else he had switched to a more appropriate program. What lay around us was hardly evidence of peaceful activity. He held out his huge, iron right hand, and I saw that each finger was a muzzle.

"You want to shoot a friend?" I asked, wafting gently over the porcelain heap. "Well then go ahead, brother. Shoot, and may it do you good."

"A Japanese spy!" he barked, blasting at me with all five fingers. Pieces of wall fell but I, still hovering calmly above him, lowered my voice box so it wouldn't be hit. Thickening the bottom half of the cloud, which was myself,

I pushed a chunk of computer the size of a chest of drawers, and it bore down on him, carrying with it an avalanche of rubble.

"An attack!" he yelled. "I'll draw their fire! For the fatherland!"

"You're so dedicated," I said, then turned myself into all cloud, and in the nick of time, because there was a boom and the mountain of debris burst into flame. My self-sacrificing interlocutor stood in blue fire, blazed then blackened but with his last breath managed to shout "For the fatherland!" before he came apart. His arms fell off, his chest split from the heat, revealing for a moment a curiously primitive tied bundle of copper wire, and finally his head went, popped open, and was completely empty, like a walnut shell. But still he stood, a pillar of embers which finally collapsed for good into ashes.

Although I was a gas, I felt the heat beating from the ruins as if from a volcano. I waited a minute, spread along the walls, but no new candidate for conversation stepped from the flames, which leaped upward so fiercely, the ceiling lights, those that were still in one piece, began to crack, and bits of tubing, glass, and wire rained on the rubble and it became darker. The room, geometrical and once neat, a perfect circle, was now like a scene from a witches' Sabbath in the glow of the blue flame that kept roaring upward, and the air scorched me. Seeing I had no more to learn here, I gathered myself and floated out to the corridor. No doubt the Japanese had other, reserve military centers, so this one might not be that important, but I felt I should return to the surface and tell Control what happened before I continued the reconnaissance. Nothing barred my way or challenged me. I took the tunnel to the armored door, passed through the keyhole and then the grating, and looked with pity at the warning signs I passed, they were so useless. Finally I saw the mouth of the cave glimmer in the distance. Only now did I assume an approximately human shape, having missed it—a new, unprecedented kind of nostalgia, that—and I looked for a boulder where I could sit and eat, because I felt hungry, except I forgot that as a remote I couldn't put a thing in my mouth. And I really couldn't leave such an excellent machine undefended just to get a quick bite to eat. So I put that off. I would report to Control first and then break for lunch after I stashed the remote in a safe place.

I called Wivitch but the only answer was dead silence. I checked with the Geiger counter to see if maybe there was ionized gas here too. Or possibly the short waves couldn't get out of this narrow ravine. So with a sigh I turned back into a cloud and flew high into the black sky and like a bird again called Earth. Of course I couldn't be a bird, with no air there's nothing to support wings, I only said bird because it sounds nice.

Visits

I returned from my aborted shopping excursion as if in a dream. I don't remember how I got back to my room, I was thinking so hard about what had happened in front of that department store. Having no desire to sit at the table with Kramer and the others, I ate all the cookies in the desk drawer and washed them down with a Coke. It was dusk when someone knocked. Thinking it was Dr. House, I opened the door. A stranger stood in a dark suit and with a thin black briefcase in his hand. He looked like a funeral director.

"May I come in?" he asked. I stepped back without a word. Not looking around, he sat on a chair, the one I had thrown my pajamas over, put his briefcase on his knees, and took out a bunch of typewritten pages. From his pocket he took pince-nez and set them on his nose, and regarded me awhile in silence. His hair was gray but his eyebrows black, his face gaunt, and his bloodless lips turned down at the corners. I stood by the desk, waiting, and finally he laid his card on the blotter. I read PROFESSOR ALLEN SHAPIRO, I.C.G.D. The address and telephone number were so small, I couldn't make them out, but I didn't pick up the card. I was filled with a weary indifference which was like drowsiness.

"I am a neurologist," he said. "Fairly prominent."

"Yes, I think I've read you," I mumbled. "Callotomy, the lateralization of brain function . . . Is that right?"

"Yes. I am also a consultant for the Lunar Agency. It's thanks to me that you were allowed to proceed as you have. I believe that in the present situation you should be protected but no more than that. The escape attempt was infantile. Consider. You have become the bearer of a priceless treasure. *Geheimnisträger*, the Germans would say. Your every step has been followed and not only by the Agency. To date the Agency has thwarted eight attempts to kidnap you, Mr. Tichy. When you flew to Australia, you were under observation by special satellites and not just ours. It's been all I can do to keep our own government leaders at bay. They want you arrested, put out of commission, and so on. The advice you obtained through your friend is worthless. When the stakes are high enough, the law means nothing. As long as you are alive, everyone—all the players—are stalemated. This can't go on. If they are unable to get you, they'll kill you."

"Who?" I asked, without surprise. Seeing that this would be a long visit, I took a seat, throwing a few newspapers and books to the floor.

"It doesn't matter. You have acted in good faith. Your official report was compared with what you wrote here and buried in the jar. In addition the Agency has all the tapes from Control."

"And?" I said, because he had paused.

"Some is the truth, some confabulation. But not done by design. You believed both what was in your report and what you put down here. When there are gaps in the memory, it is natural for a person to fill them in. One does it quite unconsciously. Anyway we don't really know if your right brain contains a treasure."

"Which means?"

"The callotomy might not have been an accident."

"What then?"

"A maneuver to divert attention."

"By the moon?"

"It's possible."

"Is this really so crucial?" I asked. "The Agency can always send more scouts."

"And has. You returned after six weeks. Once the diagnosis was made—your callotomy, I mean—three more people were sent."

"And they didn't succeed?"

"They succeeded in returning. All of them. Unfortunately . . ."

"Yes?"

"Their experiences were totally different from yours."

"Totally?"

"It's better for you not to know the details."

"But you know them, so you too, Professor Shapiro, are in danger," I said with a smile. He nodded philosophically.

"The scientists have a hundred different theories, but there's general agreement that the classical remotes were no surprise to the moon. The surprise was the molecular remote, your final remote. But now this too the moon is aware of."

"Which means?"

"You've probably already figured it out. You penetrated farther than the ones who followed you."

"The moon put on a show for them?"

"That's what it looks like."

"And not for me?"

"You got through the stage sets, at least partly."

"Why did they let me return?"

"In their strategic game, it was the optimal solution to the problem. You returned, the mission completed, and at the same time did not return or complete your mission. Had you not returned at all, the Security Council would have voted against further reconnaissance."

"And instead, to destroy the moon?"

"Not destroy so much as neutralize."

"That's something new to me. How is it done?"

"There's a way. Incredibly expensive, since it's a completely new technology. I don't know the details. It's better not to know them."

"You must have picked up something . . ." I muttered. "It would have to be a post-atomic technology in any case. No warheads or rockets, something more discreet. Something the moon would not be able to detect in time . . ."

"For a man with only half a brain, you're not stupid. But let's get back to the subject, that is, to you."

"You want me to agree to be examined? By the Agency? Let them give my right hemisphere the third degree?"

"It's more complicated than you think. We have, besides your report and the tapes of the mission, certain hypotheses. One says that the individual sectors on the moon are at war. That they have not united, neither for the destruction of some by others nor to plan an attack on Earth."

178

"What exactly has happened, then?"

"If we knew exactly, I wouldn't have to bother you. The barriers between the sectors definitely failed. The military games have engaged each other. It's produced unprecedented effects."

"Such as?"

"I'm no expert on this, but as far as I know, there *are* no experts on this. We're at the mercy of conjecture under the banner of, if you'll pardon my Latin, *Ceterum censeo humanitatem preservandam esse.*"

"What is it you want of me?"

"Nothing at the moment. You are, excuse the metaphor, a man with the plague before there were antibiotics. I came to see you because I insisted. They finally agreed. You are sort of a last resort. Who unfortunately multiplied the possibilities of what is happening on the moon. Speaking plainly, after your return we know less, not more."

"Less?"

"Of course less. We're not even sure that your right brain contains any critical information. The number of unknowns has increased."

"You speak like an oracle."

"The Lunar Agency transported to the moon and placed into sectors what it was supposed to under the Geneva Agreement. But the computer programs of that first generation remained the secret of the participating nations. The Agency wasn't privy to them."

"So it was wild cards from the very beginning?"

"Of course, because of the world's antagonisms. The question is, is it possible to tell the difference between a program that after a few decades derails from the safeties installed by its designers and a program *designed* to derail in a certain way?"

"I don't know. Perhaps computer scientists could tell."

"No, no one can tell except those who wrote the programs."

"Professor Shapiro," I said, getting up and going to the window. "I have the impression that you are drawing me into a web. The more we talk, the cloudier the subject becomes. What has happened on the moon? We don't know. What I experienced there, was it real? We don't know. What was the reason for this damned callotomy of mine? We don't know. Does half of my brain hold important information? We don't know. I most respectfully ask you to get to the point."

"Most respectfully. You have been treated most respectfully up to now."

"Because it was in the Agency's interest, and perhaps in the interest of others as well. Or are you telling me I was saved and protected out of the goodness of your hearts?"

"No. Goodness doesn't enter into it. As I said before, the stakes are too high. So high, that had we been able to extract what we want from you by torturing you to death, that would have been done long ago."

An unexpected thought came to me. I turned, my back to the now dark window, and smiled, crossing my arms on my chest.

"Thank you, professor. Only now do I understand who has really been protecting me all this time."

"But I told you."

"But I know better. It is *they* . . ." And opening the window, I pointed at the moon rising above the trees, a sharp white crescent against the dark blue sky.

The professor said nothing.

"It must have something to do with my landing," I went on. "With the fact that I went down myself to take what the last remote found, which I could do because there was a spacesuit and lander in the bay. They put them there just in case, and I used them. True, I don't remember what happened to me when I stood on the moon with my own two feet. I remember and don't remember. I found the remote but I don't think it was the molecular one. I remember that I knew why I came down: not to save it, which was impossible and made no sense, but to take something. A sample? Of what? That's what I can't recall. The callotomy itself I either didn't feel or don't remember, as with amnesia after a concussion, but when I returned to the ship and put my spacesuit back into its special closet, I remember how it was covered with a fine, soft powder. A strange powder, dry between your fingers, like salt, yet difficult to wipe off your hands. It wasn't radioactive. But I washed as if it had been. Later I didn't even try to find out what the stuff was, though I didn't have the opportunity anyway to ask such questions. When I learned that my brain had been severed, I was too taken up with that trouble to think about my hour on the moon. Did you hear anything about that powder? Like talcum. Anyway, I brought *something* back . . . but what?"

My visitor squinted at me through his pince-nez, poker-faced.

"You're warm," he said. "Even hot . . . Yes, you brought back something . . . That's probably why you returned alive despite your landing."

He got up and came to where I stood. We both looked at the moon, innocent and bright among the stars.

"The molecular LEMs remained behind," my visitor said as if to himself. "But, let us hope, destroyed beyond duplication! You destroyed your own although you didn't know it, when you went to the bay for your spacesuit. That activated the autodestruct program. I can tell you this now because it no longer matters."

"For a neurological consultant you are remarkably well

informed," I said, my eyes still on the moon as it went behind a cloud. "Perhaps you even know what came back with me. Was that *their* micropes, that powder so unlike ordinary sand? . . ."

"No. As far as I know, just silicon-based polymers."

"And not a virus?"

"No."

"Then why is it so important?"

"Because it accompanied you back."

"The spacesuit closet lost its hermetic seal?"

"No. Most likely you inhaled some of the particles while in the rocket, getting out of your suit."

"And they're in me?"

"I don't know if they still are. The fact that it wasn't normal moon dust we learned when you ran off to Australia."

"Ah! Every place I've been has been put under a microscope?"

"More or less."

"And . . . they were found?"

He nodded. We were standing at the window, and the moon sailed through the clouds.

"Does everybody know?"

"Everybody?"

"All the interested parties . . ."

"Probably not yet. At the Agency, only a few people, and in the clinical department only I."

"Why did you tell me?"

"You were on the track of it yourself, besides I want you to understand the situation."

"My situation?"

"Yours and in general."

"So they're keeping me under observation?"

"I don't know to what extent. There are different levels

of secrecy here. Based on what I've heard from a couple of friends, completely off the record, research is still in progress and they haven't yet ruled out the possibility that those particles are in contact with the moon . . ."

"What kind of contact? Radio?"

"Definitely not."

"Another means of communication?"

"I flew here to ask you a few questions and you're grilling me."

"You said you came to fill me in on my situation."

"But I can't answer questions to which I don't know the answers."

"In a nutshell, then, I have been protected so far by the *possibility* that the moon is interested in my fate and can step in . . . ?"

Shapiro didn't answer. The room was dark. He walked over and turned on the light, which hurt my eyes and also brought me back to earth. I pulled the curtain, took a decanter and two glasses from the bar, and poured what was left of the sherry. I gave him a glass, pointed to the armchair, and sat down.

"Chi va piano, va sano," the professor said unexpectedly. Only wetting his lips with the sherry, he put the glass on the desk and sat down with a sigh. "Human beings always proceed according to a model," he said. "In a case like this, however, there are no models. And yet we must act, because no good will come of procrastination. Nor does guesswork help us any. As a neurologist I can say this much: There is short-term memory and long-term memory. The short-term turns into long-term if there are no violent disruptions. It is hard to imagine a disruption more violent than the severing of the great commissure! Therefore what happened just before and immediately after that event does not exist in your memory. As for the warfare on

the moon, we don't even know who is attacking and who is defending. No nation will ever admit that its programmers didn't follow the directives of the Geneva Agreement, which everyone signed. But even if one of those programmers came forward and confessed, it would be of little use, because neither he nor anyone else knows what course things have taken on the moon. And you . . . are about as safe in this asylum as in a den of lions. You think I exaggerate? In any case you won't be here forever."

"A long conversation," I said, "and yet we go in circles. What you want is for me to put myself in your hands?" I tapped the right side of my head.

"I think you should. I personally doubt that it will help either you or the Agency that much, but I see nothing better."

"Your skepticism may be only to disarm me . . ." I muttered to myself as if thinking aloud. "Are the effects of a callotomy absolutely irreversible?"

"If it was done surgically, the severed white matter would definitely not grow back. But your skull, I believe, was not cut into . . . ?"

"I see," I answered after a moment of thought. "You offer the hope that something different could have happened to me. Either to tempt me, or you believe it a little yourself . . ."

"And your decision?"

"I'll tell you within forty-eight hours. All right?"

He nodded and pointed at the card on the blotter.

"My number."

"You mean we'll do this in the open?"

"Yes and no. No one will pick up the receiver. You will wait ten rings and phone again after one minute. And wait ten rings again and hang up."

"And that will mean I agree?"

He nodded and rose. "We'll take care of the rest. But now I must go. Good night."

After he left, I stood awhile in the middle of the room, staring vacantly at the curtain. Suddenly the ceiling light went out. The bulb blew, I thought, but when I looked out the window, I saw that all the buildings of the asylum were dark. Even the distant lights on the ramp to the highway were out. It had to be a power failure. My watch said eleven. I didn't feel like hunting for a flashlight or candles, so I opened the curtain and in the weak light of the moon undressed and took a shower in my small bathroom. Deciding to put on a bathrobe instead of pajamas, I opened the closet door and froze. Someone was standing there, fat, short, almost completely bald, as rigid as a statue, his finger to his lips. It was Kramer.

"Adelaide," I said but stopped because he shook his finger sharply. He pointed at the window. When I didn't move, he got down and crawled on all fours around the desk and to the window, and carefully reached up and closed the curtain. It was so dark that I could hardly see him return to the closet, still on his hands and knees, and take out something rectangular and flat, but when my eyes grew accustomed to the dark, I saw that Kramer was opening a briefcase, sorting through strings or wires, connecting something, then there was a snap, and, sitting on the rug, he whispered:

"Come over here, Tichy, and we'll talk . . ."

I sat beside him, too surprised to say anything. Kramer moved closer, his knees touching mine, and said quietly:

"We have at least three-quarters of an hour before the power goes back on. Some of the bugging devices are on batteries but they're low-tech and we have first-class screening. Tichy, you can keep calling me Kramer, Kramer will do . . ."

"Who are you?" I asked, and heard him chuckle.

"Your guardian angel."

"But haven't you been here a long time? How could you know I would come to this asylum? Surely Tarantoga . . ."

"Curiosity killed the cat," Kramer replied mildly. "There are more important things for you to think about, Tichy. For example, I would not advise you to do what Shapiro says. That would be the worst thing you could do."

I was silent, and Kramer chuckled again. He was obviously in a good mood. His voice was different, not as drawling as before, and there was nothing asinine about the man now.

"You think I am an 'agent of a foreign power,' yes?" he said, clapping me on the back. "I understand, you are suspicious in eighteen different ways, but let me appeal to your reason. Suppose you take Professor Shapiro's advice. They'll get you in their clutches, without torture, God forbid, no, in their clinic you'll be treated like the President himself. They'll pull something out of the right side of your head, or they won't, either way it will make no difference, because the verdict has already been delivered."

"What verdict?"

"The diagnosis, the results of the scientific auscultation, through your arm, leg, foot, who cares? Please don't interrupt, I'm telling you everything. Everything that's known."

He paused, as if waiting for my go-ahead. We were sitting in the dark. Suddenly I said:

"Dr. House might come."

"He won't. No one will come, don't fret about that. We're not playing cowboys and Indians here. Pay attention now. On the moon the programs of different parties have been going after each other. Who started it is not important, at least not now. To put it very simply, there's a cancer proliferating there. The mutual production of chaos, the interpenetration of weapons both hardware and software, the blows and counterblows, call it what you like."

"The moon has gone mad?"

"In a sense, yes. When the programs as well as what they created were destroyed, altogether new processes began, processes no one on Earth foresaw."

"What were they?"

Kramer sighed.

"I'd light a cigarette now," he said, "but can't, because you don't smoke. What were they? You brought back the first evidence."

"That dust on my spacesuit?"

"It's silicon polymers, the beginning, the scientists say, of an orthogenesis, the birth of nonliving organisms. What's taking place up there is no threat to Earth, and yet for that very reason the Agency sees a threat."

"I don't understand."

"The Agency stands guard over the doctrine of ignorance. There are nations that seek the end of that doctrine, of the whole business of packing weapons off to the moon. But it's more complicated than that. Different interest groups exist, and some would like to see a growing panic under the rubric of The Moon Invades Earth, so that a coalition will form, in the UN or outside it, to strike preemptively, whether in the traditional way, which means thermonuclear, or with that new quantum gravity collapsar technology, don't ask me about it now, I'll tell you later. What they want is to arm on a grand scale, a global scale, for if a true invasion threatens, it would be necessary to crush it before it begins."

"And the Agency doesn't want that?"

"The Agency itself is torn. Each interest group has its people in it. Otherwise the Agency would not represent Earth. You have become a trump card in this game. Possibly the highest."

"I? Because of my problem?"

"Exactly. Whatever information Shapiro and his crew get out of you cannot be verified, after all. Except for a few people no one will know whether they really learned something or only said they did and that they would soon announce it to the public or first go with it to the Security Council. But the announcing doesn't matter. The point is that no one, including you, will know whether they are lying or telling the truth."

"It would probably be a lie, since you said before that the verdict has already been delivered . . ."

"That's how it looks. But I am not omniscient. In any case they can't use force on you."

"But Shapiro said . . ."

"The attempted abductions? But they were arranged, Tichy, in such a way that you would not lose your life. Because if you did, no one would have anything."

"Who were they?"

"Different parties and for different purposes. First, to *have* you. Later, when such efforts were foiled, to frighten you a little, push you, soften you up, so you would run into the welcoming arms of Shapiro."

"Wait, are you saying that the Agency itself . . . that the later attacks were staged?"

"Yes."

"All right. Suppose that nevertheless I let them examine me. What would happen?"

"Bridge or poker."

"I don't understand."

"The game, the bidding. One can foresee the beginning but not what follows. It's clear that on the moon things didn't happen as they were supposed to. We're left with the question: Is or is not Earth in danger? So far everything suggests there is no danger and will be none for the next few hundred years, being very conservative. Perhaps for the next few thousand years or even million. But politics cannot think in such distant terms. We can sleep peacefully till the year three thousand. But many do not want to sleep peacefully. Many need a harmless moon."

"To do what?"

"To make sure no nation has an arsenal left there, or anything else. That the whole lunar project is defunct, the Geneva Agreement meaningless, and we all have to go back to Clausewitz."

"So either way it ends badly? If there's a true threat of invasion, we have to arm ourselves against the moon, and if there's not, we return to the old way, the Earth way, is that it?"

"That's it. You grasp the situation."

"A nice situation. And the secret hidden in my head isn't worth a plugged nickel . . ."

"You're wrong there. Depending on what result they announce from the examination of your person, different scenarios can be set up."

"Scenarios?"

"According to our computer simulation there are at least twenty. Not from the real result, of course, but from what they announce as the result."

"You don't know what that is?"

"No, because they themselves don't know yet. Even Shapiro's group is divided. You have to understand, Tichy, the lie they announce will not be a hundred-percent. They could do that only if they were an absolutely solid, sure conspiracy of professional crooks. Which they're not. They can't even rule out the possibility that you, although not learning anything from the examination about the contents of your right brain, will nevertheless join the poker game."

"How?"

"Don't be naive. What's to stop you from writing afterward to the *New York Times* or the *Züricher*, or wherever you like, and saying that they added, doctored, falsified things? Think of the uproar! Experts would come forward to defend you, to ask for new and better controlled tests. It would be a royal mess."

"If you see this all so clearly, why don't Shapiro's men?"

"But what else can they do other than persuade you to submit to an examination? We are all, despite our different roles, prisoners of the situation."

"They could kill me."

"No good. Even if you killed yourself, the suspicion that you were murdered would travel around the world."

"I can't believe it's impossible to repeat what I did on the moon. Shapiro said that they tried and nothing came of it, but surely new scouts could be sent."

"True, but that too is a labyrinth. You are surprised? Tichy, there is not much time left. We have a stalemate on the global board, with no moves to ensure peace, only different kinds of risk."

"And what do you advise me as my guardian angel?"

"To take no one's advice, mine included. I too represent certain interests, I'm not hiding it, it was neither God nor Providence that sent me to you, only a group that *doesn't* want the arms race started again."

"And what does this group wish me to do?"

"Nothing at the moment. Nothing at all. Stay here. Don't telephone Shapiro. Keep in touch with crazy old

Kramer during the next two weeks, or it might be only days, and we'll see what develops."

"Why should I believe you?"

"You shouldn't, as I said. I've given you the general picture, that is all. The main transformer was disconnected for about an hour, and now I'll take my electronic toys and go to bed, because I'm a millionaire suffering from depression, aren't I? See you later, Jonathan."

"Good night, Adelaide," I said.

Kramer crawled to the door, pushed it open, and I thought I saw someone standing in the hall who gave him a sign. Kramer got to his feet, went out, and shut the door quietly behind him. I sat there, my legs pins and needles, until the lights went back on.

Turning them off, I got into bed. Where Kramer had been sitting lay an object like a flattened ring. I picked it up. There was a rolled piece of paper stuck inside. I unrolled it. "Just in case," said the hasty scrawl. I tried putting the ring on my finger. It was gray, a dull metal, strangely heavy, maybe lead? On one side it had a hump like a lima bean with a pinhole through it. The ring fit only on my little finger. For some reason it troubled me more than both my visitors. What was it for? I tried scratching a windowpane with it. It left no mark on the glass. I licked it. Salty. To keep the ring on or not? I decided to keep it on. I looked at my watch. It was after midnight but I wasn't sleepy. I didn't even know what to worry about first. Perhaps the fact that my left arm and leg had been so well behaved, because their passivity, it seemed to me as I grew drowsy, might be a trap, a trap this time from within. I lay half-awake, or else half-asleep, I didn't know which, and puzzled over this for a long time, until it grew light. Dawn, I thought, therefore I must have managed to sleep a few hours after all, except that the light wasn't coming from the curtained window, it was coming from under the door.

The light was curiously strong, as if someone were directing a spotlight at the threshold of my room. I sat up. Something was flowing in across the floor, not water, more like mercury. It rolled in tiny balls, came together in a wide puddle that gathered around the small rug before my bed, and in the light from under the door came other rivulets of that strange metallic liquid. Now almost the whole floor gleamed like a mercury mirror. I switched on the table lamp. The stuff wasn't mercury, it had more the color of tarnished silver. There was so much of it now that the rug floated, then the light behind the door went out. I sat and watched wide-eyed. The syrupy liquid separated into drops and the drops clumped together to form a mushroom shape that swelled like leavened dough and stiffened and lifted. This had to be a dream, I told myself, and yet I didn't dare let my bare feet touch the "quicksilver," which was indeed a metaphor come true, for quick meant living and this moved like a thing alive, though not animal or vegetable. The monster changed into a cocoon, a shell, armor that was more and more humanoid, though full of holes, especially the gaping slit in front. When I tried recreating that metamorphosis in my memory, which was much later, the best comparison I could think of was watching a film run in reverse: as if someone had built a weird weapon and then subjected it to high temperature so it would melt, except that what took place before my eyes was all backward, first the liquid, then the hollowed-out body rising from it. The figure lost its sheen now and resembled a large store-window mannequin with a hairless head and face without mouth or nose though two round holes could serve as eyes. Then it turned into a woman, or not a woman but the statue of a woman, empty inside and open like a cupboard, and this statue began to extrude its own clothes, first white underwear then over that a light-green dress.

Convinced now I was asleep and dreaming, I got out of bed and approached the apparition. The green dress turned white like a hospital gown and the face grew more defined. On the head a white nurse's cap with a red silk ribbon appeared over blond hair. Enough, I thought, time to wake up, this dream is too stupid—but I hadn't the courage to touch the thing. Looking around, I saw my whole room in the light of the lamp, the desk, the curtain, the chairs. I stood undecided, then turned again to the phantom. She looked a lot like Didi, a nurse I had seen often in the garden or Dr. House's office, though was much larger and taller. She said: "Get in me, you'll leave here, take the doctor's Toyota, you can drive out because the gate is open. Get dressed and take money, you'll buy a ticket and fly straight to Tarantoga. Don't stand there like a moron, no one will stop you as a nurse . . ."

"But Didi is smaller than you . . ." I stammered, surprised not only by her words but also by the fact that she was speaking although not with her mouth. The voice came from the body which together with the white coat opened so wide, I could actually step inside. But should I, that was the question. Suddenly I was thinking very clearly: it didn't have to be a dream because of the technology of molecular teleferics which I had used myself. But if it was real, might it not be a trap?

"Size doesn't matter at night. Come on, get moving! Dress, and take your checkbook," she said.

"But why should I leave and who are you anyway?" I asked, but started dressing at the same time, not because I really intended to participate in this unexpected escapade, it's just that one feels more confident when clothed.

"I am not a person—you can see that," she replied. The voice was a woman's, however, low, warm, a little husky, I knew it from somewhere. I was sitting on the edge of the bed tying my shoes.

"So who sent you, Mrs. Nonperson?" I asked, looking up, and the next thing I knew, she had fallen upon me, that is, engulfed me, wrapped me not in her arms but in her whole body, and this happened so quickly that one moment I was sitting in my sweater and no tie, thinking I'd tied the left shoe too tight, and the next moment I was pulled inside and surrounded as if I'd been swallowed by a python. I can't describe it better because nothing like that had ever happened to me before. It was soft inside, and I saw the room through the eye openings, but I couldn't move, that is I could but only as she wanted to, she or it, though of course somebody was operating this remote for the purpose of taking me to where they were waiting impatiently for Ijon Tichy. I fought the monster with all my strength but to no avail. My limbs moved not as I wanted them to but against my will, my hand opening the door, turning the knob, even though I resisted every inch of the way. The hall was dim, lit with green night-lights, and there was not a soul about. I hadn't time to wonder who was behind this, because the who-less thing that had swallowed me, a veritable Frankenstein suit, was walking steadily, unhurriedly, then I remembered the ring from Kramer, but how could it help me? Even if I knew I was supposed to bite it or turn it on my finger as in a fairy tale to make the genie appear, I couldn't have done anything.

The front door of the pavilion loomed ahead, swinging doors, and my captive hand pushed them open. In the shadow of an old palm tree was the black shape of a car, rivers of distant light on its body. One of its rear doors opened but there was no one inside, at least I couldn't see anyone.

I got in or rather was got in, still pulling back for all I was worth, until I realized my mistake. I shouldn't pull back—that was what the operator of the remote expected. I should go instead in the direction imposed on me, but in such a way as to achieve my own ends. Bent over in the doorway of the car, I hurled myself forward, hit my head against something, passed out, and opened my eyes.

I was lying on the floor beside my bed. The curtains were gray with dawn. I raised my hand to my eyes and saw no ring. Was it a dream after all? But at what point did it begin? Kramer had definitely been here. I went to the closet where he had stood and yes, my clothes were all pushed to one side. Something white lay on the floor of the closet, a letter. I picked it up—no address—and tore open the envelope. Inside was a sheet of paper that had typewritten words, no date, no letterhead. I checked to see if the door was locked, turned on the lamp, not wanting to open the curtains, and read:

If you've had a dream about being abducted or tortured and it was vivid and in color, that means you've been subjected to a test, given a drug. They may be examining your reaction to certain substances. We aren't sure about this. The only one you can turn to besides me is your doctor.

—Slug Eater

Slug Eater. So the letter was from Kramer. He could be telling the truth or lying. I tried to remember as precisely as possible what Shapiro had said and what Kramer had said. According to both, the lunar mission had failed.

But on other things they parted company. The professor wanted me to be examined, Kramer wanted me to wait. The professor represented the Lunar Agency, or at least that's what he claimed, while Kramer didn't say anything about who stood behind him. But why hadn't he warned me about the possibility of drugs, leaving only this letter? Could there be another player in this game? Both spoke at length, yet I still hadn't been told why what my right brain held was so important. And why hadn't that poor, practically mute half of my head shown any sign of life since—when was it?—yesterday? Did I swallow something which put it to sleep? Let's suppose. But for what reason? It seemed to me that all these hunters of Tichy didn't really know what to do and were playing for time. In which game I was a wild card, maybe a high trump, maybe nothing, and each was preventing the others from finding out. Had they put my right hemisphere to sleep so I couldn't communicate with myself? This at least I could verify immediately. I took my left hand in my right and addressed it in the way I had developed.

"What's new?" I asked with my fingers.

The little finger and the thumb of the left hand twitched, but weakly.

"Hello, are you there?" I signaled.

My ring finger and my thumb made a circle that meant "Hello."

"So how are you doing?"

"Get lost."

"Tell me how you feel. Look, we have a common interest."

"My head hurts."

And at that moment I felt that *my* head hurt too. I had read enough in the neurological literature by now to know that emotionally I was not halved but whole, because the seat of the emotions is in the midbrain, which was not touched by the callotomy.

"The same head hurts *both* of us. Do you understand?"

"No."

"You *don't?*"

"Don't."

I was in a sweat from this silent exchange but decided, come what may, not to let go. I would learn something if it killed me. Then I had an inspiration. The sign language of the deaf required a lot of work and dexterity. But I knew Morse code, had known it since childhood. So I made my left hand flat and with the forefinger of my right began to draw dots and dashes. The left hand submitted to this for a while, but suddenly it clenched into a fist and punched me hard. "Isn't working," I thought, but then the hand extended a finger and began marking dots and dashes on my right cheek. Yes, son of a gun, it was answering in Morse code.

"Don't tickle or you'll get it."

This was the first English sentence I had received, albeit only by touch, from It. I sat perfectly still on the edge of my bed, because the hand was continuing.

"Jackass."

"Me?"

"You. You should have done that to begin with."

"Why didn't you let me know?"

"A hundred times, jerk. You didn't notice."

It dawned on me now, yes, that the left hand had been tapping at me quite a bit, but it never entered my head (my side of my head) that this was in Morse.

"Amazing," I tapped back, on the hand. "Then you can speak?"

"Better than you."

"Then speak. You will save me, that is, save us."

I don't know whether it was I or It who got better at this, but our silent conversation went faster and faster.

"What happened on the moon?"

"Tell me what you remember."

This sudden turning of the tables floored me.

"You don't know?"

"I know that you wrote it down. Then buried it in a jar. Yes?"

"Yes."

"Did you write the truth?"

"Yes. What I could remember."

"And they dug it up. That first one."

"Shapiro?"

"I don't remember names. The one who looked at the moon."

"Do you understand spoken speech?"

"Not well. It's better in French."

Whatever that meant.

"Only in Morse?"

"Morse is best."

"So talk."

"You'll write it down and they'll steal it."

"I won't, word of honor."

"Okay. You know some of it and I know some of it. You go first."

"You didn't read what I wrote?"

"I can't read."

"All right ... The last thing I remember ... I was trying to make contact with Wivitch after getting out of that underground ruin in the Japanese sector, but I couldn't. Or if I did, I don't remember. All I know is that later I landed myself. Sometimes I think maybe I wanted to re-trieve something from the remote, which had got into something . . . or else it had discovered something . . . but I don't know what, or even which remote it was. Probably not the molecular remote. I don't know what happened to that."

"The powdered one?"

"Yes. But . . . you must know," I suggested carefully.

"First tell yours to the end," It answered. "Sometimes you think. And other times?"

"That there was no remote there at all, or there might have been but I wasn't looking for it, because . . ."

"Because what?"

I hesitated. What I sometimes remembered was like a surreal dream impossible to put into words and which left only the feeling of an extraordinary revelation.

"I don't know what you're thinking," It tapped on me, "but I know you have something up your sleeve. I can *feel* it."

"Why should I have something up my sleeve?"

"Why, because. I'm the intuition half. Continue. You think you were looking for . . ."

"Sometimes I think I landed because I was summoned."

"What did you write in the log?"

"About that, nothing."

"But they have tapes. If you were summoned by the moon, they would know. The Agency was monitoring."

"I don't know what the Agency knows. I never laid eyes on any tapes at the base. But you must know that."

"I know more than that."

"What?"

"You lost the powdered one."

"The dispersant? Well, obviously, if I later got into a spacesuit myself and—"

"Not what I mean."

"It broke down?"

"No. They took it."

"Who?"

"I don't know. The moon. The remote was changing down there. By itself. One could see it from the ship."

"I saw it?"

"Yes, and you had no control over it."

"Then who was operating it?"

"I don't know. It had been disconnected from the ship but was still changing. Using all those different programs."

"Impossible."

"But true. And then back on the moon, down there. I was. That is, you and I were. And then Tichy fell."

"What are you saying?"

"He fell. It must have been the callotomy. There's a hole there for me. Then back on the ship and you put the spacesuit in its container and the sand fell out."

"Did I go down to see what happened to the molecular remote?"

"I don't know. Maybe. There's a hole there. The callotomy was for that."

"On purpose?"

"I think. I'm sure. So you'd come back and not come back."

"They already told me that. Shapiro and Kramer too, though not so clearly."

"Because it's a game. There are things they know and things they don't. They must have a hole too."

"But wait, why did I fall?"

"The callotomy, stupid. You lost consciousness. How could you not fall?"

"And that sand? The talcum dust? Where did it come from?"

"I have no idea."

I thought furiously. It was light now, almost eight o'clock. The lunar project failed? But in the rubble of that failure was more than senseless battles and tactics—for from it also had emerged something that no one on Earth ever programmed or anticipated. And this something had apparently taken control of the remote of Professor Lax-Gugliborc. Then lured me to land, intending evil or something else. Why deprive me of my memory? What purpose would that serve? None that I could see. Or was it to give me something? Or to tell me something? But in that case I wouldn't have needed to land. Did it give me that dust? And then something—another party—not wanting this to succeed, cut the great commissure of my brain. Let's say that's what happened. Then did the thing operating the dispersant save me? But was the point to save Ijon Tichy? Probably not. The point was that the thing that was given reach Earth. The powder, the sticky dust, was the message. No, it had to be more than information. A material thing. And I was to bring it back with me. Yes. A piece of the puzzle had been fitted in. I quickly explained this theory to my other half.

"Could be," It said finally. "They have the dust. But it's not enough."

"Hence the abductions and rescues, the persuading, visits, and nightmares?"

"To get you to submit to an examination. That is, me."

"But they'll learn nothing if you know no more than you're saying."

"True."

"But if something has arisen *there* that is powerful enough to take over the molecular remote, why couldn't it communicate directly with Earth? With the Agency, with Control, with anyone it wanted. At the very least with the men the Agency sent after my return."

"Where did they land?"

"I don't know. In any case it appears that there are opposing parties both here and there. What could have evolved on the moon, out of that cancer, that chaos? What word did Kramer use? Orthogenesis. Order out of chaos. Electronic self-organization. But to what end?"

"To no end. Like life on Earth. The hardware fought claw and fang, and the programs diverged. Some went in circles, repeating themselves, some broke down completely, and some entered the no man's land and set up mirrors and mirages . . ."

"Maybe, maybe." I felt a strange exaltation. "Yes, I can picture it. Out of the general deterioration something grew like photobacteria, viruses made of integrated circuits. But it couldn't have been everywhere, it happened only in one particular place, an extremely rare event . . . and from there it began to multiply and spread. Fine, I agree that's possible. But for some *entity* to arise out of that—no! This is pure fantasy. You can't have an intelligence coming into the world made of spare parts, broken bits of electronics."

"Then *who* took control of the molecular remote?"

"You're sure that's what happened?"

"Consider the evidence. After you left the Japanese ruin, you weren't able to contact the base, were you?"

"Yes, but I have no idea what happened after that. I tried to raise Control and also the Trojan satellites through the ship's computer to see if Control had me on its screen. But no one answered, no one. So the micropes must have been destroyed again, and the Agency didn't learn what happened to the remote. All they knew was that shortly after that I landed on my own, then returned. The rest is only guesses. So?"

"But that's the evidence. The only person who knows

more is the inventor of the dispersant. What was his name?"

"Lax-Gugliborc. But he works for the Agency."

"He didn't want to give you the remote."

"He said it was my decision."

"That's evidence too."

"You think so?"

"Yes. He had misgivings."

"You mean he feared that the moon—?"

"There is no technology that can't be figured out."

"And that's what happened?"

"I'm sure. Except differently from what he imagined."

"How can you know that?"

"Everything is always different from what we imagine."

"I see it now," I tapped in the surrounding silence. "This was no taking over of controls. Hybridization, more likely! The thing that came into being *there* joined with the thing fashioned *here* in Professor Lax-Gugliborc's workshop. One dispersion electronics combined with another that also had the ability to dissipate and metamorphose. The molecular remote, you see, contained a memory, and transformation programs, like little crystals of ice that can join together to form millions of different snowflakes. Each flake has hexagonal symmetry yet is different. Yes! I operated the remote, in a sense *was* the remote, but at the same time I was only providing it with signals telling it in which way to change. It did the changing itself, at the scene, on the surface of the moon and also below."

"Did it have intelligence?"

"I really don't know. One doesn't need to know how a car is constructed to drive one. I drove, and saw what it saw, that was all. I couldn't tell you whether it was an ordinary remote, an empty shell, or could function like a robot."

"But Lax-Gugliborc could tell us."

"Indeed. But I would prefer not to approach him, at least not directly."

"Write to him."

"Are you crazy?"

"Write so that only he will understand."

"They read all letters. The telephone is out too."

"Write, but don't sign it."

"And the handwriting?"

"I'll write, you dictate."

"It'll be chicken scrawls."

"So? Now I'm hungry, I want an omelette with jam. And then we'll do the letter."

"Who will send it? And how?"

"Breakfast first."

The letter seemed an impossible task. I didn't know the professor's home address. And that was the least of our problems. We had to let him know that I wished to see him but in such a way that nobody else would understand the message. All correspondence was examined by the best experts, so we would have to be fiendishly clever. Forget about codes. Moreover there was no one I could trust even in the matter of sending the letter. And possibly Lax-Gugliborc wasn't working anymore at the Agency, and even if by some miracle the letter reached him and he decided to see me, a horde of agents and intelligence operatives would not let him out of their sight. Also, there were probably special satellites in stationary orbit keeping my building under constant surveillance. I trusted House no more than I did Kramer. Nor could I turn to Tarantoga, whom I trusted like myself but there was no way to inform him of my (our) plan without drawing attention to him, and even as it was, ultrasensitive laser microphones were no doubt aimed at his every window, and when he bought corn flakes and yogurt at the supermarket, they were both no doubt x-rayed as he carried his groceries to the car.

After breakfast I went to the town, taking the same bus I took the first time. In front of the department store was a stand selling colorful postcards, and I looked through them and found the perfect one: it showed, against a red background, a golden cage and in it a white owl with big round eyes. I wasn't so stupid as to reach for this card then and there, but selected it with eight others, and one with a parrot, then two more. I bought stamps and headed back to the asylum on foot. The town was almost deserted. A few people puttering in their gardens, and at a car wash across from the spot where that shoot-out for me took place cars were moving slowly through water and big blue brushes. No one seemed to be following me, or watching me, or preparing to kidnap me. The sun beat down. My shirt was soaked with sweat when I returned after an hour of walking, so I showered and changed, then sat down to send greetings to friends—Tarantoga, both Cybbilkises, Wivitch, two of Tarantoga's cousins—the messages not too short and not too long, and of course with no mention of the Agency, the Mission, the moon, only pleasant, inno-cent sentiments, and my return address, why not? To make clear the lightheartedness of the postcards, I drew on each one, two black-and-white pandas for the twins, with mus-taches and ties, a dachshund with a halo for Tarantoga, and I gave the owl glasses just like the professor's, and on the bar where it was perched I drew a mouse. How does a mouse behave, especially around an owl? It is quiet, quiet as a mouse, and the professor might know that my name, Tichy, meant quiet in Czech or Russian, moreover at his place we had sat together in a cage. Writing to each one that it would be nice to see him, I could do the same with the professor, and thanked him for everything, and in a postscript conveyed greetings from Mrs. Mudstone, a subtle allusion, by anagram, to *moon dust*. If the professor didn't get it, the card would fail, but I couldn't be more explicit.

I didn't call Shapiro, and Kramer did not go out of his way to talk to me. I spent half the day by the pool. My other self, since I had come to an understanding with it, caused no trouble. At night, lying in bed, I sometimes exchanged a few words with It before dropping off to sleep. It occurred to me that it might have been better to send Lax-Gugliborc the parrot instead of the owl, but it was too late, the ball was in his court now. Three days passed and nothing happened. Twice I swung with Kramer in the canopied swing by the fountain, but he didn't talk business. Perhaps he too was waiting. He sweat, breathed heavily, groaned, complained about his rheumatism, was obviously in a bad mood. Bored, I took to watching television in the evening and reading the paper. The Lunar Agency reported that analysis of the data from the lunar reconnaissance was under way and so far revealed no irregularities or malfunctions in the various sectors. The media demanded more information, called for a hearing, for the director of the Lunar Agency and the heads of its different departments to appear before a special commission of the UN, and that a press conference be held to throw light on matters about which a fearful public was in the dark.

Russell, the young ethnologist who wanted to write his dissertation about millionaires, came to see me in the evenings. He had most of his material now thanks to his interviews with Kramer, but I couldn't tell him those interviews were worthless and that Kramer was only playing the role of a Croesus while the true millionaires, especially the ones from Texas, were dull as dishwater. Even in the asylum they had their own secretaries, masseurs, and bodyguards, and each had a pavilion to himself. They were so reclusive, Russell had to set up a special telescope on my roof to observe them through their windows. He was discouraged, because even when they were stark raving mad, what they did was unoriginal. Since nothing was happening, Russell would come down his ladder and drop in on me for some human conversation.

The prosperity that obtained after the weapons were moved to the moon had unfortunate consequences, made worse by automation. Russell called it the electronics Stone Age. Illiteracy increased, particularly since now you didn't even have to sign a check, only a thumbprint was necessary and a computer scanner did the rest. The American Medical Association finally lost the battle to save their profession, because computers gave better diagnoses and were much more patient with patients. Prosthetic sex was replaced by a simple device called an Orgaz. This was a headset with electrodes and a handgrip that resembled a toy pistol. Pulling the trigger gave you the ultimate pleasure because the appropriate place in your brain was stimulated with no effort, no exertion necessary, plus there were no upkeep expenses for male or female remotes, nor indeed the aggravations of natural courtship and matrimony. Orgazes flooded the market. To be fitted you went to special clinics. Gynandroics and other firms that manufactured synthetic women, angels, nymphs, fauns, etc., went out of business with much gnashing of teeth. As for education, most of the developed countries did away with compulsory school attendance. "Children," went the new doctrine, "should not be subjected to daily imprisonment and the psychological torture called learning." Who needs to know how many men's shirts you can sew out of six yards of Egyptian cotton if one shirt requires seven eighths of a yard, or when two trains will collide if one engineer is eighteen, drunk, and going 100 miles an hour and the other is colorblind and doing 75, if they're separated by 15 miles of track and 43 pre-automation semaphores? Equally useless are facts about kings, wars, battles, crusades, and all the other rotten behavior of history. Geography is best learned by traveling. All you have to know is the price of the ticket and when the plane takes off. Why learn foreign languages when you can put a translator chip in your ear? The study of biology depresses and depraves young minds, nor is it practical since no one now can become a doctor or dentist (after the appearance of dentautomata, about thirty thousand out-of-work dentists in both the Americas and Eurasia have committed suicide each year). And chemistry is of no more value than a knowledge of hieroglyphics. Meanwhile on traffic signs and street signs words are slowly being replaced with pictures.

Russell saw no point complaining about this state of affairs because nothing could be done. There were still some fifty thousand scientists and scholars left in the world but their average age was now 61.7. Everything had been smothered in the boredom of prosperity, and that was why, said Russell, most people were actually pleased by the prospect of an invasion from the moon, and the panic reported in the papers and on television was only to increase sales. *Mundus vult decipi, ergo decipiatur*, the ethnologist concluded, staring at the now empty bottle of bourbon. His field work was so disappointing that he had stopped aiming his telescope at the windows of the millionaires and turned it instead to the solarium where the nurses and their aides sunbathed in the nude. I thought that odd, since after all he could simply go there and look at them up close, but when I said this, he shrugged, remarking that that was the problem: nowadays one could just do that.

In the rec room of the new pavilion workmen were almost finished setting up the fants. Russell took me there one evening. You put a cassette into a fant and an image appears in front of the machine. More than an image, a whole artificial reality, Mount Olympus, for example, packed with gods and goddesses, or something more from life, a two-wheel tumbrel carrying a bunch of illustrious people through a furious crowd toward the guillotine. Or Hansel and Gretel at the witch's house stuffing themselves with shingles of gingerbread. Or a convent after Tartars or Martians break in. The idea is that what happens next depends on the viewer, who has a pedal under each foot and a joystick in his hand. You can go from idyll to bloodbath, have the gods depose Zeus, put ear wings on the heads falling into the guillotine basket so they fly away. Anything is possible. The witch wants to make cutlets out of Hansel, but you can have Hansel make cutlets out of her. The Prince of Denmark can steal the royal jewels and run off with Ophelia, or with Rosencrantz, depending on which key you push, because some fants have a keyboard. The instruction manual is a thick book but you can do without it. We tired of the fants after fifteen minutes of playing, even though we were both a little drunk, and went to bed. The asylum bought twenty fants, but they are hardly ever used. Dr. House is not happy about that. He went from patient to patient, trying to persuade them to give it a try because it's good therapy. But apparently none of the millionaires or billionaires ever heard of Hansel and Gretel or Olympus or Hamlet. Tartars or Martians, it's all the same to them. The guillotine they consider an oversize cigar cutter and silly. Dr. House worked the fants himself, probably

out of a sense of duty, mixing the Middle Ages, Shake-
speare, Agatha Christie, and volcanoes, and tried to get me
to join him, but I refused. I was still waiting for a sign
from Professor Lax-Gugliborc. Kramer too seemed to be
waiting for something, and that's probably why he avoided
me. Waiting for new instructions? But I was in a good
mood, having reached an understanding with myself.

Contact

It was the end of August already, and before turning on my desk lamp in the evening, I had to close the window because of moths. Except for ladybugs I don't much care for insects. Butterflies I can take or leave but moths for some reason frighten me. That August there were a lot of them and they kept fluttering outside my window. Some were so big I could hear their thuds against the glass. Since even looking at them bothers me, I got up to pull the curtains, when I heard a sound. A clear, sharp sound, as if someone was touching a pane with a metal rod. I approached the window, the lamp in my hand. Among the fluttering moths I saw one that was all black, larger than the others, and it gleamed in the reflected light. It backed away, then came at the window again and hit it with such force that I felt the frame shake. What's more, the moth had a small beak instead of a head. I stood fascinated because it wasn't hitting the glass at random but in regular intervals, groups of three; three dots, a pause, three dots, a pause, repeated until I realized it was the letter S in Morse code. I hesitated about opening the window. It wasn't a live thing but I didn't want to let real moths into the room either. I finally got up my nerve and I opened the window a crack, and it flew in immediately. I shut the window and looked around. The moth had lit on the papers covering the desk. It had no wings and now didn't resemble a moth at all or any other bug. It looked most like a black olive. Then it was hovering above the desk and humming. I reached for it, and it let me take it between my fingers. It was hard, made of metal or plastic. Again I heard the humming, three dots, three dashes, three dots. I held it to my ear and heard a weak, distant, but distinct human voice.

"Owl here. Owl here. Do you read me?"

I put the olive in my ear and answered:

"Mouse here. Mouse here. I read you, Owl."

"Good evening."

"Greetings." Expecting a long conversation, I pulled the curtains and double-locked the door. Now I could hear the professor perfectly. I recognized his voice.

"This way we can talk freely," he said and chuckled. "Don't worry, I'm using a scrambler of my own invention. No one will understand us. But let's stay Owl and Mouse to be safe."

"Fine," I replied and turned off the lamp.

"It was not that hard," said Lax-Gugliborc. "You did the right thing. I understood immediately."

"But how . . . ?"

"Better for the mice not to know. In the vernacular of criminals, the mouse should know that his accomplice is not a double-crosser. We have before us different pieces of a puzzle. The owl will go first. The dust isn't dust. It's silicon micropolymers of very curious structure doped with selenium so that they superconduct at room temperature. Some joined with the remains of our poor molecular remote on the moon."

"What does that mean?"

"Too soon for a definite answer. I have a few ideas. I was able to obtain a pinch of the powder through a friend. We have half an hour before the thing enabling our connection goes behind the mouse's horizon. I couldn't get in touch with you during the day. We would have had more time then, but the risk would have been greater."

I was dying to know how the professor sent me this metal insect, but I realized I shouldn't ask.

"Continue, Owl, I'm listening."

"My fears were confirmed, but in an opposite way. I figured that something on the moon would arise out of the chaos, but I never dreamed it would be something able to make use of our messenger."

"Can't you be a little more clear?"

"Not without getting very technical. I'll make it as simple as I can. It was an immune response. Not on the whole surface of the moon, of course. At one location, and from there the antibodies spread. What we're calling the dust."

"Where did these antibodies come from and what do they do?"

"From the rubble of bytes and logic circuits. Some draw their energy from the sun. Which is not that surprising because there were plenty of photoelectric materials there to begin with. How should I put it? The moon gradually built up an immunity to any kind of invasion. I'm not talking about intelligence. We conquered gravity, we conquered the atom, but we haven't conquered the common cold. If self-regulating ecosystems developed on Earth, you could say that one developed on the moon, albeit nonliving, out of that whole tangle of attacks and tunnelings. In other words the strategies of sword and shield indirectly gave rise, in their mutual destruction, and this without the intention or knowledge of the programmers, to these cybernetic antibodies."

"But what exactly do they do?"

"Well, in the first place I think they acted like the most ancient bacteria on Earth and simply multiplied, and there must have been many varieties of them and the majority perished, as in natural evolution. After a while, symbiotic species emerged. The kind that work together for their mutual benefit. But I repeat: this is not intelligence. They are merely capable of an enormous number of metamorphoses or mutations, like the flu virus, for example. But unlike earthly bacteria, they are not parasites, for they have no host, if you don't count the computer ruins that first nourished them and let them breed. The situation was complicated by the fact that meanwhile the weapons being produced by the programs still functional underwent a division."

"Yes, a division into weapons directed against living opponents and weapons directed against nonliving opponents."

"The mouse is quick. Correct. From the first antibodies that arose many years ago probably nothing remains. They evolved into—let us call them selenocytes. These joined into multicellular forms to survive, to become more versatile, much as ordinary germs increase in virulence by growing resistant to the antibiotics used against them."

"But what played the role of antibiotics on the moon?"

"An interesting question. The main threat to the selenocytes must have been those products of the military self-evolution which were designed specifically to attack and destroy them."

"You mean, they treated them as an enemy."

"Or as good target practice. Think of the artillery with which the pharmaceutical companies bombard bacteria. This accelerated the selenocyte evolution. And the selenocytes won, because they proved to be more viable. A person can have a cold but a cold can't have a person. Or can it? The persons on the moon were the great, complex systems."

"And then?"

"A most curious and completely unexpected development. The resistance went from passive to active."

"I don't understand."

"From defense the selenocytes switched to offense. They hastened, and very quickly, the demise of the lunar arms race . . ."

"That dust?"

"That dust. And when only the expiring remnant of the vaunted Geneva project was left, the selenocytes received an unforeseen reinforcement."

"Which was?"

"The dispersant. They made use of it. Not destroying it so much as assimilating it. Or, to put it better, an exchange of information took place. Hybridization took place. A crossbreeding."

"How is that possible?"

"It's not really all that strange. I too was working with semiconducting silicon polymers. Different, yes, mine were doped with rare-earth elements, but the adaptability of my dust was not unlike the adaptability of the lunar dust. There was an affinity. Similar starting materials, similar results."

"And now what?"

"That I don't know. The key could be your landing. Why did you land in the Mare Ignium?"

"The Japanese sector? I don't know. I don't remember."

"Nothing?"

"Not a thing."

"And your right hemisphere?"

"Also nothing. I can communicate with it now. But please keep that under your hat."

"I will. I'd love to know *how* you did it but won't ask. What does it know?"

"That when I returned to the ship I had a pocketful of that dust. How it got there is a mystery."

"You could have scooped it up yourself. The question is why."

"And the Agency. What does the Agency think?"

"The dust caused quite a sensation, and a panic especially when it followed you. You know about that?"

"Yes. Professor S. told me. He came to see me a week ago."

"To get you to submit to tests? You refused?"

"I played for time. There's at least one other character here. He advised me not to be tested. I don't know who he works for. He pretends to be a patient."

"There are more of them around you."

"You said, 'Followed me.' The dust is spying?"

"Not necessarily. One can carry a disease without knowing it."

"And the part about the spacesuit?"

"That's a tough one. It was put into your pocket or you did that yourself. For some reason. Just as you landed for some reason. And found something. And someone erased your memory afterward. With the callotomy."

"Then there are at least three parties?"

"It is not the number that matters but how to identify them."

"But why is this so important? Sooner or later the failure of the whole lunar project will become public knowledge. And even if those selenocytes are the moon's 'immune system,' what does that have to do with Earth?"

"It affects us in two ways. First, it means a return to the arms race, which is no surprise. Second—the surprise—the selenocytes have begun to take an interest in us."

"In the human race? Earth? Not just me?"

"Precisely."

"What are they doing?"

"At the moment, only multiplying."

"In the laboratories?"

"Before our scientists knew what was happening, the dust had got out and spread to all four corners of the globe. Only a small amount has accompanied you."

"They're multiplying? And?"

"So far, nothing. They are the size of ultraviruses."

"And they get their energy—"

"From the sun. It's estimated that there are a few trillion of them now, in the air, in the oceans, everywhere."

"And doing nothing?"

"So far. Which has caused great concern."

"Why?"

"The sense that this was planned. If you landed, there must have been a reason. But what? They want to know."

"But I remember nothing, and likewise the other half of me . . ."

"They are unaware that you are now talking to yourself. In addition, there are different kinds of amnesia. Under hypnosis or in certain other ways one can obtain things from a person that he cannot recall for the life of him. They have been careful with you lest some shock or trauma to your brain damage or wipe out completely what you may know though you can't dredge it up. Anyway our people disagree about how to proceed with the examination ... which until now has spared you much."

"Yes, I think I know where I stand in this game ... But why didn't the reconnaissance flights that followed yield results?"

"Who told you that?"

"My first visitor. The neurologist."

"What did he say exactly?"

"That the scouts returned but they'd been shown stage sets. That's how he put it."

"Not true. As far as I know, there were three more flights. Two teleferic, and all their remotes were destroyed. They didn't use mine, only conventional remotes. Equipped with special rockets, however, to shoot samples of the soil up to the ship. But nothing came of that."

"Who destroyed them?"

"Unknown, because communication was cut off early. When they landed, the area in a radius of several miles became covered with a fog opaque to radar."

"Something new. And the third scout?"

"He went, landed, and returned. With complete amnesia. He woke up back on his ship. Or so I heard. It might not be the truth. I never saw him. The murkier this business becomes, the more secrecy surrounds it. I don't know if he too brought back dust. I assume they're examining the poor man but without success, since they're still taking such good care of you."

"What should I do?"

"The situation looks bad but is not hopeless. Very soon now the selenocytes will have paralyzed the last of the moon weapons. Shorting them all out. The moon project has already been written off, not officially yet but that's not the point. A couple of top information scientists here believe that the moon has begun to take an interest in Earth. They say: 'The selenosphere has entered the biosphere.' "

"An invasion, then?"

"No, probably not, or at least not in any traditional sense. A multitude of genies were sent in well-corked bottles. They broke out, battled each other, and as a side effect microorganisms appeared, vital though not alive. It doesn't have the look of a planned invasion. Rather of an epidemic, a pandemic."

"I don't understand the difference."

"I can present this only in metaphors. The selenosphere reacts to an intruder the way the immune system reacts to a foreign body or an antigen. Even if that's not quite right, we have no other way of conceptualizing it. The two scouts who went after you had at their disposal the very latest in weaponry. I don't know the details, but it was not a conventional device, or nuclear. The Agency is keeping what happened on the moon hush-hush, but the dust clouds were so large that they could be seen and photographed by many observatories. What is more—when the clouds dissipated, the ground was changed. Holes had formed, craters, but completely unlike the moon's typical craters. This the Agency was unable to keep secret, so it said nothing. It was only then that headquarters began to see that the more strong-arm the methods used for reconnaissance, the more strong-arm the counteroffensive would be."

"So there you are . . ."

"No. Because we are dealing not with an adversary or enemy, but only with a kind of giant anthill. Such strange theories have occurred to me, I won't even repeat them. But our time is up. Stay put. As long as they don't go completely mad, they'll leave you alone. I'll be away for three days, will talk to you Saturday at this time if I can. Keep well, intrepid Missionary."

"Until then," I said but don't know if he heard me because there was no answer. I took the olive out of my ear and after a moment of thought wrapped it in tinfoil and hid it in a box of chocolates. I had plenty to think about. I opened the curtains before I got into bed. The moths had left, probably drawn by the bright windows of the other pavilions around the garden. The moon sailed through white, feathery clouds. "We've done it this time," I said to myself, pulling the covers up to my head.

Next morning Kramer knocked at my door while I was still in bed. He told me that yesterday Padderhorn had swallowed a fork. The man had swallowed cutlery before in order to kill himself. Last week he swallowed a shoehorn. They did an esophagoscopy on him—and gave him a new shoehorn a foot and a half long but he pinched someone's fork in the dining hall.

"You came to talk about flatware?" I asked politely.

Kramer sighed, buttoned the top button of his pajamas, and sat in an armchair beside my bed. "No . . ." he said in a surprisingly weak voice. "It's not good, Jonathan."

"Depends on for whom, Adelaide," I replied. "In any case I have no intention of swallowing anything."

"It's really not good," Kramer said. He folded his hands over his stomach and twirled his thumbs. "I'm afraid for you, Jonathan."

"Don't be," I said plumping up my pillow behind my head. "I am well protected. Do you know about the selenocytes?"

I took him by such surprise that his mouth fell open. Then his face grew stupid, the face of a millionaire who had nothing left to fantasize about.

"I know you heard me. And perhaps you know about the selenosphere too? Yes? Unless your rank is not high enough for you to be privy. Did they tell you about the sad fate of the quantum collapsar weapon in the last missions? About the clouds above the Mare Ignium? But no, that they wouldn't tell you . . ."

He sat staring at me wide-eyed and breathless.

"Do me a favor, Adelaide, and pass that box of chocolates on the desk." I smiled at him. "I like something sweet before breakfast . . ."

As he didn't move, I hopped out of bed and got the box myself. Getting back under the covers, I held it out to him, but keeping my thumb over the piece in the corner.

"Go ahead."

"How do you know?" he asked in a hoarse voice. "Who . . . ?"

"No need to get upset," I said, not too clearly because I had caramel on the roof of my mouth. "What I know, I know. And not only what happened to me on the moon but also the troubles of my colleagues."

He had difficulty breathing. He looked around the room as if he were there for the first time.

"Transmitters, secret lines, antennas, modulators, yes?" I went on. "There's nothing here except that the showerhead leaks a little. Needs a new washer. Why are you surprised? Can it be you don't know that *they are inside me?*"

He sat speechless. He wiped the sweat from his nose. He tugged on an earlobe. I watched him with sympathy.

The chocolates were good. I had to be careful to leave enough in the box. Licking my lips, I said, "Adelaide, move, speak, you're making me feel bad. You were afraid for me and now I'm afraid for you. You think you'll be in trouble? Perhaps, if you behave, I can protect you, you know with *whose* help."

I was bluffing. But why shouldn't I? The fact that these few words had so dismayed him proved the powerlessness of whatever power he represented.

"I promise not to name names so I won't get you into further trouble."

"Tichy . . ." he finally groaned. "For God's sake. No, it's not possible. That's not how *they* work."

"Did I say how? I had a dream, that's all. Didn't I tell you, I'm clairvoyant."

Kramer suddenly decided. Putting his finger to his lips, he left quickly. Certain that he would be back, I hid the box of chocolates under my shirts in the closet and had time to shower and shave before I heard him knock lightly. He wore a white suit and under his arm held a large bundle wrapped in a towel. He drew the curtains and from the bundle pulled apparatuses that he positioned with their black funnels pointed at all the walls. From a black box he plugged a cord into a wall socket and fiddled with something else, wheezing, because he was really quite fat, his belly altogether authentic, and was probably pushing sixty. Face flushed, he knelt and struggled with his electronics, then finally straightened with a grunt and a sigh.

"Now we can talk," he said.

"About?" I asked, putting on my nicest shirt, the one with the blue collar. "But you first. You might want to tell me about the gray hair I've given you. After your boss assured you I was as insulated here as a fly in a bottle. But say what you like, speak, confess, unburden yourself. You'll see how much better you feel."

And suddenly, apropos of nothing, like a poker player who wins the pot with a pair of threes, I tossed off: "What division are you in, the fourth?"

"No, the first—"

He stopped himself.

"What do you know about me?"

"Enough of that." I sat on a chair, its back in front of me. "Surely you don't think I'm giving you something for nothing."

"What do you want to know?"

"We could start with Shapiro," I said pleasantly.

"He's from the LA. That's a fact."

"And more than just a neurologist."

"He has another job."

"Go on."

"What do you know about the selenosphere?"

"What do *you* know?"

It occurred to me that maybe I'd overplayed my hand. If he was a secret agent, it didn't matter for whom, he wouldn't know that much. Scientists didn't usually involve themselves in such activity. But this was an unusual case, so I could be wrong.

"Enough of this hide-and-seek," said Kramer. He was desperate. His white jacket had patches of sweat under the arms. "Sit here next to me," he muttered, getting down on the carpet.

We sat as if to smoke a peace pipe, in the center of a circle of gizmos and wires.

Da Capo

Before he had time to open his mouth, the drone of an engine could be heard above us and a great shadow swept across the garden and windows. Kramer grew bug-eyed. The throbbing faded, then returned. A helicopter hung just above the trees. There were two reports, as if someone had uncorked enormous bottles of champagne. The helicopter was so low, I could see the people in its cabin. One of them opened the door and shot another flare downward. Kramer jumped up. I didn't dream he could move so fast. He rushed from the room, his head down. From the helicopter something shiny fell and was lost in the grass. With a roar the machine lifted and flew off. On his knees in the high grass, Kramer opened a container no larger than a soccer ball, took out something, an envelope, and tore it open. The message must have been important because the paper shook in his hands. He looked in my direction. He was pale, changed. Again he read the paper, and stood. He crumpled it in his fist, put it in his pocket, and slowly crossed the lawn, not bothering to take the path. He came back in and without a word kicked one of the antibug devices. Something in it crackled and there was a little blue smoke from it. I still sat on the floor, and Kramer stamped on his equipment and tore at the wires as if he'd gone insane in earnest. Finally, out of breath, he took off his jacket and sank into the armchair. Then he looked at me as if seeing me for the first time, and grunted.

"I just lost my temper," he explained. "They'll retire me. Your career too is finished. Forget about the moon. You can send a postcard to Shapiro. Care of the Agency. They'll still be there for a while, out of inertia."

I said nothing, suspecting some new trick. Kramer took a large plaid handkerchief from his pocket, mopped his brow, and regarded me, I thought, with a mixture of pity and resentment.

"It started two hours ago and is going like a house on fire, everywhere. Incredible. We're pacified, all right, here and overseas and from pole to pole! The global loss—trillions of dollars. Including space, because the satellites were the first to go. Why are you gaping?" he added, irritated. "Haven't you figured it out? I got a letter from our Uncle Sam . . ."

"What does it say?"

"You think we're still playing? No, my friend, the game is over. Sit down and write about your adventures, the Agency, the Mission, whatever you like. Maybe it will be a bestseller. And no one will touch a hair on your head. But don't put it off, or the guys at the Agency may scoop you. They may already be starting their memoirs about the old order . . ."

"What has happened?"

"Everything. Did you ever hear of Sim Wars?"

"No."

"Core Wars?"

"Aren't those computer games?"

"Ah, you see, you do know! Yes. Programs that destroy other programs. They were thought up back in the eighties. They were unimportant then. An amusement for programmers. Viruses and counterviruses. DWARF, CREEPER, RAIDER, DARWIN, and a hundred others. But here I am giving you a lecture on cybertronic pathology." He grimaced. "This has cost me my health! And now I fill you in instead of looking for a new job!"

"Uncle Sam sends you letters by copter? Isn't the post office working?" I asked, still sniffing for a trap.

Kramer took out his checkbook, scribbled something across a check, made a paper airplane out of it, and sailed it onto my lap.

"To the Missionary: a souvenir from Adelaide," I read. "What are you getting at?"

"That's all it's good for. Uncle sends his greetings, of course. There is no post office. There is nothing now, nothing." He swept his arms in a circle. "All gone! It started two hours ago, didn't I tell you? Doesn't matter who's to blame. Your professor too is out of work. Nice old man! At least I bought a house in time. I'll grow roses, vegetables, for barter. No more banks now either. It's stuffy in here . . ."

He fanned himself with his checkbook. Then he looked at it with disgust and threw it into the wastebasket.

"Pax Vobiscum," he spat. *"Et cum spiritu tuo."*

I began to understand. He wasn't pretending.

"Those viruses?" I asked slowly.

"Yes, my brave little Missionary. This is your work. It was you who brought that clever dust to Earth. Now they can either give you the Nobel Peace Prize or have you shot for treason. I wouldn't pin your hopes on a Nobel, but you've definitely made it into the history books. You brought humanity a plague, whether of doom or deliverance is up to the historians to thrash out over the coming years. You'll be in every encyclopedia."

"Maybe together with you?" I suggested. I still didn't know exactly what had befallen us, but Kramer wasn't playacting, I'd have bet both halves of my poor head on that.

"There was another program then, WORM," Kramer went on sadly. "You have to realize that nowadays a person in my profession has to have a higher education. Those days are gone when it was enough to be a beautiful woman, go to bed with someone, photograph a stolen document in the bathroom, and it's back to Washington. No, first you need a Ph.D. in math, then information theory, then your specialty, and it's half your life in school before you can even begin."

"As a spy?"

"Spy." He turned the word over in his mouth as if it was sour, and snapped his suspenders, which were deep blue with white stars. "I am a civil servant in a special section and privy to the highest matters of state. The word *spy* is an insult to me. But it doesn't matter anymore. From WORM and programs like it came the theory of information erosion—you know about it?"

"A little."

"So. It turned out that information erosion wasn't the invention of some professors of computer science but had been used by bacteria four billion years before, give or take a few hundred million. They were the oldest cells, the first, each with its own program, and they fed on each other and off each other because there was no one around yet to get herpes or cancer. But our great scientists somehow didn't see the connection. They were too full of their own knowledge. The theory was tested only a few times, in the context of secret battles between consortiums, each trying to paralyze the others' computers. Software warfare. You've heard of that, I think?"

"But it was a long time ago."

"Forty, maybe fifty years. That's precisely why now we are undone . . . Because except for clubs, kitchen knives, and pistols there are no weapons that have not been computerized! Everything became programs, chips, processors, and it's for that reason. Have you tried to use the phone?"

"Not today. Why?"

"The telephone system is out, too. The viruses attacked everywhere at once! Did you listen to the radio?"

"No. I don't have one."

"They aren't intelligent. That was clear from the beginning. They have as much intelligence as any other virus. But the erosion capability is phenomenal!" He squinted at a van Gogh on the wall, fiery sunflowers. "But why am I here talking to you? Maybe I'll take a walk, or hang myself. On these wires."

He kicked the nearest gizmo.

"What seems a great mystery from the front is as plain as potatoes from behind," he said. "Did we send the best weapon-creating programs to the moon? We did. Did they improve themselves over x years? And how. Did they go at each other hammer and tongs? Of course, it couldn't have been otherwise. Who won? As always, the side that packed the most punch in the least space. The parasites won, the molecular midgets. I don't think they've even been named yet. How about *Virus lunaris pacemfaciens?* All I want to know is what made you land there and bring back that dogood plague? You can tell me now—privately, because it makes no difference to the governments. Not anymore."

"*All* programs have been destroyed? Computer memory, everything?" I asked in a daze. I was beginning to see the scope of this.

"Yes, Missionary of pestilence. It puts me in mind of Poe's Red Death. Not that you spread it intentionally, because how could you have known? We are thrown back to the first half of the nineteenth century. Technologically speaking and in general. Except that there were cannon then. We'll have to pull them out of museums."

"Hold on, Adelaide," I interrupted. "Why the nineteenth century? After all, there were fully equipped armies then . . ."

"You're right. Our situation is without precedent. Like after a quiet little atomic war where the whole infrastructure goes up in smoke. The industrial base, communications, banking, commerce. Only simple machines are left, yet no one has been hurt, not even a fly. Although actually that's not true. There must have been plenty of accidents, but without the media we remain uninformed. After all, newspapers have not been printed on a hand press for a very long time. Forget the editorial offices. Forget our cars too. My Cadillac is no more."

"It was a company car, wasn't it?" I observed. "Not your worry . . ."

"True," agreed Kramer. "The poor will be on top now, the Fourth World, because they still have the old Remingtons, maybe even muskets from 1870, and of course spears and boomerangs. Those are now the weapons of mass destruction. We could not withstand an invasion of Australian Aborigines. But come, there is no reason now not to tell me: Why did you land on the moon?"

"You think I know." It began to sink in, how small I had become, how insignificant my situation. "But I don't. I'd happily give you five percent of my royalties from that bestseller if *you* could tell *me*. After all your studies you should be better than Sherlock Holmes. It's elementary! You know the clues as well as I do . . ."

He shook his head in a melancholy way.

"He doesn't know," he told van Gogh's flowers, which the sun had just reached. They cast a yellow light over my unmade bed. My legs hurt from sitting cross-legged, so I got up, took the bottle of bourbon hidden in my closet and some ice cubes from the refrigerator, and poured for myself and for him. I proposed a toast to the memory of the arms disarmed.

"I have high blood pressure and diabetes," Kramer said, turning the glass in his fingers. "But one drink won't hurt. So be it. To our dead world!"

"Why dead?" I asked.

We drank. Kramer choked, coughed a bit, put the glass down, and rubbed his face. I noticed he hadn't shaved well. In a weak voice, as if he'd aged ten years in a moment, he said:

"The higher one has gone with computers, the farther he'll fall. They ate every single program." He slapped his pocket where the letter from Uncle Sam was. "The end of an era."

"Why? There are antivirus programs . . ."

"Medicine is useless when the patient has died. Anyway there are no more programs of any kind, on land, in the air, at sea, in space. Even to deliver this letter an old Bellem was used, because the new models won't move. It began a few minutes after eight . . . and those idiots thought it was an ordinary virus."

"Everywhere at once?"

I tried to imagine the chaos in banks, airports, offices, hospitals, computer centers, universities, schools, factories . . . and couldn't.

"No one knows for sure because there's no communication, but from what I've heard, yes, everywhere at once."

"How is that possible?"

"What you brought was in a dormant form, like spores. The spores multiplied in chain reaction to achieve a certain level of saturation in the air, water, everywhere, and that specific concentration in turn activated them. The weapons programs on the moon must have been the best shielded, so with ours on Earth it was like taking candy from a baby. Total bytocide. With the exception of living things, which on the moon the spores never had to deal with. Otherwise they would have butchered the lot of us, along with the antelopes, ants, sardines, and grass. But enough! I'm tired of talking . . ."

"If it is as you say, everything will start again from the beginning—in the old way."

"Of course. In six months or a year they'll find an antidote for *Virus lunaris bitoclasticus,* and the world will proceed to the next mess."

"Maybe you won't lose your job."

"No, I'm through," he said firmly. "I'm too old. The new era will require new training, new courses. Antilunar information theory and so on. They'll probably heat the moon by thermonuclear means, sterilize it, and even if the cost goes into the trillions, it'll be worth it not to have to worry."

"Worth it for whom?" I asked. This Kramer was an odd character: he kept saying goodbye but didn't get up to go. Maybe he was just unburdening his heart because I was the only one in the asylum who knew who he was. Maybe, with his broken life, he should see a psychiatrist.

"What do you mean, for whom? The armorers, the industrial-military complex. Everyone. They'll go to the libraries for old blueprints, rebuild some classic machines, rockets, and then turn to the dead computers. Because the hardware is perfectly preserved, like mummies. Only the software is kaput. Wait a couple of years. You'll see."

"History never repeats itself exactly," I said, and poured him another bourbon without asking. He tossed it down and didn't choke; his bald head reddened a little, that was all. Little flies played in a ray of sunlight coming in from the window.

"The damn flies survive," Kramer muttered. He looked at the garden where patients in colored bathrobes and pajamas were shuffling along the paths as if nothing had happened. The sky was blue, the sun was shining, the wind made the big chestnut trees sway, and the fountains made little rainbows with their spray. While one world was perishing, departing to an irrevocable past, the new world was not even in diapers yet. I didn't share this insight with Kramer, it was too banal. I just poured him the rest of the bottle.

"You want to get me drunk?" he asked, but drank. He put down the glass, stood at last, threw his jacket over his shoulder, then hesitated, his hand on the doorknob.

"If you do remember . . . you know what . . . write to me. We'll compare notes."

"Compare notes?" I said like an echo.

"You see, I have my own theory."

"About why I landed?"

"Yes."

"Tell me."

"Can't."

"Why not?"

"It wouldn't be right. Oath of office, duty, and all that. We sat on opposite sides of the table."

"The table's gone. Don't be such a stickler. I give you my word I'll keep it to myself."

"Sure! You'll put it in your book, then swear that your memory returned."

"All right, a deal. Six percent of my royalties."

"You'll put this in writing?"

"Of course."

"Twenty!"

"You're crazy."

"*I'm* crazy?"

"I've begun to figure out anyway what you'll tell me."

"Hm."

He frowned. You could see that with all the high-level courses he had taken, he hadn't learned enough. I decided he wasn't really cut out for his profession but I didn't tell him. He was retiring anyway.

Kramer let go of the door and went to the window, then sat on the edge of the desk and scratched behind his ear.

"So you tell me," he said.

"If I tell you, you don't get a cent . . ."

Behind him the garden was green. Old Padderhorn came down a path in his wheelchair, an enormous shoehorn in his hand. He held it like a flag. The orderly pushing the chair was smoking one of his cigars. Several steps behind them walked Padderhorn's bodyguard, in shorts, muscular, with a bronze tan. He wore a wide-brimmed panama and his face was hidden behind a comic book. The holster on his loose belt slapped against his thigh.

"Speak or go, old friend," I said. "You know that whatever I write, the Agency will deny it . . ."

"But if you name me as your informant, it could mean unpleasantness for me."

"The money will make the unpleasantness less unpleasant. I'll name you if you *don't* tell me. Anyway, I think you should get professional help. Your nerves are shot. It's quite obvious. You can't hide it."

He was silent, a broken man. The corners of his mouth twitched. I felt sorry for him.

"You won't quote me?"

"I'll change the name and your appearance."

"They'll know me even so."

"Not necessarily. Do you think it was only you they sent to stick to me? But this whole thing was your side's work, wasn't it?"

He was indignant.

"We have nothing to do with the Lunar Agency. They were the ones!"

"How and why?"

"I'm not sure how but I know why. It was so you wouldn't make it back. If you died there, things would remain the same."

"Not forever. Sooner or later . . ."

"That was the point, it would be later. They were afraid of the report."

"Let's suppose. And the dust? How did it get into my suit? How could they have known about the dust?"

"They didn't know, but Lax-Gugliborc had his fear. That's why he fiddled with the dispersant."

"You learned this?" I was surprised.

"His assistant belongs to us. Lauher."

I remembered my first meeting with the professor. He had indeed said that one of his colleagues was a spy. It put everything in a different light.

"The callotomy, that was them too?"

"I don't know." He shrugged, added, "And you will never know. No one will ever know. When the stakes are that high, the truth no longer exists. All that remain are theories. Different versions. As it was with Kennedy."

"President Kennedy?"

"The stakes here were higher. The whole world! There's nothing higher. Now write what you promised . . ."

From the drawer I took a sheet of paper and a pen. Kramer stood at the window, his back to me. I signed the document and handed it to him. He looked and was surprised.

"You made a mistake."

"No."

"Ten?"

"Ten."

"All right. It's my turn. I'll tell you. The dispersant was *supposed to* draw you to the moon."

"You're telling me it was Lax-Gugliborc? I don't believe it!"

"Not the professor. He didn't know anything. Lauher knew. To the fifty-odd programs he added one. Not hard to do for a programmer."

"So it was your side after all."

"No. He was also working for a third party."

"Lauher was?"

"Yes, but we needed him."

"All right. The dispersant called me. I landed. But what about the sand?"

"An unplanned factor. Unforeseen by everyone. If you can't remember that moment, no one will ever know. Ever."

He folded the paper in two, put it in his pocket, and at the door turned and said:

"So long."

I watched him walk toward the main pavilion. As he disappeared behind the hedge, my left hand took my right hand and shook it. I can't say I was thrilled by this gesture of support. But life must go on.